From Within

Written by Brian Delaney

Published by KOBA Media, LLC – Colorado
ISBN-13: 978-0997867305
ISBN-10: 0997867302

For my beautiful wife, Alli and our children.

You are an amazing woman, wife, and mother. Thanks for all the support for my idea to start writing.

Table of Contents

Chapter One

Early October 2036

"Government intervention and taxes breeds government intervention and taxes," the deep voice was booming from the speakers. "People are polarized and fed up across all political beliefs with the American government. Most every group with any stance politically has the feeling of being betrayed. Protests are constant and many times violent. Even those who demanded higher taxes are feeling the pains of their wishes. Unemployment is at a record high. Businesses are failing, with many already gone, because they can't operate at a loss. The government instituted a higher minimum wage at the same time as instituting higher corporate taxes. Those that demanded the increases didn't seem to realize that most businesses, big and small, even their local 'mom and pop' shops they frequented, are...rather, were corporations. They are gone now. Many decided that laying off their few workers would help keep them alive. It did for a while. Many soon realized they were working too hard for too little or no reward, just to save their businesses.

Cashing in on their assets in the business seemed like the better option. It should also be realized that a business owner might not necessarily be rich. Many business owners who operate their business as a corporation still make the average American yearly wages and sometimes even less. The average business operates at a loss for about the first five years before reaching profitability."

Marcus Braden sat in the dimly lit room watching himself on the large flat screen centered on the office's side wall. He studied himself. He had thick dark brown hair that was beginning to gray around his ears. He could still see the defined lines on his face and crow's feet protruding from the corners of his eyes. All of this made him raise an eyebrow and nod his head at the realization of his aging. No matter how much the makeup artists tried to hide them, he still noticed. He wore a custom tailored midnight black suit with white vertical hairline pin-striping that helped slim his thickening midsection. He wasn't a young man anymore and his metabolism wasn't what it used to be. He still felt like he kept himself fairly healthy. He was tall, six feet three inches. Even with his co-anchor bringing her chair to the highest setting, his entire head still appeared to be above hers on screen. He glanced at the others in the room. Kenneth Wellen stood leaning against his desk. He was the senior producer of the news program Marcus anchored. Kenneth was slightly squinting, staring intently at the screen. His thin lips were pressed together in a look of disappointment. Kenneth stood about an inch shorter than Marcus, which still made him a tall man. His hair had turned completely silver years earlier. His figure had always been slim. He was usually described as 'tall and skinny.' Marcus's glance continued to Ava, his co-anchor. Her face was buried in her phone. She was petite and had long flowing blonde hair. She was very attractive. Between her looks and her slight northern European accent, she held viewers attention well. Ava had immigrated to the U.S. from the Netherlands. The widespread economic collapse in Europe caused the Netherlands to strengthen their practice of socialism as an attempt to shield themselves from the collapse and Ava's father took his family as far away from it as he could.

Marcus was still speaking on the screen, "Along with the corporate taxes were higher individual income taxes. The saying became that the rich could afford the higher taxes to help the country out. With failing businesses and the rich bowing out of the work world, because they had the money they needed to live without work, the higher taxes didn't yield the desired result. This, of course, is ignoring our country's history where lower taxes encouraged business and economic growth and brought in higher tax revenue. We are repeating the policies of the New Deal that put the 'Great' in Great Depression. So, the middle class's individual incomes now begins to bear the higher taxes as well. "Trickle down" now means to many that the government's failed tax policies trickle down to cause failure for the whole country. In reality, the more the government stays out of business the better business does. Likewise, the more the government gets involved, the more businesses and individuals suffer. As you know, some areas of the country people have come together against misrepresentation by politicians and created new states. It's difficult to track how many breakaways have happened since there is constant debate on their legitimacy. The last report I saw said the number of states has nearly doubled. That doesn't include areas that broke away and didn't consider themselves a part of, and made no effort to join another state or even form their own local government. They simply refuse to pay more taxes, well...rather, they simply refuse to pay any taxes at all. They don't see why they should pay a government that doesn't represent them. In a speech to supporters, Mikey Johnson, the recently elected governor of California posed the question of whether or not these break-away regions are still being considered a part of the United States. He also reiterated in the speech that he preferred to leave any armed encounters with the break-away regions off of the table for the time being. The military has been cut so drastically due to the poor financial situation that some experts have said that even if needed, the U.S. military could provide little to no assistance within the U.S. or anywhere in the world. Governor Johnson's state is host to numerous regions that has given up any affiliation to California. The Golden State has dealt with bankruptcy and higher taxes much more comparatively to the rest of the country for decades. For the rest of the country, around two-thirds of the average person's income is going to the government to fund America to be a welfare state. The longer so many people collect all these government handouts, the more the economy is going to be drained and cause more people to be in a position to be eligible for handouts. The sad thing is that most of these people would be fine if the government hadn't started meddling in the financial affairs of businesses and the people. I'm Marcus Braden and this has been 'A Moment with Marcus.'"

"And...and I'm Ava Van Boer." Ava had paused briefly, sounding confused. "Thanks for joining us tonight on WWNL, the Worldwide News Link." She didn't end with her typical sign-off. She hadn't expected Marcus's ending speech. His 'Moment with Marcus' was generally a brief opinion about a news piece they had covered during the broadcast.

As the program's credits began to fade onto the screen, Ava's face was still visible to viewers. Her head was bolting back and forth looking past the cameramen, searching for Kenneth's reaction. Kenneth usually hung around behind the scenes during the broadcast. Her light-blue eyes were stuck wide-open; her mouth had dropped open immediately after her sign-off line.

The upbeat instrumental credit music came to an abrupt stop and the screen went blank. Kenneth dropped his T.V. remote onto his desk breaking the silence in the room and let out a long, forced sigh. The sound caused Ava to look away from her phone for a moment. She quickly glanced at Kenneth and Marcus and then bowed her head back down towards her phone.

"Marcus...," Kenneth began, peering off beyond his blank T.V. "Marcus, ya know, many of the VP's up top aren't too happy with this stunt you pulled last night."

"Well Ken, the truth isn't always popular," Marcus returned.

"Huh? Truth!?"

"Yes Ken, it's the truth. I could have spoken those things on the show as a prediction five, maybe even ten years ago. I saw this coming. A country can't survive as a welfare state. Eventually, the job providers are driven to the ground with their pockets turned out."

"That's your opinion. Not everyone sees it that way. Anyways, I think management is getting pressure from the government for us not to cause any panic. There is way too much violence already out there due to this financial crisis."

Marcus jumped in chuckling, "Oh, I see. So, they are wanting to censor us now!"

"Let me finish!" Kenneth nearly yelled trying to gain control of the conversation. His temper was rising and he was becoming visibly frustrated. "The VP of operations is tossing around the idea of having every one of your ending segments reviewed, I'm guessing by me before you go on each night. It's not censorship!"

"Ken, if I may?" Ava's soft voice surprised Kenneth since he forgot she was still sitting there. "If this is all about Marcus's ending segments, why am I here? Can I go?"

"Ava, you are here because you lost it while we were live. We need you to keep your composure no matter what is going on. What if there's a major crisis that breaks while you are on? We need you to keep it together through it all. You won't always be able to review everything before you read it live. You know that. We want people to turn to our network. If they turn us on and it looks like we don't have a clue, they'll be changing the channel in no time flat! That's all for you. You can go."

"That's not a problem. It won't happen again," Ava's face was searing and clearly revealing her embarrassment and anger on being called out. She quickly got up, grabbing her phone off the armrest of the chair. She disappeared into the hallway, avoiding any eye-contact with Kenneth and Marcus trying to conceal the embarrassment.

"Where was I? Oh yeah, they want to review your segments. Well...they are thinking about it. You are lucky they aren't talking about firing you. Maybe they are, I haven't heard anything about it, though."

"Fire me?" Marcus chuckled. "I'm contracted for another four years. I worked out a deal that would cost them more to get rid of me than it is to keep me. You know once I made it to the big leagues I wasn't going to take whatever deal they throw down first. They scouted me out which gave me the ace up my sleeve."

"Yes yes, the 'ace up my sleeve' line," Kenneth made quotation symbols with his fingers from both hands to mock him. "You've been saying that line for the last ten years. You know they could just keep you on staff and not put you on air, don't you?"

"Yeah, they could do that. But, I don't think they will. Every time I take a vacation the ratings go down. Sure, you have Ava as the pretty face to watch, and, not to brag, but I've become a household name in news. People aren't up in arms over my speech. They were talking about it over the radio on my drive in this morning. They say it's generating real conversation and debate about ways to fix the country and I think the phrase was 'It's about time someone in the media told us how it is.' You just watch Ken, the VP's will be eating up all the increased ratings and will be telling you within a week to have me keep 'telling people how it is.'" Marcus made quotation symbols with his hands mimicking Ken from moments ago.

Marcus knew he was putting Kenneth in a lousy position. They had been friends and colleagues for years. They started off together as interns after college for a local network in a small market area in western Nebraska. They were both out of place in the slow and easy-going farm region. They quickly became friends and as the years went on they piggy-backed off of each other to move up the ranks in bigger markets. One would get hired at a better location and would help bring the other up with him shortly after. There were only a few years and a couple locations their working relationship of partnered career-progression didn't go as planned. They were simultaneously hired at different locations and had to part ways. After a couple more jumps to higher markets, they wound up together again in the top news market of New York City. Kenneth was always a behind-the-scenes type. A hard-worker. Always ambitious to become the leader where ever he was working. Marcus was a smooth-talker. A hard-worker like Kenneth. He was handsome and used that to his advantage to get his face on screen as much as he could. He wasn't cocky by any means. He knew things weren't just going to be handed to him. He put in any extra effort he could, even if it was outside his job description. He was raised that way. His father had owned his own business, a grocery store. Marcus spent many weekends and summers learning from his father. His father didn't give him any advantage over other employees other than giving him the job. His father was purposely a very strict and ungenerous boss so that his son would work harder and stand up for what he deserved. Before long, his work ethic was ingrained in his DNA. The major news networks must have seen all the same things in both of them because it didn't take long for both Kenneth and Marcus to be scouted and quickly hired by Worldwide News Link.

They both peered intently at each other, as if in a duel. Eventually, Kenneth gave in, letting it be known with another long, forced sigh.

"Marcus, work with me here. You and I have been friends for a long time. I know we don't see eye-to-eye on anything political anymore. But..." he paused, trying to think of what he wanted to say. "But...I don't know. Your speech isn't the view of the company. And you know I've become fairly active volunteering with political groups...groups that have the complete opposite view of what you said. I'm just torn. I don't want to have to come down on you every time you have another speech like last night."

Marcus thought Kenneth was sounding whiney. He also couldn't gather what Kenneth was trying to say.

"Ken, what are you getting at? How was my segment opinionated? I was just calling it as I see it. Well, rather, I was calling it as it is! How does our company, which is supposed to be non-biased news have a view that disagrees with what is actually going on? And haven't you noticed those groups you volunteer with are now just as angry as everyone else because they can't afford to live with taxes at the levels they are?"

Kenneth jumped in to respond, "What you said was...grim, to say the least. As far as the groups I'm a part of, well, I've been looking for a different one. One that hasn't lost it's focus on what they are supposed to be doing."

"Grim? Have you been out in the world at all in the past year? The country seems to be on the brink of collapse and possibly civil war. We already have plenty of civil unrest and like I said in my segment last night, there are people rioting somewhere in the country every day! Come on Ken! Can't you see that the focus of your groups...their goal is what is bringing our country down? It's much more than grim out there."

"Alright Marcus, I don't have any more time to deal with this today. The way this seems to be going and knowing how stubborn you can be, I'd imagine we'll be having another conversation brought down by the VP's tomorrow morning."

"Ok. So be it," Marcus said while shrugging his shoulders.

Marcus casually strolled out of Kenneth's office. He still could not quite grasp what Kenneth was trying to say. It seemed that there was more to that conversation than what was on the surface. *Why would WWNL be so adamant about certain news NOT making a broadcast? Why did Ken seem so antsy? What does he think is causing all the problems around the country?*

"Still with us?" Ava asked with a chuckle. Marcus was caught off-guard with the question because he was so busy in his own head as he walked down the stairs from Kenneth's office into the studio's office area.

"Ha..of course," Marcus said with a forced laugh of sarcasm.

"So...if I may ask, what was your segment all about last night?" Ava asked. "I mean, aren't all these problems just being exaggerated and escalated by a very small amount of very extreme people?"

"I wasn't making up anything I said last night. There are real problems going on in this country. You and I are reporting the same news every day. And label these people as extreme? All they want is a return to America as it was and was meant to be. Ava, we are driving this country, full-bore, towards the same cliff that your country, the Netherlands, and the rest of Europe drove off of just less than ten years ago. Can't you see all the similarities going on here? Just last week, our government took over the assets of two large charity organizations because they said it was necessary to help the people. Why couldn't those organizations continue handling charity the way they already were? The government just drove them into the ground. That's the same thing that happened to your family!" Marcus's volume was continually rising and he realized it and paused. He wasn't sure if he struck a wrong chord with speaking about her family's past situation.

Ava's father had been an owner of a quite lucrative

bread bakery on the outskirts of Amsterdam. The government took over his operation as it was considered a "necessity to the social and economic strength of the country and quite assuredly the whole European Union," or so they told him. He and his few business partners were reassigned to lower management positions. In less than a year, the governments operators took the profitable business and turned into a pit that needed government subsidies to survive. Within a few months, the previous owners were taken out of management altogether and offered positions on the production lines. They had been blamed for mismanagement. Eventually, the government's propaganda machine was claiming the company was mismanaged by the previous owners and was teetering on the edge of total collapse and because so, it had to be taken over as a necessity for the factory could continue to operate, only with government help, of course. The old owners became despised by people in their own town; there were even some of their employees who had been involved and victimized in the whole scandal who bought into the propaganda and hated them even though they had been there all along and knew the true sequence of events. All of the old owners left the country. Ava was in her last year of school when she had been uprooted and dragged along to the U.S.

"Oh Marcus, we are better off in America than we were in the Netherlands."

Marcus noticed that bringing up the subject didn't seem to bother her. "Better off because the U.S. government didn't intervene in your lives so much? Didn't used to anyways. Or, better off financially? Your father's company distributed throughout all of Europe. I don't see how they are better off here...unless he has another successful business here?"

"Better because the government doesn't intervene like they did back home. No, they aren't better off financially, but money isn't everything. They are both working in retail. The government here isn't taking away businesses like they did to my family in the Netherlands," Ava replied.

"How not!?" Marcus burst out. "What about the two charities that got swiped away last week!?"

"Those were charities, not businesses. That money they had now will be given to those who need it by the government," Ava said.

"Yes, they were charities. However, people work for those charities to manage and run them. Also, what about the people the charities were helping? Now, they are apparently out of luck. And, if those people had depended on the charities rather than the government, doesn't that just now cause all those people to depend on the government too? The two charities' employees will now have to find new jobs, but that is doubtful for most of them with the way the economy is and how many businesses are closing up shop. Once the government starts doing what it did last week, it only escalates the problems of government dependence. The government doesn't produce anything to get money, they tax, and apparently they just confiscate now as well without any due process of the law. We'll be seeing more and more of this kind of atrocious and shameful activity in the coming months, you just watch."

Ava seemed to be done with the conversation. She muttered something Marcus could not understand and then turned back towards her desk to continue reading news briefs. He wondered if she ended the conversation because she felt defeated or if he had been too harsh with his tone. Marcus sat down at his desk and silenced ensued.

Their desks were the most exquisite and well-built in their department. They had been special ordered and hand-made. They were a deep red oak and rustic cherry wood with a fine finish that made their rear-section of the office floor stand out compared to the short cubicle partitions that occupied the rest of the floor. Ava and Marcus were the faces of the whole broadcast and were therefore treated with distinction. They were even privileged with having their workstations located away from the main entrance in the back of the office area with their own key card locked entry door from a back hallway. They received this privilege in the event that any visitors made it to the main hallway or in the department and past the receptionist. If they had been situated front-and-center they were sure to be consistently interrupted by visitors expressing their recognition and loyalty to watching the show. Their two desks sat across from each other facing opposite directions. Kenneth had planned it as such since the goal was to show both anchors on screen as good friends that always acted professionally. Ideally, sitting next to one another during the work day up until the broadcast would help them to get along. Had they been separated in their own offices, they would also not be an example to their fellow co-workers. Being situated amongst everyone else in the department partially forced them to get over and not publicize any differences they might have. It worked for a few years until they began to notice their differences in personal beliefs.

They were, however, not close friends. They remained cordial to one another. They even would spend time together outside of work at gatherings thrown by co-workers or themselves or local events they both happened to be in attendance at. They considered each other not much more than acquaintances. Mainly long-time co-workers. They both recognized their strong belief differences, which, for one reason or another kept them from opening up to each other as long-time friends would have after this many years of knowing one another.

The conversation they had just ended had been the deepest beyond the surface they had spoken to each other since the first year of working together. It was Marcus's observation that Ava had held some conflicting views with herself. He noticed over the years that even with her disgust of what happened to her family and many others in Europe, she had supported and voted in favor of steps that would progress the United States in the very same direction that had been the collapse of Europe. He had tried over the years to get her to see the contradiction in thinking, but she seemed to want to remain in the contradiction.

Marcus decided he wanted to end the conversation on a good note. He rotated in his chair back towards Ava.

"So, how's that boyfriend of yours? Are we going to get to meet him sometime soon?"

"Oh," Ava began and then turned to face Marcus, "he's pretty busy with his company down in the financial district. I doubt he'll try to make time to come around here. I'm sure he'll join me at the next company gathering."

"Well, good. Can't wait to meet the lucky guy," Marcus returned.

Ava smiled and turned back to her desk. Now satisfied with how the conversation ended, Marcus turned back around.

Marcus sat at his desk the rest of the morning and into the afternoon reading over news briefs he and Ava were to cover in the evening's broadcast. His stomach prompted him to look up at the set of clocks on the wall. It was a large, five-foot by six-foot digital panel that kept New York time at the top-center and then had a dozen or so other large city times from around the world that would cycle through another set of cities every five or six seconds. Marcus used the clock often as a time-waster. He would try to count out the seconds to figure out if the display changed cities every five seconds or six seconds. While doing so, he often came up with an idea for what to cover in his 'Moment with Marcus' segment. This time, he only looked at the panel briefly to notice it was a few minutes after 2 p.m., which meant it was well over an hour after he normally went to lunch. He knew his stomach would completely occupy his thoughts until it was satisfied.

*****

Marcus sat in the corner of the cafeteria that was situated in the lobby near the main entrance of the WWNL building. He didn't eat there too often. Today he had not felt like walking anywhere out of the building to the slowly diminishing selection of restaurants that peppered the street. There were many he liked to frequent that were no longer in operation. His stomach dictated that he stop here as it was the closest location he deemed to have decent food. Marcus stared across the mostly-empty dining area. It was late for lunch and too early for dinner so the crowds were elsewhere. He noticed the visible cold outside as he glanced out of the large windows that made up one entire wall of the cafeteria. People quickly passed by at their New York pace, covered in large coats and scarves and woolen hats. It had been unusually cold for early October during the last couple of days in the northeastern states. Marcus looked forward to the following week when temperatures were forecasted to return to normal.

Marcus was deep in thought while he ate. He pondered whether or not he should challenge Kenneth's threat with his topic for the closing segment later on in the evening. He had numerous subjects he could speak on, especially after reading the morning briefs that had been piled on his desk. One, in particular, had caught his attention. It was a report about a quiet decision made in Congress that had been sped through a vote in both the House and the Senate the previous evening. The decision gave the government the power to manage private businesses that were considered by a congressional committee to be an infrastructure necessity. It appeared to Marcus that the government was posturing for more takeovers like they did with the charities. He thought of pointing out the decision to Ava but figured the "I told you so" wouldn't be well-received. He knew she'd be reading the same brief soon enough anyways. Marcus wondered what businesses would be considered an infrastructure necessity. Looking down at his plate he thought food-distribution would probably be one of the ones taken over.

Then it'll all be bland bread and processed government cheese.

He wondered if he was becoming too cynical with everything going on in the government. Perhaps all these politicians over the years that led us to this point had good motives and morals. *But why lead us this far when you see it's only causing destruction? Why work so hard to recreate historically failed systems?* Marcus concluded that he was not a cynic. *A realist acknowledges the facts and pays attention to history.* He also concluded that he'd lay low for a couple of weeks before he would 'tell it how it is' in his segment again. There were sure to be plenty of developments to talk about in a couple of weeks. With that thought, he gathered his tray and made his way through the maze of empty tables and chairs towards the exit. He placed his tray on the trash bin near the cashier's station.

"Have a good day, Mr. Braden," the clerk said cheerfully.

Marcus only slightly recognized the clerk but understood that the young man probably recognized him from his show rather than his attendance in the cafeteria, which was rare. He returned a kind response and a wave and strolled briskly to the elevators. On the journey back to his desk, he made no acknowledgment of anyone or anything around him. He remained inside his own head contemplating the same question, over and over.

Why lead us this far in the same direction when it's only causing destruction?

Chapter Two

October 2036

The early morning fall air was crisp and cold. Leaves were well into their transformation to yellows and rustic oranges. Will began packing the few items he had brought along. He meticulously rolled his sleeping pad as tightly as he could. He was pressing out any sign of air with one knee while supporting himself with the other against the frosted grass. He then moved on to his sleeping bag and rolled it up in the same manner.

Will had chosen this particular weekend to be alone. The gloomy news of the state of the country that seemed to be around every corner permeated into his mind and drew him into a somber mood. Will needed the time alone to shake off the mood before interacting with anyone. He threw some of his camping gear into his Jeep and took off into the Sierra Nevada mountains early on a Saturday morning. It was his favorite hideaway. Less than an hour drive from his hometown of Oakhurst, California, Will would park his rusting earth-toned Jeep Cherokee off a lesser traveled dirt road not too far from the well-beaten, paved pathway that led to Yosemite National Park. He would slide the Jeep in between two tall pines he easily recognized and would then drive further in about half of a mile, dodging trees within a few inches of his side mirrors and leave his Jeep out of sight from anyone passing by on the road. From there he would hike a few miles deeper into the woods and up a small mountain. The hike would take several hours to reach his destination. He always made his camp in the same location.

In previous stays on the mountain, Will had dug and built up a fire pit next to a large fallen pine tree that he could sit on to enjoy the warmth from the fire. In one direction it held a perfect view of the snow-capped peaks of Yosemite in the distance. In the other direction, he could see down into the lower foothills and then, on a clear day, beyond into the valleys of central California. He kept this spot a secret because as soon as he left the dirt road he had never seen anyone else nor a trace that anyone had been there other than himself and he gladly planned on keeping it this way. The alone time out in the rawness of nature reenergized him.

As Will picked up and swung his pack around his side and onto his back, he turned and looked up at the high peaks. He thought to himself that he would not return again to his hideaway until the following spring. He had other locations he preferred for his wintertime outdoor activities. He continued his pause and scanned over the mountains in the distance, admiring their beauty. He let out a sigh and noticed the moisture from his breath in the air, swirling outwards and fading away. He turned back to his camp and did a quick scan to be sure nothing was left behind and then started his trek down the mountain to return to his Jeep.

Will enjoyed the journey down just as much as he did hiking up. His eyes would be darting back and forth discovering new mysteries hidden amongst the trees with each adventure he took to his secret location. He would imagine what these woods were like several hundred years back. Maybe even several thousand years back. *Were there tribes that hunted here? Was this even a thick-wooded mountain back then*? Will always thought he belonged in a different century, perhaps when new settlers were pioneering across the west. He wondered how well he would have managed knowing how many had perished on their journey westward in search of fortune.

Will's hunger began to control his thoughts as he rounded one of the final switchbacks coming off of the mountain. All he had brought for his breakfast was a granola bar that he had eaten earlier when he began to pack up his camp. He always brought a spare as emergency food if he got lost or stranded from an injury. He assumed getting lost would never happen since he knew the woods so well from exploring. However, some of the most experienced outdoorsmen become prey to injury from unexpected falls or even wildlife. He chose not to eat his spare granola bar as this was not an emergency. The several hours it took to climb up was cut in half on the descent. He had figured if his timing was correct, and it usually was, he would arrive home in time for a late lunch. For Sunday lunches his mother usually made a large pot of hearty chicken and rice soup and grilled-cheese sandwiches for the whole family and many times a house full of guests as well. His mother, Beth, knew he would be returning from his camping trip around that time. The thought of the food made his stomach ache and grumble. He decided to think of other things to take his mind off of the food.

His thoughts began to fall back to the state of the country and his situation. Even though it was the depressing news is what drove him out into nature, spending some time out allowed him to keep a neutral mindset on the situation now. He thought of the chain of events over the past few years and how it had molded his life. Will had been packing his things in his college dorm room after finishing up his sophomore year when he received a call. His uncle broke the news to him that his father had been killed in a car accident. His father had been a long-time head pastor at a small church in Oakhurst. His father had taught him everything. Will knew he was basically a clone of his father. It was after the funeral that Will drove up into the mountains with his dress slacks and shirt and black tie still on. That was the first time he came upon his secret camping spot. Will's father had always known about the somber moods that would bring Will down for a time because he also dealt with them. Many times his father gave him the advice to drop everything and go out into the wilderness to get rid of the mood, knowing how much Will enjoyed the outdoors.

Will had every intention of returning to college for his junior year, however, the economy determined differently for him. His father had kept a life insurance policy that allowed them to keep their home that was nestled on a few acres outside of town. However, Will's mother's income from working in a local gift shop that featured all-things Yosemite National Park was not enough to pay for the rising tuition costs. Will had spent a week later in the summer in San Jose looking for a job to pay for tuition on his own but found many of the retail businesses around his campus had recently become vacant or couldn't afford to take on an employee. They weren't able to survive an economic downturn caused by major tax increases and forced costs by the government, especially when most of their clientele were students who were home for the summer. The few offers Will received were very low paying, under-the-table, part time jobs that even if they could have covered tuition, they would have never covered his living expenses as well. The work situation in his hometown of Oakhurst quickly mirrored the bigger city area of San Jose. Will had no choice but to stay living at home. He was now twenty-four years old and there was no end in sight to the economic turmoil that plagued the country and college could not be seen on the distant horizon. Will eventually came up with the idea to be a handy-man around town. It didn't pay all that well but it helped he and his mother get by. He became a jack-of-all-trades when it came to repairs. He did carpentry, fixed household appliances, plumbing, and whatever anyone asked him to fix. He could usually figure out some make-shift way to fix something.

Will arrived back at his Jeep. He noticed the splattered bits of mud spreading outwards from his tires. He knew he should wash it but since the Jeep was multiple shades of green, brown and rust he figured it would blend in and go mostly unnoticed by others. Will placed his pack in the back seat. He stood with the driver's side door open remaining still and quiet, turning his head from side to side listening for any distant noise. It was his ritual prior to starting up the vehicle. He always liked to be sure no one was nearby on the dirt road when he arrived at it, emerging out of the forest. He was satisfied and climbed in. The Jeep rumbled to a start and he began maneuvering back and forth out of his tight parking space and slowly made his way back towards the road. He kept his window down and music off just in case he might hear any vehicles. He paused about fifty feet back and shifted his head back and forth examining both directions of the dirt road. He again was satisfied he was alone and crept forward and slid through the two tall pines.

As he arrived back onto the highway that led to Oakhurst he noticed his fuel gauge. He had just under half of a tank of gas. He knew he shouldn't be driving this much. It was only a year ago that gas prices reached record-setting highs. Taxes on oil companies were at a record-setting peak. Every part of the process of making gasoline was taxed in some way. The government stopped allowing the oil companies to drill in new areas and supplies lowered. The government stepped in and set price controls which caused the oil companies to operate at a loss. Some of the CEO's stopped taking pay and then stockholders stopped taking dividends so employees could be retained and still get paid. Regardless, within six months mass layoffs began. The government began subsidizing the oil companies to keep them afloat. Company presidents could be seen in the news making statements against the government telling them if they stopped trying to run their business, thousands would have been able to keep their jobs. The government fired back that their intervention by subsidizing the companies was the only reason their companies were still in operation. Will had followed the situation in the news and couldn't understand how the government officials didn't see that it was all their intervention that caused the mess in the first place. He figured the false lower gas prices couldn't last forever. He tried to keep his Jeep full as much as he could afford. He also kept a ten-gallon container filled that he stored at home. Will noticed the time and figured he would fill up on gas later that day knowing his mother and other family were over by now waiting for him with lunch ready.

Will also remembered Lea would be over this Sunday as well. His thoughts lingered on Lea. She was a beautiful young woman that he had grown up going to school and church with. He had never talked to her much while they were younger. It wasn't until he ended up at her family's house to work on their furnace the previous winter that they started talking. Lea's parents, Alejandro and Juana, practically threw her in the basement with him after he began looking at the furnace. They kept trying to initiate a relationship between them ever since that day. Alejandro and Juana even became friends with Will's mother, which was why they would be at his house today for lunch.

Will turned on to the long rock and dirt driveway that curved back and forth through a patch of old oaks and pines and continued along the side of their ranch-style home. He could see through the front window and into the living room as he drove up. He saw Lea. She had her deep black hair pulled back into a pony-tail. He could tell she had put on make-up on what he thought was already perfect bronze toned skin. Her eyes radiantly highlighted. He had figured that the effort was for him and a smile formed on his face as he parked alongside the house.

*****

Will watched out the front window as Lea and her parents piled into their car and took off down the drive and out of site. Will was thinking it was time that he should sit Lea down and tell her how he felt. He was nearly one hundred percent sure she felt the same way, however, he considered she might just be overly polite and could just be respecting her parent's desires for her. Will's mother was walking past the front room and glanced over and noticed Will still staring out the front window.

"Oh my! Is that smoke I see coming from your ears?" she said.

Will chuckled at his mother's question.

"Yeah, I suppose I'm doing some thinking." He was still staring out the front window.

"Well, if you gave me three guesses as to what you were thinking so hard about, I would guess the same thing all three times," her tone raised at the end of her sentence suggesting that she was prying for more information.

Will turned from the window and saw his mother disappear into the kitchen.

"You'd probably be right all three times," he yelled out so she could hear him.

"Well I think she is an excellent choice. Your father would be very proud and happy for you," she yelled back.

Will chuckled again, this time to himself. His mother always amused him.

Will's mother, Beth, was a kind, humorous and very strong woman. She had been strengthened over the many years by her faith in God and her husband's encouragement. She had endured several miscarriages before and after Will's birth as her and her husband tried to build a family. The many losses took a toll on her but she recovered with the help of her husband, the community, her faith, and her responsibility to raise her baby son. Beth had a natural intuition that allowed her to read others quite well. Her son was no exception. She could read him better than anyone else. Beth was quite an extrovert and it showed by how often her home was full of guests. Will did not mind, although he did enjoy his alone time. He knew he had the nearby wilderness for that.

Chapter Three

The sounds of voices chattering and ice clinking against glass filled the large private theater. A man who appeared to be in his late 30's stood next to a tall cocktail table. Next to him was a blond woman. She leaned against the table staring down at her drink, swirling the ice around every few seconds. They appeared to be a couple. He wore a tuxedo, as did every other man in the room. Just like every other man in the room, the only item worn that was unique was the watch. They were all very nice tuxedos, however, the layman's eye might think they all had the same designer. She wore a formal gold colored dress. It appeared to be made by a special designer. There were reflective adornments that peppered the dress which made the wearer appear to sparkle under even the slightest amount of light. As with every other woman in the room, everything about her dress and jewelry was unique. Large and bright diamonds were common throughout the room on the ears, necks, and wrists of the ladies. There was probably more money in clothing and jewelry in the room than most could hope to save in a lifetime.

The man's gaze concentrated on different clusters of people around the large room. He listened to each group and then turned his head to focus on the next, hoping to hear subjects of his expertise that he could walk over to join in on. She appeared bored. Occasionally, others in the room would walk up to the two and talk with the man about important sounding topics. As they approached she would look up with a smile and appear interested but she was still not. She wanted to be entertained beyond what this party was offering. Perhaps it wasn't the type of people she had expected. Maybe she had been to so many similar parties that they no longer gave a rise to any excitement in her.

A buzz from a speaker clicked on and a familiar microphone tapping sound from a sound test pounded from the speaker. "Ladies and gentlemen," a man across the room began to speak and the chattering voices ceased. "I'm glad you are all enjoying yourselves. We must now begin the business portion of our gathering. The final preparations over the last couple of years have now brought us to within mere months of implementation."

The room erupted into applause. The man with the golden lady now attached to his arm made his way through the groups of people to the microphone.

"Indeed," he said, leaning into the microphone.

The woman was now smiling next to him. No doubt she was eating up the fact that all attention was on her man.

"I commend you all on your patience. We have been planning for this for decades. I must tell you," he built in a dramatic pause, "the planning is over." His volume was quickly rising. "It is now time to put this plan into action!"

The room, once again, erupted into applause.

Chapter Four

WWNL interview
Late October 2036

"For our feature on this evening's news Marcus is speaking with a local business owner right here in Manhattan. Marcus?" Ava said with a smile.

"Thank you, Ava. I'm here with Ralph, owner of The Gourmet Grocer. Ralph is among New York City's many grocery business owners that have recently been contacted by the government about oversight and management changes that go into effect this coming week. Ralph and the other grocers will now have nearly every business decision going through a government committee. Ralph and many of his customers are worried that the government will start instituting rationing on food. Ralph, what is your take on all of this?"

"Thank you, Mr. Braden. Well, I believe the only reason that the government chose to basically take over the grocery business is because they want to control what gets out to the public. I see no other reason to choose this industry over any other." Marcus noticed Ralph was very well-spoken. He very much preferred his interviews to go smoothly like this one was.

"Ralph, if you don't mind me asking, how's business? I only ask because one might think that the reason the government would do something like this is to keep a failing business afloat."

"Yes, it would be logical to think that since that has been a past practice of our government and other governments around the world. However, the grocery business is doing fine. People will always need food and as long as owners and management of a company know how to run a grocery store, then they should have no problem keeping a sustainable revenue. Honestly, profits have been down but, we still have profits. With the shaky economy, there has been businesses closing and our inventory variety has decreased. Thankfully, there are alternative products we still have. Some are cheaper, but there are still options. To me, these actions by the government are nothing more than steps toward an ultimate goal of a complete takeover of my business and all grocery stores."

"Ralph, were you aware of the decision in Congress about a month ago that increased the government's power to manage businesses that they considered to be a necessity to the country's infrastructure?"

"Uhh...no, Marcus, I don't believe I knew about that." Ralph raised an eyebrow.

"Well, I'd like to remind folks that a little over a month ago, WWNL reported on the matter along with a story about the government confiscating the assets of charity organizations. Ralph, you may not have noticed much in the news because Congress pushed this item through both the House and the Senate all in one evening. To me, it sounds like they didn't want the public to know.

"Yes," Ralph chimed back in. "It must've been pushed through really fast because I always watch the news and I never saw anything on the matter."

"Yes, Ralph, it's very unfortunate," Marcus said as he turned from Ralph to look into the camera. "It was only a few weeks ago I made some comments on the decisions. Our viewers will remember that I predicted that very soon we would see government takeovers happening. I, however, predicted food distribution would be the first to go, with the intent being the trucking companies that distributed the food around the country. I did not imagine that grocery stores would have been taken over, but I suppose they are a part of food distribution to the public. For our viewers, what is your opinion? Is the prediction that the government will start rationing food like Ralph and other owners think is a possibility, something for the public to worry about? Go onto WWNL's website to weigh in on the matter. Thank you Ralph for taking time to be here with us. Stay tuned to WWNL throughout this week and next for more on how the government will utilize this new power they voted to themselves. I'm Marcus Braden reporting from on the street in Manhattan. Back to you, Ava."

Chapter Five

WWNL Interview
November 2036

"Many of our viewers will remember our guest today as we followed his steady rise to infamous business success. Son of European immigrants that fled economic crisis a few decades back. Marek Dominski, now one year shy of 40 years old, is the CEO of Dominski International. His company's beginnings were from the long time Wall Street investing icon, The City Mutual. Since Mr. Dominski's takeover in majority ownership and becoming CEO, the company has seen a mass expansion unprecedented by most financial experts. During the long-term market recession, Mr. Dominski's company has watched their stock prices skyrocket."

Marcus turned from a camera and readjusted in his seat. The camera panned out. He now faced Marek Dominski. Three cameras sat across from them. Their two chairs sat angled towards the middle camera. Marek sat straight and confidently. He appeared comfortable and natural in front of the camera. He had one leg propped up on the other and laid one arm across his lap. This made his expensive A. Lange & Söhne watch easily visible to Marcus and the cameras. Marcus had glanced at the watch many times as he and Marek chatted prior to the interview beginning. He guessed it cost no less than $110,000 for the artful masterpiece. Marek had neatly trimmed dark hair. It appeared there wasn't a single strand out of place. His custom-tailored suit and power-red silk tie were probably priced just as much as the watch.

"Welcome, Mr. Dominski."

"Thanks for having me again, Marcus. Always a pleasure," Marek said. He had only a slight accent remaining. Having spent most of his life in the U.S., his speech had acclimated greatly compared to his parents. "Remember Marcus, you can call me Marek. I think I've told you that every time I come on your program." Marek and Marcus both chuckled.

"Marek," Marcus said with emphasis referencing the previous comment, "the U.S. is entering its' sixth year of an economic depression and your company has only been succeeding, seemingly untouched by the poor economy. How is this possible?"

"Well," Marek began with another chuckle, "we certainly don't always succeed. I know our stock price probably makes it look otherwise, but we have our failures. I just make sure that our successes more than outweigh the failures. We are an international, multi-industry conglomerate."

"That's a mouthful," Marcus added.

Marek continued without skipping a beat, "Even if there was worldwide economic collapse, there will still be some industries that do well. We have diversified investments across so many companies and industries that there is no way for me to remember them all. Pharmaceuticals in the U.S. and Europe, manufacturing in Southeast Asia, mining in Russia and China are some of our major ones."

"What makes you so confident in the places you invest? How do you know they'll be a success?" Marcus asked.

"I've built a time machine," Marek joked. He and Marcus laughed. "No, it just takes lots of research. Research on the company's history and their goals and plans for the future. Research on the individuals that run the company. We try to learn absolutely everything we can. There will always be risk. There is no way to avoid it. We aim to minimize it with education."

"About a month ago, I interviewed a grocery store owner," Marcus said. "His particular industry is seeing a government takeover. What are your thoughts? Any worries?"

"Obviously, there are worries and questions anytime something like this happens. My company has dealt with some of these issues with governments around the world. Is it a buyout? Is it a managing takeover? Is it industry wide or is it just the one company?" Marek asked the questions hypothetically. "Each situation could mean a different thing. Yes, most of the time it means a loss in some way for the ownership, but there are a few rare times that the stock stays strong. Again, we research everything we possibly can. I have many people with retirements in our mutual funds or that own some of our stock that I must consider as well in making a decision to hold or sell our interest."

"Marek, what do you think this means, not just for the investor, but for the citizens of the U.S.?"

"Honestly, my gut tells me we shouldn't worry. Dominski International doesn't have anything in the way of grocery stores, but we do have some stake in the food industry. We have heard the rumors of the expansion of the federal government taking over more in the food related industries and Dominski International has made the decision to continue to hold all these assets. We obviously will monitor the situation, but that is business as usual for us. Currently, all legislation coming out of Washington is for power of managing authority. Those situations usually don't hurt stock prices. I imagine they are just trying to prevent more people becoming unemployed."

"Interesting points. I have my worries, however," Marcus said.

Marek had a big smile. "Oh, I know Marcus. You've made that quite clear in your newscast."

"Good to know you watch the program," Marcus shot back with a smile. His eyebrows furrowed as he became serious, "It's just the quick and secret actions done by congress to accomplish these overreaches doesn't add up for it to be for protecting the industry and jobs. If they are acting to protect, why not make it public?"

"You make interesting points as well. I look at it more from the business perspective, though," Marek answered.

"Marek, always a pleasure to have you on the program. I know our viewers love to follow you as well. You are a hero in the business world."

"Too kind. Thank you. Always a pleasure to be here," Marek said with a smile.

"Before we go," Marcus said as he pointed to Marek, "any hot stock tips for our viewers?"

Marek peered off beyond Marcus for a moment and then answered with a shrug of his shoulders, "buy low, sell high."

Chapter Six

February 2037

Will sat on the aging couch in the living room with his legs propped up on the ottoman. Frayed fibers lined the edges of the pillows. They had given under pressure as many bodies over the years had plopped their weight down on the couch. His legs were draped with a thick blanket quilted by his mother. Another one of his mother's quilted masterpieces was wrapped around his shoulders. Heavy curtains completely covered the large picture-window that viewed out the front yard and beyond to the beautiful mountain views. Had the curtains been hung aside, a view of the distant moonlit high mountain peaks could be seen through the clear night sky. Even with the curtains being drawn shut, the icy winter air still pierced through the large picture window as if it were a fog bank slowly creeping into a mountain valley. A fire flickered from the room's side fighting back the cold while providing some warmth and low light. A wooden lamp sat upon a matching wooden end table beside the couch providing sufficient light to the half of the room opposite of the glowing fireplace. The other half of the room where the fireplace was located still housed dark corners only briefly lit by the flickering flames.

Will stared down at an outdoor survival book in his lap. It was well-worn as this was not his first time reading it. When he wasn't reading the book it was stored in his rusty Jeep for his mountain excursions and it always traveled with him up the mountains in his pack, which contributed to the rough edges and rounded-off corners. Along with the book, he religiously followed the author online. He would watch all his videos he posted about survival and Will would practice different survival techniques on his trips out in the woods. He quickly shut the book and glanced up at the clock. He had to hold his gaze and narrow his eyes for a moment before his eyes readjusted to the distance so he could tell the time. He guessed that he had been reading for a couple of hours. He decided he should start his ritual of readying himself for bed. He wanted to get an early start on the next days tasks.

Will's mother had decided to spend most of the winter at her brother's house in town. Will and his mother's home was just outside of the city gas lines and their heat was from a large propane tank. With fuel costs at an all-time high, the two had decided this arrangement would work best. Beth's brother, David, was away from his home most of the year with his job sending him all over the country and all over Europe as well. He liked the idea of his sister watching after things for him. Beth had been allowed to stay on at the gift shop. The owner, Mr. Jacobs, knew she and her son depended on the income and was fine keeping her and a couple of others in his employ as long as customers still came through. It was also to their advantage that Will had used his skills to fix things at the small store and at the owner's home from time to time. From her brother's centrally located home, Beth only had a short walk to work and didn't have to drive at all to get anywhere around town.

Will was comfortable with chopping firewood for most of his heat and only running the central heating system to keep it warm enough to prevent the water pipes from freezing and cracking. He split his time in between his own home and his relatives. Many of his jobs were in town and staying at his uncle's was quite convenient. He also enjoyed taking charge of his own house. There was always plenty to do on their large property and at the house. Will always had a running to-do list in his head.

Will thought of Lea as he readied himself for bed. He had finally worked in a time to be frank with her about his intentions. At the beginning of winter, they had decided they would be together. This made him smile as he thought about that long evening conversation. In the midst of the collapsing civilization around them, she had the power to free him from his gloomy moods.

Will unrolled his sleeping bag onto the couch and unzipped it open. He moved his hands back and forth over the length of the bag smoothing it down flat. He switched off the lamp and picked up his pillow from the side of the couch. With one single movement, he placed it down while he swung his legs up to the couch and fell down into place on the sleeping bag. He zipped himself in. The remnants of the fire was a slowly pulsating glow. There were no more flames to be seen. Will watched the glow slowly fade as his eyes grew heavy. Each blink grew longer and longer as the minutes passed. He finally gave in and fell fast asleep, not realizing how much his life would soon be quickly changing.

*****

The next morning Lea woke early. She had spent the previous afternoon and evening with her parents reorganizing their store of home-canned fruits and vegetables and then turned their latest purchase from the local butcher into home-made beef jerky. Lea's mother, Juana, had come up with the recipe on her own and it was an instant family hit.

"Oh, it's nothing," Juana would blow off compliments. "I'm sure the recipe is stuck in my brain from something my mother taught me."

"Mom! You told me you never made beef jerky with your mother!" Lea always challenged back.

It was a fruitless argument that happened anytime a compliment came on the popular recipe. She wanted her mother to get credit for something so pride-worthy and for her mother to stop being so modest about it.

With the previous day's activities keeping her at home rather than hanging out with Will, Lea had turned in early which was why she awake now during the dark of the early morning preparing her breakfast. Lea carefully picked up her freshly toasted bagel from the toaster with the tips of her thumb and finger and dropped it on her plate. She quickly put the tips of her fingers in her mouth to cool the sting from the hot bagel. She took the knife and meticulously spread cream cheese on one half of the bagel and then spread peanut butter on the other half. It was a morning favorite of hers. She started doing the combination of cream cheese and peanut butter because when she had only one of the two, she would always crave the other once done.

Lea sat in the kitchen with the t.v. across in the living

on with the volume low. She could hear a door open from down the hall and wondered if she had the volume too high. Her father, Alejandro, stepped around the corner with his morning eyes mostly closed.

"Uhhhgh," He moaned. "Lea? Why are you up so early?" He slightly stumbled over his words as his body was not quite awake yet.

"I went to bed too early so now I'm up for the day. Am I being too loud?" Lea answered.

"No, I couldn't hear you. I woke up and was getting a drink of water and noticed the light coming from under our bedroom door and thought we accidentally left it on. I'm going back to sleep..." His sentence trailed off and he turned around and dragged his feet as he went back down into the dark hall.

"G'night," Lea whispered loudly as he had turned to go back to bed.

Lea only heard a grunt in return. She turned to look at the clock on the microwave and figured Will was probably not even up yet at this hour. She knew he was up early many days but was not sure of his plans for this day since they did not spend the evening together as was becoming their custom. Lea kept looking down at her fingers. They were worn rough from the packaging and vacuum sealing work from the previous day. She guessed they packaged around six dozen bags of the jerky. It was the most they had ever done but they all knew it still would not last them until their next jerky making day.

Lea finished her breakfast, placed her plate by the sink, and then switched off the kitchen light. She maneuvered her way across the room to the couch in the living room by the dim light of the TV. She turned the volume down still further since she was now closer but still kept it up enough so she could still hear. She was sitting on the edge of the couch leaning forward towards the screen with her legs crossed. The leg still on the ground was anxiously bouncing up and down. Lea was watching the ultra-early morning news broadcast which was re-runs from the late evening news from the night before. Her mind would wander occasionally to chores or Will. Her attention was jolted back to the broadcast when she realized it was live and the familiar voice of Marcus Braden, the normal evening news broadcaster, was speaking quite emotionally on riots.

Marcus on in the morning? Riots?

Lea would hear news of riots on a regular basis these days, however, it would still always concern her since her small hometown was situated on a well-traveled road.

"The state of unrest in our country can no longer be downplayed or ignored," Marcus's voice rattled the speakers. Lea pushed the 'volume down' button down a couple of times and moved off the couch and knelt in front of the TV so she could still hear and not wake her parents.

Chapter Seven

WWNL Breaking News
February 2037

Marcus quickly shot up in bed. The ringing phone in his dreams eventually roused him enough to make him realize the ring wasn't only in his head.

"Hello?" Marcus's hoarse voice cracked as he answered with a question. He took a few sips of water from the glass that sat on his nightstand to help his voice return to normal. He recognized the voice on the other end as a member of his news crew but couldn't remember his name. It must be this man's turn on the midnight shift to monitor for any breaking stories.

"Marcus, I know it's late or early...whatever, but the VP's want you in. A lot happened in the night and they want you on first thing in the morning to report it."

"What's happened?" Marcus's mind was racing through the possibilities. He hadn't worked the day before and turned in somewhat earlier than his usual the evening before and wondered what he had missed. As he thought about it, he realized he didn't watch the news at all the previous day.

"What didn't happen last night? Everything you've been talking about is happening. It's all gonna change. Just get in as soon as you can and I'll bring you up to date."

"Be there within the hour," Marcus quickly answered and hung up, not listening for anymore. *Everything you've been talking about is happening*. He understood the meaning and what was about to unfold.

*****

Marcus tipped his coffee mug all the way up above his face to finish the last few remaining drops. He held out the mug and let James fill it up again from the freshly made pot from the studio office break room. Marcus noticed the name badge hanging from his neck right as he walked into the offices. He remembered after seeing 'James' that he hated to be called 'Jim'.

"I'm sure you saw how much the markets dropped," James said.

Marcus hadn't but he didn't say anything.

"The House and the Senate held emergency sessions last night. Unanimous votes. Even the President has already signed it," James rattled off as he held out the press briefs sent over from the WWNL reporter in Washington D.C. James continued to speak as Marcus began to read the reports.

"They put a stop to trading just before market close. No after hours trades could go through. The government is taking over everything they can. Food companies, farms, distribution, oil companies, utilities, a slew of other major companies that have lots of employees...even banks!" James exclaimed and his eyes widened at Marcus.

"It has media outlets listed in here," Marcus glanced up at James with his eyes as he spoke. His eyes returned to the pages and James answered.

"I saw that. Wait 'til you get to the part about the private company they are contracting to run all this. It's some new corporation that apparently has all the means to implement this and they are already prepped to begin. This plan had to have been in the works for a while if they are ready to go with this. This is what you've been saying, Marcus!"

"We need to be pushing this information all day before they stop us. Where's Ken?"

"He should be in soon. I called him after talking to you. Do you really think they'll try to stop us?"

Marcus looked at James and nodded his head. Regardless of their political opinions, Marcus knew the bosses and Ken couldn't let the biggest news story pass by the network because it didn't support their views. However, if the government would soon be running things he thought that they might be inclined to let their unpopular actions go unannounced. Marcus considered that he would have to convince Ken to get on board with operating how they wanted regardless of what the government dictated to them. He would convince Ken and then Ken would have to convince the V.P.'s. Marcus ran the scenario through his head.

I hope it goes that easily.

*****

Marcus sat at his desk in the nearly empty office. It was much quieter than during the day. All that could be heard was the continuous hum of fluorescent light bulbs and cooling fans on computers. He flipped through the pages of the report and scribbled down notes on another page. He was startled as James slammed down more papers next to him on the desk.

"As if that wasn't enough," James said as he pointed to the pages Marcus was flipping through. "Increased rioting is happening pretty much everywhere. There's bits and pieces of these documents already on the internet and it's causing panic."

"Sounds like the beginnings of a revolution," Marcus returned.

"A revolution," James spoke the word as if it were an epiphany he was having and nodded his head slowly. After a brief pause as he stared off towards the big clock on the wall he spoke again, "Well, you are all set to be on the six-thirty broadcast. Whatever we get on there we'll loop throughout the morning so people will get it as they wake up across the West. We'll cut in with you if there's anything else that breaks on this. It's Ken's plan. Just got off the phone with him again. He should be in any minute now."

"I'm pretty much ready. I'll review what you just gave me to get some specifics." Marcus glanced at his watch and saw he had thirty minutes.

*****

"The state of unrest in our country can no longer be downplayed or ignored." The urgency was clear on Marcus's face and in his voice as he spoke. "If you are just joining us, the news of the government taking over the majority of the private sector has brought the country to a violent revolt. A couple of months ago the House and the Senate made the decision to increase their powers by taking over key management decisions in businesses they considered to be vital to the country's infrastructure. It now appears that was not enough for them. Farms, all food companies, all distribution, oil companies, all utilities, transportation, media outlets, many financial institutions, many other major employers...these are now all owned and controlled by the government and now all these citizens no longer own their businesses and can no longer make any decisions for them. The legislation also creates a private corporation that will run and manage everything under government guidance. It also states that the company will have military and police units to aid in the transition. There are reports from our WWNL teams across the country that some of these military units are already in place in large cities and have been working through the night to stop rioting and even stop protests before they begin. To clarify for everyone, this decision went through the House and the Senate late last evening and was passed unanimously and signed just hours ago by the President. These private soldiers were already in place and are reportedly stopping anyone protesting in opposition to the legislation, including peaceful protests. I'm being told we already have the text of the legislation posted on the main page of our website, which is listed on your screen. We'll bring you any information on this company that the government has contracted, including the name, as soon as we learn. Oh...and I'm just learning that the name of this company is Central Management Authority, Incorporated. They must have tucked the name in one of the final paragraphs of the legislation. Well, there you have it folks, Central Management Authority. That is the private company that appears to be the new governing authority of the United States. Please, everyone, be safe and be careful. There is widespread violence all over the country. Stay tuned to WWNL."

*****

Marcus left the studio to return to his desk. They had finished the live broadcast and he stayed to review it as a recording was edited and re-aired. Any other major news that morning from around the world would be sent out live and then the recording of Marcus would be broadcast again. Kenneth considered this news 'too big' to let any other network get higher ratings. Marcus kept his head buried in a stack of papers as he slowly walked back towards his desk. He sat down and continued reading the legislation. Just about every paragraph he read caused him to either shake his head or sigh in disappointment or do both. Someone clearing their throat with the intention of getting Marcus's attention startled him. He looked up and was surprised to see a well-dressed man sitting on the edge of his desk not even a foot from him. The man appeared to be younger than Marcus but still had graying hair on the sides of his head with dark black hair covering the rest. The man was shorter than Marcus, but most were against Marcus's height. He noticed he had the rough hands of a working man which didn't match the custom tailored suit which was typically worn by a lawyer or executive in this town.

Marcus opened his mouth and was just about to speak when the man began before he could.

"Puts a bad taste in your mouth?" The man pointed to

the stack of papers Marcus was holding and then extended his hand to Marcus. They shook hands but Marcus had still not spoken. His mind had been so focused on the news and the coffee was losing its effectiveness and exhaustion was beginning to set in. The well-dressed man broke the silence again. "Hello, Mr. Braden. I've been paying close attention to your work for quite a while and I think you and I should have a talk. I'm Thomas Allen."

Chapter Eight

Lea frantically dialed Will's number for the third time and again for the third time she only heard the ear-piercing tone and message that all circuits are busy and to "please try again later". She threw her phone down onto the couch next to her in frustration. The too-happy tone of that lady's voice didn't help her frustration. She figured there wasn't any way that many people were on the phone in the middle of the night jamming the network. *It must be shut down on purpose*, she thought. This worried her but also caused her to start running through scenarios in her head about how she could get to Will and his mother. She stood from the couch and began to pace back and forth in her living room as worst-case scenarios were running through her head. *What if riots happen here? What if we can't get food from the grocery store? What if I can't find Will? What if something has happened to Will?* She decided that worrying like she was currently doing wasn't going to solve anything and then sat back on the couch. She grabbed the remote and switched over to local news and began to nervously bite her finger nails.

*****

Will awoke to his phone alarm in the still-dark early morning. He sat leaning forward rubbing his eyes and face and greatly considered setting another alarm and getting a little more sleep. He began fumbling in the dark attempting to find the extra layers of clothing he laid by the side of the couch knowing it would be quite chilly in the early morning hours. After spending a couple of minutes putting on the extra layers of clothing, having to take a shirt off and turn it around and try again, he reluctantly switched on the lamp. He then switched on a small radio that sat next to the lamp and made his way to the fireplace. He moved the spark guard aside and brought his hand an inch over the coals and ash searching for heat. He took the fire iron and began poking at the coals hoping to see some red color to rebuild the fire with. He found a few and moved them together and began placing kindling on top. There was a small metal box filled with wood shavings and a couple of newspapers that sat on the edge of the tile by the fireplace. It flickered to life and Will placed some larger pieces of wood surrounding the flames. Once the fire was to a point that Will considered it self-sufficient, he placed the last remaining larger log that was in the house on top and replaced the spark guard. Bringing in more wood was one of the items on the running list in his head.

Will checked the time on his watch and wondered if Lea was awake this early. He went to his phone and typed out a message to Lea and hit send. He went to the kitchen to make breakfast, setting the phone down on the countertop.

He settled on cereal. It wasn't like he had many options.

They hadn't kept this house stocked with groceries. Most of the food he and his mother bought were kept at his uncle's house in town. There had been many mornings when Will was staying at their own house that he had dry cereal. He wasn't as prompt as his mother at replacing things like milk. Luckily, there was still some milk this morning. Maybe just enough for one more bowl tomorrow morning.

After washing his few dishes in the sink, Will returned to the living room to put his shoes on. He glimpsed his phone out of the corner of his eye as he passed it. He remembered he had texted Lea and stepped back and grabbed the phone to check for a response. A frown formed on his face when he noticed the warning message that his text was never sent in the first place. He attempted to send it again. The same warning message appeared and his face scrunched up further in frustration. As Will glanced up to the status area at the top of his phone's screen to check for service, the words "martial law" became a fleeting sound from the radio that distracted him from the phone. Still shoeless, Will quickly knelt by the radio and turned the volume up with one hand while slipping on his shoes with the other.

It was a morning talk show. Phrases such as "government corporation", "contract law enforcement" and "rationing" confused Will. What are they talking about? He had tied his shoes and stood up, beginning to think the two hosts were discussing imagined scenarios. It made Will think of the "War of the Worlds" radio broadcast from the 1930's and the panic it caused and how some people committed suicide over the fictional story. Will stared into the fire as he continued to listen to the broadcast.

The longer Will listened the more he started to believe

they may be talking about real news stories. Will decided to turn the t.v. on to the morning news to see if there was anything similar. He knew the radio talk show hosts could ramble on for hours about the most insignificant news story or their general suspicion of the intentions of most politicians. He tuned into one of the network's morning news broadcasts. They were covering all the same things he had heard on the radio. He quickly switched to a different network to find the same coverage. He recognized one of the locations in the footage they were showing. It was a few blocks from where he went to college in San Jose. Large generator-powered lights illuminated people burning buildings, overturning cars, and openly fighting what he thought were some oddly dressed SWAT officers. They were wearing the typical black tactical wear, but they also had blue and white patches on their chests. There was also a blue and white striped armband around each bicep area and a long blue and white stripe down the side of each leg. The news camera was not close enough to see what the chest patch had written on it but Will assumed it said 'SWAT'.

Will suddenly had a slight feeling of worry and fear overcome him. He wondered if there was any of the violence and chaos happening in his town. He immediately decided he wasn't going to wait to hear about it on the news and started gathering a few things to go get his mother and Lea and her family. With everything happening in the bigger city areas there would be no way they'd cover anything happening in Oakhurst.

Will went to the coat closet and grabbed the 12-gauge that sat on the top shelf along with a box of shells. He then went to the closet in his room and pulled a plastic tote that he used to organize and store all of his camping gear. On top was a gun case that held his Glock .45 caliber pistol. He grabbed it and an open box of bullets and then returned to the living room. He had kept his pistol magazine only loaded with about 6 or 7 bullets to not keep the spring compacted too much so he filled it the rest of the way. He took the guns to his Jeep and laid the shotgun against the front passenger seat with the barrel face down against the floor. He placed the pistol in the center console so both guns would be in easy reach if needed. Will looked around the property. An orange glow was beginning to lighten around him. He got in the Jeep and backed up from the side of the house and the continued reversing until he was in front of the door to the house.

Will stepped back inside the house and looked around to see if there was anything else he could think he might need if things took a turn for the worse in their little town. He knew he already had a first aid kit in the Jeep so he didn't get the one that was in the house. He filled two bottles of water in the kitchen and then figured he'd be fine with what he had. He hoped it wouldn't take too long to get to his mother and to Lea's house. As Will was rushing back out of the house he paused at the closet where he had retrieved the shotgun. He looked up at the .270 hunting rifle and decided to take it as well. He grabbed a box of bullets for it and a baseball bat that leaned against the back corner of the closet. He imagined the craziness he saw on the news and considered how mobs of people could get desperate and irrational when they wanted what you have. He wanted all the protection he could get if that is what he would encounter. The rifle and bat went on the floor of the back seat of the Jeep.

Chapter Nine

"Mr. Braden? Are you okay?" Thomas Allen questioned.

"I...I'm sorry," Marcus stammered. "I'm exhausted already for the day and my mind is elsewhere and you surprised me. I didn't even see you there when I walked up to my desk."

"I know," Thomas said with a chuckle. "Your face was buried in those papers." Thomas paused for a moment and looked down at the papers on Marcus's desk before beginning again. "Well, like I said I'm Thomas Allen. I'm not sure if you've heard of me or my work. I'm President of the American Rights Foundation. We call it the ARF."

Marcus cut him off, "Oh yes. I knew I recognized you. I've read some of your books and I read your online editorial from time to time."

"Good to hear," Thomas answered. "Before I get too much into what I want to talk to you about I would like to know what you think of my work. I think I already know the answer based on what I've seen you say on your segment. Are you generally in agreement with my writing?"

"Yes, of course. That's a good assessment of my work," Marcus said.

"Excellent. Is there a more private place to talk? I had hoped when I found your desk it would be inside of an office." Thomas glanced around at the open room. No desk in the area had any privacy.

"It's just the way all news offices seemed to be designed. There's a conference room out the back entrance," Marcus motioned to a door, "just down the hall."

*****

"Listen, Marcus, I hate to be so direct, especially since we just met, but I'm just going to put all the cards on the table for you. My organization has been anticipating what's happening right now for years now. I think you have too on some level, based on what you talk about on your program." Marcus nodded and Thomas continued, "We have had plans in place and now it is time to implement them. Given the current scenarios that are playing out, we think you can be a key element to fighting this."

"How so?" Marcus's eyes narrowed with some confusion.

"I don't want to go into too much detail here. I'd like you to come to my ranch in upstate in the next few days and you can meet some more people from The American Rights Foundation and we can go over some ideas. I know you are going to be quite busy here as our country begins to deconstruct." Thomas placed a card on the large conference table next to Marcus. "When you think you have some time to get away for about half a day give me a call."

Marcus slipped the card into his pocket.

"This seems a little vague," Marcus said.

"I know. But you now work for who I consider an enemy of my country. All news outlets are now controlled by the CMA. I'm not saying that I don't trust you. I just don't trust where we are to give you details here."

"A ranch, huh? Are you a rancher or the President of a big organization?" Marcus asked with a raised eyebrow and a half grin.

"Both," Thomas answered with a big smile. "I do most of my work with the Foundation from my home. I do my writing from home. It gives me plenty of time to oversee my ranch as well. Of course, I have many hands doing a lot of the day-to-day but I still am out fixing fences and feeding animals quite often. It's a part of my roots. My father left the ranch to me after he passed. Can you believe that he was the only black ranch owner in the entire county for his whole life?" Thomas didn't give Marcus any time to answer the question. "I think I might still be the only black ranch owner in the county. I've never kept track of that statistic like my father did. Anyways, most of the leadership for the Foundation is here in New York City and they like to join me on the ranch for meetings and such."

"Sounds nice," Marcus said. "You really aren't going to give me any more information?" He attempted to get anything more out of him.

Thomas shook his head and pointed to Marcus's pocket. "Don't wait too long. Give me a call in the next few days. With the violence that is happening, you might need to wait that long so it's safe enough to get out of the city. I think the CMA will forcefully settle the mobs down for the time being. People are either revolting or panicking quicker than I thought they would."

"How are you getting back to your ranch?" Marcus asked.

"I came in by air. I'll just need to make sure my route back to the building the helicopter is parked on is ok. There is no way of knowing what is going to happen to private aviation and airspace in the coming days, but if need be, I can send the helicopter for you when you come to my ranch. Given your prominent face and now your connection with the company that is taking over the country, I think you'll have some options to get to my ranch on your own. When you call, though, just let me know what you think from your end about road travel and we'll compare to our end and if it's looking bad then you'll come by helicopter. Don't hesitate to ask for it. People are going to be getting desperate and desperate people have the potential to do horrible things. Marcus, you need to keep all of this to yourself. Don't tell any co-workers, supervisors, and not even any friends. We can't be sure of what kind of people these are. I'm pretty sure we don't have the rights and freedoms we did yesterday. We all need to be careful."

*****

Marcus sat back at his desk considering what Thomas had said before leaving. *We think you can be a key element to fighting this...I'm pretty sure we don't have the rights and freedoms we did yesterday*. Marcus had predicted the government would take control of so many things but he wondered why a government corporation took over everything. *Was Thomas suggesting a total remaking of the United States? A completely new government? What did he and his foundation think was going to happen? What plans did they have for him*? Marcus was frustrated that he had to wait to ask all of these questions and to get the answers.

Chapter Ten

Will sped down the road towards town and slowed down to the speed limit as he reached the edge of town. The sun was fully above the horizon now. He tried calling his mother without any success as he left the house. He was pleasantly surprised to see things appeared to be normal here. Passing the grocery store, he noticed a couple of people jogging into the store. He wasn't surprised at that. News of bad weather approaching made people rush to the store so news of chaos nationwide would most certainly do the same. He made a mental note that once he got to the others and once they decided what they were all going to do, that he wanted to make a stop at the grocery store for some extra food, as long as he had someone else with him to watch after the Jeep full of weapons. He didn't want someone seeing them in his Jeep and decide that they needed them.

Will turned onto the street where his uncle's house was. He figured it was still early enough that his mother wouldn't have walked to work yet. They were close together so he could always drive there next. He pulled into the driveway. His mother opened the front door as he was getting out of the Jeep.

"Well, I'm guessing you've seen the news?" His mother asked as he walked up to her.

"Yeah, on the radio. I wasn't sure if it was real at first so I checked every news channel and it was all showing the same stuff. What do you think we should do? I was thinking we all would get back to our place where there are fewer people around. There are riots and looting all over the country and I think it is bound to happen here too if it is so widespread like they are saying on the news. Our place seems like a good place to hold up. It's not on a main road."

His mother was smiling. "I think you are right. What do you mean by 'we all'?"

"Oh..uh...well, I was meaning Lea and her parents too. That is if you are fine with it? You know I've stored up a bunch of survival food for an emergency."

Her smile widened and she put a hand up to stop him. "Yes, I am fine with it. I was thinking all the same things. Are you going over to their house?"

"I was going to right after I talked to you. There doesn't seem to be any cell service so I can't call them. Have you tried your phone? He asked.

"I don't have any service either," She answered.

"It's weird. I don't understand why there wouldn't be any service at all."

"I don't either. You should go over there now. They are probably all still home. I'm going to gather some of the things I have here. I need to go by the store to let Mr. Jacobs know I probably won't be in until we figure out what is going on around the country."

"Things look quiet around here. Nothing like what I was seeing on the news." Will said. "I brought some guns just in case. Do you want one to have with you?" Will asked.

"No. I actually am already carrying your uncle's pistol." She opened her coat part way to reveal the holstered pistol. "I've had it by my bedside since I've been staying here alone some nights. I'll carry it with me as I run to the store and then head home.

"Good," Will said and then hugged his mother. "I'll go now to see if I can get Lea and her family to come out to our place."

"Be careful. Don't get involved in any rioting," Beth said to her son.

"Mom!" Will shook his head and chuckled. "I'm not out looking for a fight. I'm trying to make sure we all get someplace safe to hunker down."

"I know. I know. I'm just being a mother. Your mother."

*****

Will pulled up to Lea's house and parked on the street. The driveway still had vehicles in it. Will hoped that meant everyone would still be home. Before Will even reached the driveway as he walked towards the house Lea came bursting out of the door running full speed to Will.

"Whoa!" Will yelled out unintentionally as Lea crashed into him with a big hug.

Lea looked up at Will and spoke quickly, without any pause. "Sorry. It's just with all the news and I haven't been able to get a hold of you all morning. I was worried."

She gave him another tight squeeze and then stepped back quickly, looking at his side.

"Why do you have that on your waist?" She asked with a quizzical look on her face.

"It's my pistol. I don't want to take any chances. People are acting crazy on the news and that could happen here too." He answered in an almost rehearsed manner. "I have more guns in the Jeep. I just covered them with some blankets and locked it so I think they should be fine. Are your parents here too? I have something I want to talk to you all about."

"Yeah, they're here. They slept in, but they are up now. I just told them a little bit ago what has been happening and they are watching the news right now," Lea said.

Will and Lea walked inside the house and found Lea's parents parked in front of the t.v. Will had gotten to know Lea's parents quite a bit over the last few months. Alejandro had retired fairly early in life. About fifteen years earlier, he worked in maintenance for the county and had gotten injured. A fellow co-worker had backed a truck into the maintenance shop and ran into Alejandro as he worked on a different truck. He received a moderate insurance payout. He was unable to work for the better part of a year while he recovered. During his now abundant free time he decided to invest the insurance money. He gave most of it to a money management firm, knowing they would need to be conservative in order to have money during his recovery. He took a small chunk to try his chances in the stock market. He studied and studied and studied every investment he chose to make, no matter how big or small. The studying paid off as his account value continued to rise and rise.

He returned to work ten months later and was beginning to contemplate retirement. He had never imagined a scenario in his life where he'd be retiring so young. He continued investing, being successful across his diversified self-managed portfolio. He didn't even spend a full year back at work before departing. Now newly retired, he adjusted his thinking and decided to stop being risky. They shifted all their money into the safest modes of investment they could think of. In addition, they stayed living the same way they always had. They had many discussions about upgrading their living situation and decided if they were going to stay retired that they should stay in the same house.

"Mr. and Mrs. Navarro?" Will asked to get their attention.

Without taking his eyes off of the t.v., Alejandro said, "Will, I've told you many times to call me by my white American name, Al."

Will laughed, "Sorry...Al."

"Alejo! How can you joke at a time like this? Hi, Will. It's good to see you. I'm glad you came over today." Juana said. "Lea was so worried. I think she was having a panic attack."

"I can believe that," Will said as he smiled and winked at Lea.

Lea smacked Will's arm.

"Ow! What was that for?" Will asked jokingly.

Will enjoyed the light humor in the room. It lightened the mood. He loved Alejandro's sense of humor. However, in light of the events unfolding around them, Will still wanted to steer the conversation more serious.

"So...Al...what do you think about all the violence happening?"

"It's scary and crazy. It seems quiet here still. Small

town where most people know most people, so it makes sense." He finally turned from the t.v. and looked at Will, "I do think it will happen here too eventually. If not by people that live here then it'll be those people." He pointed to the t.v. "They are panicking is what's happening. They are looting because they are scared and they don't feel prepared for whatever is going to happen now that we are under martial law."

"I heard that mentioned this morning but didn't know if it had happened for sure," Will said. "I think you are right that the rioting and looting will be here in our town too. That's why I came here. I think you three should come stay with us at our house. I just talked to my mom about it and she had the same idea as me."

Alejandro looked to Juana. Having been married for years they could communicate without speaking quite well.

"We'll need to talk about this first, Will," Alejandro said and Juana nodded her head as he said it.

"I understand," Will answered and Alejandro and Juana stepped out of the living room.

Lea turned down the volume of the t.v. and turned to Will, "Do you really think it will get that bad here?"

"I do. To be honest, I'm surprised that it isn't like that now. Some of the places they are showing on the news are small towns and it looks no different than the riots and looting they are showing in L.A. What do you think of my idea? Our place is isolated and all of us together could keep good watch over things."

"I like it. Of course, I am a little biased." Lea winked at Will as she answered, "I'm not sure how my parents are going to feel. I could see them going either way on this. They definitely won't like leaving our house empty for so long."

Will smiled and answered, "I'm glad you like the idea. Maybe you could help influence your parents if they are leaning towards staying here. Yes, I am biased as well wanting you there but I really do want your whole family to be safe. I really think it's going to get rough. If people begin to flee the big cities then I think they'll head for the hills." Will held up his fingers to make quotation marks. "Our little town is the hills to some people and to others it'll be on the way to the hills. Desperate people fleeing their homes might see the chaos as a reason to loot and riot. Just the fear of the change that has happened already is probably part of the reason people are rioting and looting in the bigger cities. Our property is off the main road. I don't think people will easily happen upon it."

Lea stared pensively towards the floor. Will noticed she appeared sad now and attempted to comfort her. After a few minutes of asking more questions and thinking through some of Will's answers, she began to come to terms with the situation for the time being. Her parents called her back to their room where they had been discussing the idea of holding up at Will and his mother's home to get her opinion. Will turned the volume up on the t.v. so he could hear if there was anything new being reported.

Chapter Eleven

Will and Alejandro finished packing Will's Jeep with as much as they could fit. Alejandro and Juana took a little more convincing from Lea and Will to make the decision to go. What brought them to the decision was food. Will told them he had quite the store of survival food. He let them know he was into survival and prepping and had at least a year or so supply of food stored up. He had been buying it over the last several years and had also won a few months supply worth in an online contest on a survival blog he read. The long stretch of the poor economy caused him to increase his planning and prepping. The news had continued to discuss that morning the possibility of rationing under martial law and Alejandro wanted to make sure his family could eat. The economy was already in bad shape and he couldn't imagine it improving at any quickened pace with everything that was happening.

They moved on to loading one of the other vehicles in the driveway. Will and Alejandro kept having to remind Juana and Lea that a lot of the basics would be at the other house already. It wasn't like they were taking some tents out to the middle of nowhere and everything needed to live for a long period of time would need to be brought. Will said they should definitely take heirlooms and valuables too. If need be, they could always make a trip back to their house. Lea made sure that all their food, including the jerky they had just made the day before, was packed in the car.

Juana was in tears as she got into the car. Will and Alejandro had been discussing a lot of different scenarios as they packed up the vehicles. They hoped for the best but planned for the worst. All the talk of worst case scenarios made Juana quite upset. Discussion on strategies for a stop at the grocery store is what had finally brought the tears. She couldn't believe that they wanted to bring guns to the grocery store. They had also talked about scoping out the parking lot before entering it and once there having two people guard the vehicles while the other two went in armed. Alejandro had to remind her what they had seen on the news that morning and had said that the evening before no one could have imagined what would happen through the night and this morning. They had watched suburban America turn into what looked like a war-torn middle-Eastern country in only a few hours.

*****

Wanting to get a look at the situation before entering the parking lot, their two-vehicle convoy slowly passed the first entrance into the grocery store parking lot and turned onto the side street to enter from the next parking lot access. Will had only seen a couple of people rushing into the store as he drove into town that morning, but now it looked as if half the town had arrived. It didn't look quite like the chaos the big city stores were seeing. There was a little more order to things.

Will thought to himself it must be the slower small town life and the fact that most of these people know each other.

Will pulled into the parking lot and turned around and pulled his Jeep into a spot that was facing out towards the entrance they just drove in. He motioned for Alejandro to pull next to him facing the same direction. Will wanted a quick route out of the parking lot if the people began rioting. He was anticipating with the amount of people rushing to the store due to the news that some of the basics people like to keep on hand might already be out of stock. If that was the case, Will figured people might turn to violence like crowds would do on Black Friday, regardless of whether or not they knew the people around them. They all got out of the vehicles and grouped together in between the two.

"Alejandro, I think you and Juana should stay out here while Lea and I go in and get whatever we can off of our list," Will said as he held up a piece of paper.

Alejandro glanced over to the store entrance and then back to Will and Lea, "Are you sure it's going to be safe in there for her?"

"It looks a little crazy in there but it doesn't look like people are being violent. I think it gets worse on Black Friday. We'll stay together and move quickly. Plus, I have my pistol." Will pointed to the weapon holstered at his side, "I don't think anyone will mess with us."

"Okay," Alejandro said reluctantly but still nodded his head in agreement.

"I think you two should just stay in your car for now

and keep a hold on your shotgun. I can give you my shotgun to have in your car too." Will opened up the passenger door and grabbed the shotgun and handed it to Alejandro.

Juana gasped and threw her hands up to her face. She was beginning to tear up again.

"This is too much. How could things be like this!" She cried out hysterically.

"Juana, it'll be alright. We are just trying to anticipate the worst case scenario. We don't really think we'll need to use these guns but we want to be prepared," Alejandro said as he pulled his wife closer to him and hugged her.

Alejandro and Juana got back into their car and set the shotguns resting against the seat beside them. They watched Will and Lea quickly walk into the store. Alejandro brought his window down a few inches and had Juana do the same. Alejandro kept his head on a swivel. His eyes went from mirror to mirror and out all the windows in a continual pattern. He told Juana to keep watch as well and to let him know if she saw anyone approaching their car.

Only a few minutes after Will and Lea disappeared into the store, they heard some shouting. Alejandro darted his head around and scanned the area of the parking lot he thought he heard the commotion. He couldn't tell exactly what was happening due to all the cars in the way of his view. He could see the tops of heads as people were rushing around. He told Juana to stay in the car and that he was going to step out to see if he could get a better view. He stood up outside his car and held the shotgun low with both hands. He was in between his car and Will's Jeep and hoped no one would see the gun. Now that he was standing he could see more of the disturbance. There were many people gathered around a small area. People were pushing and shoving each other and the shouting was escalating. He noticed six large 4x4 vehicles, an assortment of lifted trucks and Jeeps, lined up on the back lane of the parking lot. He thought they were parked there to be ready to leave quickly like he and Will had done at this other entrance. He didn't recognize any of the vehicles. Having lived in this small town for many years he would recognize any of those if they were from the area.

As he focused on the fighting, a shot rang out from the direction he was watching and a cacophony of shouting and screaming instantly filled the air. The sound of the firing gun caused him to duck his head. He quickly turned to get back in his car and saw a man standing across from him outside Juana's door, holding a large knife.

*****

Will and Lea had a single cart and were rushing up and down the aisles, remaining side by side the entire time. Just as Will had thought, most of the items they had on their list were already gone from the store. As he saw some items he hadn't thought of, he would toss them into the cart. Whatever they could get would lengthen the store of survival food he already had. Most of the survival situations he imagined were more regional. The blogs he would read would base their advice on natural disasters or war zones and how people reacted to those situations. Will never imagined martial law for the entire United States. *What does that mean for the possibility of more food arriving at this store*? He always imagined state and federal aid eventually coming to the rescue after some point and returning things back to normal. It made him think of the history lessons on occupied areas during World War II. It took years before anyone came to the aid of the occupied people.

Lea was surprised when Will started loading large bottles of alcohol into the cart. He loaded an assortment of different liquors from the bottom shelf.

"What could you possibly need all that for!?" Lea asked with a baffled look on her face.

Will motioned for them to continue down the aisle as he answered. "Lots of things. Who knows how long this will all take until things are back to normal. We can use alcohol to help with sickness, cleaning, trading, and many other things."

"Huh. I would never have thought of any of that," she said.

"Just wait until you see what else I hope to buy," Will said and winked at Lea.

Once they had gathered everything that they could find that was on their list, they joined one of the many lines waiting to pay. As they slowly moved forward they heard a loud bang that came from outside. Will and Lea looked at each other both wondering if they had just heard a gunshot. They didn't have a view outside through the main entrance from where they stood so they couldn't look to see without leaving the line and neither wanted to part from each other with how hectic is was in the store. The consistent noise from shouting and rushing of people made it hard to tell if it was a gunshot that they heard. However, Will was pretty sure that it had been. Though, he didn't think it was a shotgun.

As they finally made it to the cashier, Will pointed to the cigarettes that encompassed the display, "Can I also get a bunch of cartons. Camels or Marlboros, I don't really care."

The chaotic sounds continued outside and Will thought he heard another shot. It could've been anything he considered with all the noise.

"I didn't know you smoked, Will," the cashier said.

Will was surprised that the cashier called him by name. He hadn't looked at the lady yet because he was still thinking about the shot and also that he wanted to remember to buy cigarettes. It was Mary, his mother's friend.

"Oh, I don't. They are for a friend. Listen, Mary, if you already haven't done so, you should probably make sure you get some of this stuff too." Will swept his hand pointing from one end of the store to the other. "Who knows how long all this rioting and stuff will go on."

"I think we'll be okay." She leaned in and lowered her voice, "The manager let us set aside some things for ourselves. Plus, he said that new government corporation is going to be coming into town sometime really soon. He said they are going to be rationing out food. He wanted us to get everything we needed before they came in and took everything. He said that technically he was supposed to close the store and wait until they got here to handle everything in the store. Are you all going to be fine?"

"Yes, thank you," Will answered. "I think we'll be set for now. And thanks for the information. We'll make sure to get set up with rations too when that group comes into town." Will paid and helped reload the cart.

As they walked towards the exit Lea whispered to Will, "Why didn't you tell her we had a bunch of food at your house?"

"I don't want too many people knowing about it. The

more people that know the greater potential people will want to have some if things get worse," Will whispered back.

"Good point. So, I understand the alcohol but you are going to have to explain the cigarettes."

"Well," Will began and paused for a moment, "it's a luxury item. If they start rationing, which Mary just confirmed that they are, I'm sure cigarettes won't be a priority to be shipped around the country. People are addicted to these things and their value will skyrocket. We could use them to buy something we need."

"How on Earth do you even think of these things?"

Will laughed, "It's stuff that has happened during wars or other big disasters. I read about this kind of thing on the prepping and survival blogs I read. People theorize what could happen on a much larger scale. On one hand, I hope that buying them is worth it. On the other, I hope I wasted my money and things don't get that bad."

They exited the store and turned to the right towards where they had parked. They both stopped abruptly. All they could see was Will's Jeep. Alejandro and Juana's car was gone.

"Will?" Lea said with an anxious tone in her voice.

"I don't know," was all he could say back to her.

Will had Lea push the cart as they approached his Jeep. He had his hand ready on his pistol. There was a deep crimson pool on the ground to the side of where the car had been. Once Will had seen it, he turned to Lea who noticed a moment after him. She put her hand to her mouth as tears began to flow down her cheeks and she began screaming.

Chapter Twelve

Kenneth stood at the head of the large conference table with his hands up on his sides. He was scanning the group as people shuffled into the room trying to find a spot to stand in the space that was left.

"Alright everybody, please settle down," Kenneth yelled out as an attempt to quiet the packed room. "There are a lot of rumors floating around and I'm going to try to clarify things as best as I can for everybody. Yes, we will be moving quite a bit of our operations to a smaller town in upstate New York."

The room immediately erupted in displays of every emotion imaginable. Kenneth could see people nodding to each other with big smiles spread across their faces. He could also see people throwing their hands up in frustration. Some were yelling at him. There was a woman in tears that pushed her way through the crowd towards the door.

"Please, people!" Kenneth was yelling again. "I'm just the messenger on this. As you may or may not know, we are partially controlled by the new government entity...or corporation, whatever they are." He was no longer yelling as the room had mostly settled down again, "It's about as clear as mud. Anyway, the CMA, as they are calling themselves, are asking us to implement some of our disaster and safety plans. You may have heard that fires have been started in some of the buildings on our street and the surrounding blocks. The CMA wants us all to be safe and also for us to have continuous broadcasting. The streets are pretty dangerous right now with the rioting. The CMA has told us that they will have security posted on the streets by the end of the day to help combat the problem. Not everyone will be moving. The transition will take about a week. A very minimum crew will remain here. Well, they will remain here unless there is an emergency here. In that case, we may have to give over full control of the broadcast to one of our affiliates at a different location. The CMA has also told us that we will have plenty of assistance in the transition..as far as travel goes."

Many began to ask questions and many others began talking to each other again. Kenneth didn't have the answer to most of the questions he received. Too many similar questions kept getting asked over and over. He was getting frustrated.

"Listen! I've told you all that I've been told. There is plenty of work to be done. We can't stay in here all day asking questions. You'll find out more as I find out more. I just had a meeting with all of your immediate supervisors before this. They'll have more information on what you should be doing for the rest of the day. Marcus, are you in here?"

"Right here," Marcus put up his hand. He had been one of the first in the room for the meeting and was standing off of Kenneth's right-hand side near the window.

"Marcus, follow me after this meeting. I have an assignment for you."

*****

Marcus had to quicken his pace to keep up with Kenneth, which was difficult as he was still overly exhausted.

"You are going to be all over the place, Marcus. The CMA has things they'd like us to cover."

"I'm sure they do," Marcus said in a sarcastic tone.

"I know you don't like this. I don't like it either. But, what can we do?"

Marcus didn't answer. He wanted to but he couldn't think of anything to say that Kenneth would agree with.

"So the CMA has started to set up some camps around the country. They want you to go and do a story on one to show what they look like."

"Camps? What, they already have concentration camps for dissenters?" Marcus asked.

Kenneth, surprised by the response, shot a glance over to Marcus.

"I'm just kidding," Marcus quickly added. He then thought that maybe he shouldn't joke about that.

"From my understanding, they are being put in place because of all the rioting going on," Kenneth said. "They are anticipating people fleeing the big cities and trying to seek safety. I guess if you get too many people showing up in small rural areas without the infrastructure to support them then there'll be more problems."

"It's still odd that they are already building these and

we aren't a whole day into the announcement of all these changes. I couldn't have told who the CMA was yesterday. I couldn't have told you who they were when I got here to work this morning. If they are building massive camps around the country to support people bugging out of cities, it means they already had everything they needed in place."

"I'm with ya, Marcus. There is way too many things like that. For example," Kenneth lowered his voice to a whisper, "they gave us a box full of I.D. badges for everyone that we are supposed to hand out today. How'd they get everyone's information and pictures to have those ready? Someone up top must've known about this beforehand. They already knew we had contingency plans for relocation. They ordered us to move on those plans."

"Huh," Marcus was processing all the new information and didn't say anything more.

They arrived at Kenneth's office and Marcus was handed a packet that Kenneth picked up off of his desk.

"This has the details for what you'll be doing for the story. You should probably go home and get cleaned up and get some rest. You'll have a helicopter that you'll be paired with for the time being. I think they want you back sometime in the middle of the night to head to the camp. All the details are in the packet. I think you have a long day tomorrow. There's more than just the camp to cover tomorrow. Like I said, it's all in that packet."

"Anything else?" Marcus asked as he opened the packet and flipped through.

"Nope," Kenneth answered and Marcus turned to leave. "Oh wait," Kenneth yelled as Marcus reached the door, "your new badge is in the back of that packet. You'll need that from now on, especially traveling with the CMA.

Here is a phone as well." Kenneth picked up a small cell phone from out of a box that sat on his desk and tossed it to Marcus. "They said cell service to the public is very patchy right now but these phones they gave us are supposed to work no matter what." Marcus had his own phone in his hand and looked down at the screen and saw he currently did not have service. He frowned.

"I can see the writing on the wall, Ken," Marcus said as he started to back up out of the office. "They are going to fly me to one of these concentration camps not to do a story, but to drop me off and leave me there for good," Marcus chuckled and all Kenneth did in response was shake his head at him.

*****

Marcus placed his new cell phone in his desk drawer and closed and locked it. He didn't care if they couldn't contact him at his home or on his own phone. He'd be returning soon enough anyway to catch the flight to the camp. He thought of the new phone as if it were disease infested. He hated that he was now working for the corporation that stood for everything that he was against.

Marcus walked back to the conference room for the third time that day and saw it was empty again. He went in and closed the door and walked up to the window. He could see the uniformed CMA troops down on the streets below. It looked as if their presence was keeping the violent crowds away for the time being. He pulled the card Thomas had given him earlier out of his pocket and stared at it. He wondered if he should update him on the fact that he'd be out of the city the next day and also update him on WWNL's move out of the city. He checked his cell phone and noticed he now had a few bars of service. He dialed Thomas's number.

Chapter Thirteen

Alejandro was staring straight into the strange man's eyes. He still had the shotgun held low but was ready to bring it up quickly. He wasn't sure, but he thought the man couldn't see the gun in his hands.

"What kind of supplies do you have in here?" the man asked in a demanding tone. "It looks like you are packed pretty full."

"It's no concern of yours," Alejandro answered.

The man chuckled and opened Juana's door and she gasped. Alejandro quickly raised the shotgun in response and pointed the barrel directly at the man's face. His face quickly morphed from a look of controlled calm into a look of wide-eyed surprise and rage.

"You don't want to do that," the man said. He lifted his chin in the direction of the group of vehicles on the opposite side of the parking lot. "We have quite a bit more than one shotgun."

"I think they are a bit occupied at the moment to come to your rescue," Alejandro quickly said back. The man narrowed his eyes. He was obviously becoming angrier and was trying to find a way to gain control of the interaction. "Just step back," Alejandro said.

He kept the shotgun steady. He felt nervous and had expected to be shaky but he knew the stakes could be his wife's life. Adrenaline flowed through him, heightening his senses. The man didn't move back. The man started glancing down at Juana and then back at him. Alejandro was sure the man would be able to see the shotgun that Juana had sitting on her left side. He was hoping the man wouldn't drop down behind the car. If he did, then Alejandro would no longer have a clear shot at the man. Juana would be in between them and there was no way he would shoot in that situation.

Just as Alejandro was contemplating the scenario, his fears unfolded before him. The man dropped to his knees and yanked Juana out of the car and held her in front of himself. Juana screamed and the man held his knife in front of her face and told her to be quiet.

"Alright, this is how this is going to go now," the man said as he slowly rose from his knees, pulling Juana up with him. He had his right arm up to Juana's neck with his forearm tucked under her chin now. The knife was in his right hand which put it next to the left side of her face. His other arm was placed across her middle, holding down both of her arms. He held tightly to her right wrist. "You are going to lay down that twelve gauge. Put it on the hood of the car and then you walk back by the trunk. I think it's obvious what will happen if you don't do everything I say." He briefly moved the knife to her throat and then repositioned his forearm back under her chin.

Alejandro still held the shotgun steady at the man's head. The man was a least a whole head taller than Juana and there wasn't much he could do to hide completely behind her. Alejandro's mind was racing. He wasn't sure how much time he had before the man went through with his threat. Although he could aim clearly at his head, he still didn't like the fact that the spray from the shotgun could still easily hit Juana. How he wished for slug shells to be in the gun rather than the buckshot he knew was in it. He thought he might aim high. However, if he missed, it could be all over for Juana as well, and it would be by his hand.

Alejandro was beginning to feel defeated and slowly began to lower the gun. It had only been seconds, ten at the most, that had passed since he lost the upper hand on the situation. He wished he would've pulled the trigger the second the man went for Juana's door. He wished Juana had the other shotgun ready in her hands while she sat in the car. Why did she dislike holding guns? He had taught her plenty about use and safety. He wished he had a pistol or a high caliber hunting rifle. He wished too much. Wishes weren't going to do anything for them now.

"DO IT NOW OR SHE GETS HER THROAT CUT!" the man shouted at him. Juana had tears continuously flowing down her cheeks.

Alejandro's arms hung low now. All of the adrenaline and confidence had drained from him. He moved towards the front of the car. He dragged his feet, never lifting them a single millimeter. He lifted the shotgun with both hands and set it on the hood, keeping both hands on it. He stared into Juana's eyes, tears forming in his. He shifted his eyes to the man. He lowered his brow as his face shifted from sadness to pure rage. Before letting go, an idea sparked into his mind. A plan was forming. He needed to get the other shotgun. The man had not seen it when he grabbed Juana. He slightly lifted and rapidly pumped the shotgun until all the shells were expended.

The few red cartridges were rolling across the hood and falling to the ground. The man chuckled at Alejandro's actions.

"Now move away from it. Get back by the trunk," the man said, no longer shouting.

Alejandro lifted his hands from the shotgun and said, "let her go now."

"MOVE," he shouted. "I'll let her go when I want to let her go. Maybe I take her with me. She feels pretty nice against me. Get away from the gun. I will cut her throat," the man raised his voice with the threat.

Alejandro stepped backward. He hadn't anticipated the man taking Juana as he formulated his plan moments ago. He would have to be fluid in his actions, conforming to whatever happened as this continued forward. He moved around his open driver's door as he stepped towards the rear of the car, never taking his eyes off of the man and Juana. He slowed as he was abeam the open door. He wanted the man to let go of Juana and make a move for the empty shotgun on the hood. He also thought this would be a good time for Will and his sidearm to return. He contemplated that if he made a move for the shotgun in the car, it might prompt the man to let go of Juana and scramble to get the shotgun on the hood and then have to crawl around on the ground to get the shells to load it. He would regain the advantage then. The worst case scenario would be that he does something to Juana first before getting the gun. He had to do something.

To Alejandro's surprise, the man pushed Juana away from himself. He still held on to her wrist firmly, but she was no longer his shield. This was Alejandro's opportunity. If he didn't act now the man would soon have a loaded shotgun and would still have Juana and Alejandro assumed he'd be dead. Juana might die too but Alejandro feared more horrors would come to Juana if she wasn't immediately killed in this situation. The man bent down and picked up a shell that had rolled near him and then moved towards the hood of the car. Alejandro lunged onto the driver's seat of the car and quickly pulled the shotgun from the passenger side. This move made the man panic. It was clear he wanted to pull Juana in front of him again but he also wanted to get the shotgun and load it. Still holding Juana's wrist, he yanked her downwards and she tumbled onto the pavement. He now had the shotgun and was loading the single shell. His left hand was holding his knife up against the fore-end of the gun so he could still hold both weapons. His right hand was pushing the shell in.

Alejandro rocketed back out of the car. He swung the barrel up. The man had fumbled only for a moment while loading the shell. He was now bringing his barrel up towards Alejandro. Then came a loud boom. No, it was two loud booms. The report of both shotguns going off nearly simultaneously. Alejandro dropped to his knees. The adrenaline and shock of what just happened caused a feeling of numbness in his fingers. He had a continuous ringing in his head probably due to the same reason. The man across from him now lay on his back, gripping one of his shoulders. The shotgun and knife he had held were now laying next to him. Alejandro was starting to regain his senses and could hear the man grunting in pain through the ringing in his head. He patted himself as he still knelt on the ground. It appeared he was uninjured.

There was still a lingering numbness about his body from the shock of the intense situation that just played out. He couldn't comprehend how he was not hit. The spray of the other shotgun must have gone over his head by only a couple of centimeters. He thought if he was any taller, the spray of metal would have scalped him. It had looked like he was staring down the other barrel just moments ago. The sound of Juana crying refocused his attention. He set down his shotgun as he stood to check on her.

"Juana! Are you okay?"

As soon as Alejandro asked the question the man sat up. Blood dripped from his shoulder wound. He was no longer holding the wound because he had his knife again. The wounded arm lay slumped in his lap. Without warning, he raised the arm with the knife and quickly sliced downwards toward Juana. The knife sliced a large gash across her forearm and she screamed in pain. Alejandro had wished he never set his gun down. In less than a second, he made the decision to lunge at the man rather than return to his shotgun a few steps back. He figured a return to the gun could mean more time for the man to continue slicing at Juana with his knife. Alejandro brought his foot up. With all the force he could bring together he slammed it against the man's face. His head whipped back and blood spewed out of his mouth. The knife flew from his hand and slid away. The man's head cracked against the concrete.

The man quickly rolled over and pushed himself up. He swayed slightly from side to side, dazed from the shot and the kick to his face. Alejandro could see blood dripping from the man's nose. His teeth were red and his bloody mouth dripped down the front of his lip. The man must have realized he would never regain any control in his attempted theft and he bolted towards the back of parking lot where the convoy of trucks were parked. Alejandro grabbed his shotgun and started to lift it to aim. He stopped part way, realizing the shot would be wasted.

The man was too far out of range for a shotgun. He was going in between cars, bumping into them in a delirium-like state as he made his getaway.

Alejandro returned to Juana. He set the gun within arms reach as he knelt by her. He carefully lifted her hand from her bloody forearm. She was bleeding, but not to the amount that would make him worry that she might bleed out quickly. She immediately replaced her hand over the laceration.

"I'm going to get something from the car to wrap around the cut," Alejandro said.

Only a moan came in reply as Juana continued to cry. She sniffled several times as the tears flowed. Alejandro went to the car and quickly returned with a t-shirt he pulled from a suitcase. He folded the shirt a few times, making sure the folded amount would be large enough to cover the whole cut. He wrapped her forearm with the shirt and tied it tightly, leaving just enough give in the shirt for her arm to not go completely numb.

As he helped her stand, Alejandro was surprised to see his neighbor, Mike, approach them. He was holding a baseball bat and his eyes seemed stuck wide open as they darted between the pool of blood on the ground and Juana's arm.

"Al! What's happened?" Mike questioned, still with the look of shock covering his face.

"We were attacked by one of the group from the back of the parking lot," Alejandro pointed to the convoy of vehicles. "I need to get her to the emergency center right now. Lea will be coming out of the store soon. Can you tell her where we went?"

"Yes, of course," Mike answered as he helped Alejandro get Juana into the passenger seat of their car.

*****

Juana had mostly calmed as they began their drive. She had not spoken much during the whole event. She lifted the shirt from her arm as much as she could to look and it turned out to be a mistake. Seeing the severed flesh and the oozing blood caused her to panic again.

"Juana! Juana! Just keep putting pressure on it. We're almost to the doctor," Alejandro yelled over his wife's crying and moaning as he tried to focus on the road.

He was driving as fast as he ever had through the small town. The car bounced and creaked. The tires squealed as he turned corners too quickly. Alejandro was inexperienced in the race car style driving and ended up in the opposite lane a few times. Fortunately, there weren't any other cars driving in the opposite direction and the drive to the emergency care center was only a few minutes through the town. Juana continued to wail in pain as she held the now blood-soaked shirt tightly against her forearm.

Chapter Fourteen

Thick pine forest peppered with leafless maple trees passed below. Marcus stared down out of the helicopter. He could see a road a few miles to the north that their flight seemed to be paralleling. Patches of snow from a storm that had passed the area about a week earlier could be seen through the trees on the forest floor. There seemed to be a haziness blanketing the land. Marcus wondered if there were fires from rioting somewhere near the area they were over. The monotony of the flight paired with the constant hum of the helicopter's engine caused Marcus to doze off every once in a while for a few minutes. The seats were a cushy leather and they seemed to pull Marcus closer as if in a giant bear hug. He had slept for around six hours or so before having to ready himself for another long day. Six hours seemed sufficient for him to last another day. He had been a little annoyed at the hurry up and wait situation of the morning. They had all arrived on time, yet they all sat around for an hour and a half before their flight began.

He awoke after one of his couple minute long naps and

looked away from the window towards his cameraman, Blake. He was across from Marcus and sunken low in his chair in a deep sleep, mouth hanging open. Blake was Marcus's usual cameraman when he did on-location interviews or stories. He wasn't much for conversation, though. Blake was all business. He would typically only speak to Marcus about work related items such as camera placement for an interview. To Marcus's left sat two CMA employees. One in a suit and the other in a military or SWAT-like uniform. It was mostly black with some blue and white decorations. Marcus took note of the CMA uniform and patch. He thought it was another interesting fact that Thomas would like to know. The suit's name was Anthony. He had told Marcus that he would be accompanying him anytime he would be doing stories on the Central Management Authority and their operations. Another tidbit for Thomas. Marcus thought Anthony looked like the kind of guy that would push you into the tiger pad at the zoo for his own entertainment. Maybe it was his disdain for the CMA that made him immediately dislike him, however, Marcus did think Anthony had a constant evil grin pasted on his face.

Marcus turned back to the window on his right. He figured they were in far north-eastern Pennsylvania. The suit had told him they'd be a little ways northwest of Manhattan. This particular CMA refugee camp wouldn't be ready for a couple of days. Anthony wanted to cover this one first because it would be mostly quiet. Marcus was to leave the location out of the story since it wasn't ready yet. Next, they would fly to a regional supply depot for all the area camps. They would round out their day covering CMA buses gathering people in Philadelphia and then the camp west of Philadelphia that would be accepting all the new refugees. Marcus could see the good in having camps to relieve rural areas from being flooded with refugees. At the same time, he thought of it all as a self-fulfilling prophecy. Take away the people's government and the complex system the country lived on and then, of course, you would need somebody like the CMA to swoop in and save the day.

The thick forest stopped abruptly and fields of tan dormant grass began to fill Marcus's window. Marcus straightened himself in his seat as the outer portions of the camp came into view. There was row after row of large white tents. They almost looked like the type that people rent for weddings. Each tent had a large black sign with a letter and number painted in white hung above the tent's opening.

"Pretty impressive isn't it?" Anthony yelled over the engine noise.

"How is this already set up?" Marcus ignored the question and asked his own.

Blake awoke from the yelling and was now looking out of his window down at the camp. He quickly reached into his backpack that sat in between his legs and produced a small camcorder. He started filming the camp from the air as they arrived.

"Some of our country's leadership had anticipated the government failing and disintegrating so they put the whole work in motion," Anthony twirled his finger in the air as he yelled in reply.

Marcus nodded his head in response and turned back to the window. They were descending quickly now and he reached down and tightened his seatbelt. He could see crews of workers putting up fencing and others still erecting tents. He thought the camp looked mostly complete other than a little bit more perimeter fencing. It made Marcus wonder if the fencing was to keep out or keep in. There was no telling how many more tents were going to be put up. He saw a dozen or so eighteen wheeler semi-trucks that workers were entering and leaving carrying supplies. He figured some could still be completely full.

A few minutes later they all ducked out of the helicopter and regrouped in front of a tent about fifty yards away. The whine of the helicopter's turbine engine winding down along with the whump whump whump of the slowing blades could be heard as they all stretched their arms and legs by the tent.

"Most of the construction should be complete by day's end," Anthony said as if he read Marcus's thoughts. "Tomorrow the staff will be here unloading more trucks with supplies to run the camp. After the camp is supplied, probably next day, this camp will be ready to accept people and be fully operational."

"Well," Marcus said and then paused for a moment, "...things sure do move fast with you guys."

"When plans are made and set in motion, there's no stopping us," Anthony said, widening the permanent grin on his face. "You two should start getting some basic footage of the camp and workers finishing up things. I'll find you two in a little bit and we'll go over what should go in the newscast."

"Go over?" Marcus asked. "You don't want us to do our thing? We are pretty good at it."

"We can compare notes. No offense. I know you are professionals, but WWNL is now technically a subsidiary of the CMA. As a public relations matter, coverage of the CMA needs to be monitored. You understand, I'm sure. I guarantee WWNL wouldn't want any unfavorable publicity without a fine tooth comb meticulously analyzing everything possible to make them appear in the best light possible."

Marcus raised an eyebrow. "Are you anticipating these refugee camps will give the CMA bad publicity?"

"Oh, no. Of course not," Anthony quickly answered. "I was just saying as an example. Anyways, like I said, I'll find you in a little bit." Anthony turned and went inside the tent. Marcus could tell that he seemed a bit annoyed.

Marcus and Blake spent the better part of the next hour walking around the camp recording footage of people working on tents and fencing. They went in the tents as well to record sleeping areas, bathroom facilities, and kitchen and dining. Marcus was quite impressed with how nice everything seemed. Everything was brand new. He had pictured in his mind old tattered military materials. A government that couldn't even support to maintain its' own military and many agencies and programs could somehow afford to build brand new miniature cities all over the U.S.

"This is just all too weird," Marcus said to Blake.

"How so?" Blake asked.

"Just a week ago I never would have pictured refugee camps being built everywhere across the country. Now we are walking around one. It's surreal. Why did the government...rather, a government corporation, have all of this stuff?" Marcus asked as he looked around shaking his head.

"I always figured the government always had this stuff on hand," Blake answered. "Maybe it was all FEMA equipment."

Marcus and Blake were several tents down from the tent that Anthony had disappeared into earlier. They saw him walk out of the tent and look around while putting a phone to his ear. A moment later Marcus felt the CMA phone in his pocket vibrate. They began walking towards Anthony as he answered it. Anthony spotted them and they both hung up.

"Where would be best to do the story portion of this?" Anthony asked as they approached each other.

Blake answered before Marcus could, "Back at the studio would be ideal since we aren't doing this live. But, we could film in one of these tents. Either way, the editing will be done back at the studio. I assume this won't be airing tonight?"

"It could if we get done quickly enough," Anthony said. "We can film in one of these tents. I have a couple of the staff to film too. PR stuff. You can't edit here?"

"We could," Blake said. "It would just be a lot more difficult for a story of this length. We have much better equipment at the studio. All we have here is a laptop. Most of the time we have a van full of equipment when we do off-site work and that equipment isn't the most fun to work with."

Anthony looked towards the ground and nodded his head. "Fair enough. I'll be heading back with you to the WWNL offices anyways. I'll sit in on the editing to make sure everything is in the CMA guidelines. Once we are done with that, I'll need to see Kenneth."

Anthony turned around and motioned for the two of them to follow him into the tent. Marcus and Blake both looked at each other with questioning looks on their faces. Blake shrugged his shoulders and then headed for the tent and Marcus followed. As he ducked through the door flaps, he was taken aback by what he saw inside. Two large box trailers from semi-trucks were parked inside. Sets of stairs had been placed at the back opening. The inside of the trailers were lined with computers and other equipment. Large bunches of cables packed with ethernet and power cables were run out of the back of the trailers and then back towards the opposite side of the tent. Marcus assumed they went to generators and probably satellite equipment for communications. Sitting at the workstations that lined the inside of the trailers were military personnel. At least Marcus assumed they were military. They weren't wearing the black SWAT-like uniform that he saw on the man earlier in the helicopter. They had regular camouflage fatigues. As Marcus focused a little more on the people in the trailer, he could see the blue and white CMA patches on their arms. All of them had sidearms on their waist.

"Marcus, come with me for a moment," Anthony said and gestured over to the side of the trailer. "

They walked over beside the trailer. Marcus was surprised to see that there was no one else there. He wasn't sure why, but he had expected others to be there. He was beginning to feel nervous and like his jokes to Kenneth about being held prisoner at a camp were about to come true. Anthony turned around and clasped his hands together.

"Marcus, we need to get some things straight and make sure we are on the same page," Anthony said as he started to pace a few steps back and forth. "You've been very vocal on the show about your opinions. WWNL has given you quite a bit of leeway."

"Not to brag," Marcus began, "but I'm a bit of a household name when it comes to news. There's some freedom that comes with the popularity of the show. Some of that popularity comes from people that want to hear my opinion."

"Right," Anthony answered. "However, you now work for the Central Management Authority." He emphasized the name as if it were the most important title known to man. "We aren't exactly going to be running things the same way WWNL did. Like I told you earlier, we are going to want things to go through our filter before it's broadcast across the nation. Times are different now. The country is in a state of emergency. There will be a process that needs to take place to get the country on track. We don't need a population of opposing views hindering that process. Do you understand?" Anthony didn't leave any time to answer before asking another question. "The CMA's process of doing business isn't going to be a problem for you, is it? Don't get us wrong, we want you to be involved. You are a voice and face people trust. But, a voice that causes problems for us will need to be replaced."

Marcus's mind was racing through the whole conversation and now he needed to answer. He had figured something like this would come up. It was obvious that he had some level of distrust of Anthony. It was obvious what his opinion had been because he had been spouting it on the show for years. He was surprised they even wanted to attempt using him over someone else who didn't have a publicly established position with an opposing stance. He thought of Thomas and what he had said. *We think you can be a key element to fighting this*. Whatever Thomas had meant in saying that, he was pretty sure he shouldn't stand his ground to Anthony and the CMA at this first opportunity and blow whatever the plan was. He had to fight his own strong, instinctual desire to open his mouth and blurt out his opinion.

"Oh, I'm on board with you. The opinion portion of my news program is just all part of the show." Marcus felt a little nervous. He hoped it didn't show. "We've got a country to get on track and I think we should all work together to get it done."

Marcus must have pulled off the lie. It was revealed when Anthony's face transformed from the permanent evil grin into what looked like a genuine smile. Marcus smiled along with him and nodded his head.

"That's great to hear, Marcus. You are going to make my job a lot easier. Things will be much smoother this way."

Marcus continued to smile as Anthony guided him back to where Blake was still waiting. Blake raised an eyebrow at Marcus and lifted a palm upwards in a questioning gesture. Marcus waved him off as if there was nothing to talk about.

"We have a couple people for you to interview," Anthony said as he handed Marcus a piece of paper. "These are the questions we'd like you to cover. They are grouped together for each person."

Marcus could see three groups of several questions each. "Are these people familiar with these questions. It's always nice for the interviewee to not be surprised. People are usually more well spoken and professional when it's done that way."

"Oh, of course. These people have all been specially chosen for this and they know all the items to be covered," Anthony answered.

*****

Blake and Marcus spent the next forty-five minutes interviewing the three CMA employees. Marcus thought they all did really well on camera. It wasn't surprising to him, though. He thought they were all well-versed at their propaganda. They recorded Marcus's portion of the segment as well. Anthony had provided a script for that. Marcus was disgusted by it but did his best to hide the emotion. It felt too scripted and fake. He wondered if his usual viewers would catch on.

They repacked their gear into the helicopter and climbed back in. Ten minutes later they were climbing steadily out of the camp southward. The next stop was near Philadelphia at the regional supply depot for all the area camps. Marcus leaned back in his seat in thought for the whole flight. He was torn inside. On one hand, he felt good about gathering information for Thomas. On the other hand, he felt like having to go along with what Anthony and the CMA wanted was turning him into a coward. He was brought out of his thoughts as the helicopter began its descent.

Marcus was surprised by the size of the warehouse. It seemed to go on for acres. He wasn't sure why anything surprised him anymore. The CMA's operation seemed so massive and complex that it had to have been planned for years in advance. There was no way all this had begun this same week. He again wondered where all the funding came from. *Had the government been hiding all this money for years and years?* He made mental notes of all he was learning. He had to get to Thomas's as soon as possible to relay all this information.

Chapter Fifteen

Thomas adjusted in his chair. He and Marcus sat across from each other in Thomas's dining room. The little portion of the ranch that Marcus had seen so far made him realize it was more of a military stronghold than a working ranch. Scattered all over the walls were typical novelty western decorations. Cowboy hats and boots were hung on the walls. Picture frames were lined with tattered rope. All the furniture was made with natural wood, unstained like any modern style would be.

Marcus had been able to get a personal day upon returning from the long day filled with CMA public relations. Kenneth had quickly signed off on it, however, Marcus thought he looked too stressed and preoccupied to even realize what he was doing. Marcus had heard that Kenneth spent that entire day making arrangements to move the studio to one of the tent towns. It made him wonder if they'd be put up at one of the refugee camps or if they had a whole separate plan for them. He dreaded the move. He had hoped they would be taking over a hotel to live out of while working out of a small town studio. He enjoyed city life. He had every convenience he wanted within walking distance. Perhaps this wealthier older version of himself was becoming more high maintenance, but he didn't mind if that was the case.

"And you are fairly certain they were military?" Thomas asked.

Marcus had spent around fifteen minutes filling in Thomas on everything he could think of since they last met. The WWNL ID badges, WWNL's pending move, the camps, the depot, Anthony, and especially his conversation with Anthony.

"CMA military. I'm one hundred percent certain. At the first camp we visited in northeastern Pennsylvania and the one outside of Philly. Both of those camps had the massive tent that was like an administrative headquarters. Both had uniformed and armed personnel. Get this," Marcus said excitedly as he leaned forward on the table, "I'm pretty sure that supply depot had military equipment. You know, weapons and ammunition and stuff. There was about half of the depot they didn't want us filming. I was still able to see some of it."

"Hmm," Thomas grunted as he sat back in his chair. "I'm beginning to wonder if our estimate of their capabilities is falling a little short. We've known some of what you told me. We've had some people inside the CMA for some time now. It was all super secret government projects up until the last few weeks." Thomas now leaned forward against the table and cocked his head to the side in thought. "You know, Marcus, our insiders only have access to so much information. I think unless one is running the CMA, most of their personnel is purposely kept in the dark on operations not pertinent to their immediate work. Having someone in your position," Thomas now had a growing excitement in his voice, "someone who gets to travel from place to place and see the behind the scenes, so to speak, could gain us a lot more information." Thomas slowly lifted his head and appeared like he had just discovered fire for the first time.

"Wasn't that the plan all along for me?" Marcus asked curiously. He was now puzzled in what they had originally wanted him for if Thomas was coming up with this new plan on the fly. "You said your group had me pegged as a key element in fighting this."

"Well, the plan was for you to start announcing the CMA's plans on the news. We are ready to hack into and hijack all the major news outlets," Thomas said which caused Marcus to raise an eyebrow. "I think it would be better to have you keep up the disguise and gain more information before we go with the original plan."

What have I gotten myself into? Marcus thought.

"You still want to hijack the news and have me tell people what the CMA is doing? That seems risky to me. I'd think they'd be putting a price on my head for that. Anthony said a lot without actually saying it."

"Yes, it would still need to be done. We need the people on our side. I know there'd be a risk for you. That's a question you'll have to ask yourself and a decision you have to make on your own. But, do it sooner than later. The ball is already in motion. We want you, Marcus. You are America's household name in news."

Marcus leaned back and sunk deep into his chair. He let out a long sigh. This is not what he had in mind. He had thought about this kind of thing before, but now it was real. It was right before him. His brother was the soldier, not him. This was dangerous. He would have to be a spy, not just acting, but living out a lie. Then, when they decided, he would have to put his own face on TV in opposition to this giant machine. His neck would be on the line. Thomas could see Marcus's apprehension and thought he needed to give him some guiding words.

"Marcus, you are a key element to fixing our country. You've reached something many people seek and toil for their whole lives. You have fame and fortune. What good will those things be if the country continues on the same course? Is that fortune even yours anymore? Remember, they took over banks. Can they do whatever they want with your money? Will all that hard work be erased? I'm not just talking about money. Even those without that wealth, there is freedom, liberty, their rights! They have ownership in this country. Under the CMA's plan, will they have that? I certainly doubt it. You said they are micro-managing you to make sure the public only hears what they want them to hear. You will have to throw away all of your beliefs in what this country stands for so you can start taking the shovels full of what they will be feeding you and everyone else. Sure, a lot of what they will be saying and doing will appear promising and tempting. It will only be a means to an end. A candy trail leading to a hidden pitfall. Now is the time we must act. Now, Marcus! The fight will only get harder and the battle more complex as time goes on. Yes, we are asking you specifically to take a huge risk that could result in harm to you or even death. But, the alternative is to live out the death of our freedom. You'll be living the life they choose for you. You must do this, Marcus."

Marcus was energized by what Thomas said but still had his uncertainties. "I...I just don't know. I know I don't want the alternative. I just need to think this through. We don't know for sure what the CMA's plan is."

"You are making excuses," Thomas retorted curtly. He paused for a moment and then sighed. "I'm sorry for that," Thomas said more calmly. "Forgive me, Marcus. I know this is a lot to ask. Take some time to think about what I've said and think about the plan. See what you can learn about the CMA. I am ninety-nine percent certain I am right on their motives, though, I've been following their moves for several years now. You need to learn it for yourself."

"I think...that would be good," Marcus said as he nodded his head. He started to feel guilty. There was a spark of shame forming somewhere deep inside. How could Thomas, an older man, have so much confidence and bravery facing this situation? Why, after all his brave speeches on the news program, did he back off in the face of opposition? *Is that all I am? Talk*? He wanted to stand up tall and say he'd do it without any trembling of his hands; without any doubt in his mind.

*****

Thomas left the subject alone as they wandered around his ranch awaiting other leadership to arrive so Marcus could meet them. They covered only a small portion of the large property. Surrounding the complex of Thomas's house and other buildings was mostly wide open fields of grass. Just like the fields Marcus saw from the helicopter the day before, the grass was mostly tan and dormant. Although walking amongst the grass, he could see hints of green from new growth pushing through. Marcus could smell smoke on and off as they walked around. He could tell it wasn't like campfire smoke which he would be able to tell the different woods like pine or oak, but it was a dirty smoke smell. He was reminded of burning plastic or almost like the smoke emitted from welding. He figured there must be a town nearby that had rioting overtake it.

As they approached the house Thomas explained what the other buildings were. One was a large workshop. It held ranch equipment such as a tractor, woodworking tools, fuel storage, and many other necessities for a working ranch. There was a barn and feed house and an oversized garage. Thomas had an addiction for vehicles, it seemed. They walked through the garage and Marcus must have counted a dozen vehicles.

They headed back to the house after leaving the garage. They needed water after the lengthy walk. They heard a helicopter approaching and Thomas figured it would be the few that lived in Manhattan. Thomas and Marcus waited in the front room for all the other guests to arrive. Thomas warned Marcus that since everyone for the Foundation would be here, they would probably talk some business. They would have to talk privately without Marcus to decide if everyone would be fine with him sitting in on that portion of their gathering. As everyone trickled in, the introductions began. Of course, being a nationally known face and voice, the introductions seemed one-sided to Marcus.

The group shifted to the basement where it was a more comfortable setting along with an extensive selection of bourbon at the bar. Marcus remained in the front room for a short time while it was unanimously decided that Marcus could hear any American Rights Foundation business that was discussed during the evening. Marcus had feared that most everyone would try to convince him the same as Thomas had on his duty to the country and their foundation. Thomas must have mentioned during their private talk that he already spoke with Marcus on the subject because no one else brought it up. It was really a relaxed setting, especially with the bourbon flowing. Things did turn serious for a while as Thomas relayed the information about Marcus's trip to the camps and supply depot. Marcus filled in bits and pieces as Thomas told most of the story. As most were done asking questions on the new information, Marcus decided he'd bring up some of his own questions.

"Do you suppose the government has been hiding all the money to fund this operation? I mean...everything was brand new. They have full staffing. Up to date technology. The government couldn't afford to maintain its' desired levels of military staffing for the last decade."

Thomas answered, "We think that the government had some role in the funding, but only very little. From what we have gathered from our inside people, there is a separate group that is behind this. We think they provided most of the funding. We are nearly one hundred percent certain it is a group of very wealthy individuals who would like to attain the governing power for the country. Some in this group very well may be some of the politicians behind dissolving the government. It is all too secretive for our insiders to know anything more."

"The government really hasn't been dissolved, has it?" Marcus asked. "The CMA is just a government corporation. The powers and responsibilities still lie with the government."

"Where are they then?" someone in the group asked.

"Exactly," Thomas said. "Where are they? What you say Marcus is technically true. However, it seems like all of the politicians have skipped town. There's no word from them or from their staffers. There hasn't been a peep out of the President. The rumor out of Washington is that the President skipped town too. They are all riding this out in places unknown. Maybe inside hidden underground bunkers."

"That or they are the ones behind the CMA," another from the group said. "They either handed over the reins and bolted or they just changed titles and they are trying to take the people out of the American government and restructure as a totalitarian system. What is happening is the perfect way to do it."

Marcus would normally be right in step with this crowd and the conversation. His fears that were brought on hearing Thomas's plan made him wonder if it was just conspiracy theory chatter. Yes, his predictions on what the government had been doing had come true, but now he wondered if it was the government's fault. Were they right in their actions? Was it his inner fears of this fight growing? Was this his brain's subconscious method of trying to snuff out the spark of shame? His mind raced through the timeline of events and his previous analysis of government policy. Did government intervention cause the decay of the American economy or was government intervention brought on by economic decay? Was it clearly black and white like that? Marcus knew he needed more time to sort through everything. He couldn't make a decision tonight. Having had a few bourbons might make him feel more courageous or possibly irrational than if he were sober.

The conversation slowly morphed away from business talk back to general party conversation as everyone's second and third drinks were consumed. Marcus got a few of the Manhattan crew's contact information before the night wound down. He thought it might be all for nothing if he was about to leave New York City for a tent city in some isolated location. Marcus looked around the room as the party calmed. Most were now seated, talking in smaller groups quietly. He thought it was surreal. This all seemed too normal. Normal for just a week ago. Now the country was like a puzzle that had been pulled apart and tossed in the air. Everyone was specks on the pieces wondering where they were all going to land.

Chapter Sixteen

Lea sat in an old vanity chair that she had turned away from the mirror to face the bed. The chair's frame was made of a worn brass. The seat's padding had been compressed too many times over the years to expand back to it's intended shape. The chair paired with an old wooden vanity. The corners were worn down from years of use and being moved from location to location and perhaps people brushing against it. The mirror had a few nicks scattered around which made it look like missing pixels on an old computer screen. The set was most certainly an heirloom that had been passed for two or three generations. Juana lay in a deep sleep. Although her mother's wound seemed to be closing up as best as it could only a few days after the incident, the toll of the experience had exhausted her. She was also taking some fairly powerful pain medications which amplified the exhaustion. The medication made her appear at peace while sleeping. It was a different story during her waking hours. Her face would hold a constant look of pain and agony.

The doctor at the emergency center had held off on using antibiotics. She said in her opinion, they arrived quick enough for the staff to clean the wound hastily enough after the cut happened and apply a topical antibacterial ointment that it should be sufficient to prevent infection. The wound was stitched and wrapped in a clean bandage. The doctor didn't like to give antibiotics for preemptive use. She had explained that decades ago antibiotics were prescribed in an almost careless manner which had resulted in many strains of antibiotic resistant bacteria. She further explained that rate of mortality for children and the elderly had skyrocketed for nearly a decade. Regardless, she said they should not hesitate to return for a prescription at any signs of infection.

Lea had severely heightened levels of stress over the last few days after seeing the pool of blood outside the grocery store where her parent's car had been parked. Her screams and tears that day were not just the fear of the unknown. They were the screams of a grieving daughter who lost her mother too early in life. Her mind had immediately gone to the worst. There was little Will could say or do to calm her down.

Alejandro and Juana's neighbor, Mike, had waited around for a few minutes for Lea to return before curiosity got the best of him. He wandered to the back of the parking lot to see the group that accompanied the large convoy of vehicles parked in the back. He kept his distance knowing what happened to Juana. He turned back to watch for Lea as often as he could. He could see the group stealing food from people as they returned to their cars from the store. They were also smashing car windows to get anything else they wanted. It was a scream from behind him that made him realize he hadn't looked back in a minute or two. He saw Lea and another person standing by the spot Alejandro and Juana had sped off from. He bolted back across the lot towards them. He relayed the story of what happened and it helped to calm Lea down some. She was still worried knowing that her mother had been hurt.

Now Lea sat watching her mother sleep in the spare bedroom at Beth and Will's place while she drowned in her own anxiety. Her mother was beginning to develop signs of an infection. There was an expanding swelling and redness now visible beyond the bandage on her arm. She had a slightly elevated temperature. They called the doctor that morning to tell her the news and she said there was no need to bring Juana in, just to send someone for the prescription of antibiotics.

Will and Lea's father, Alejandro, had taken on the task. Their absence that morning paired with the news they had been hearing the last few days added to Lea's anxiety. Every news report from every channel was filled with stories of violence and death. It seemed that a panic settled in over most people which led to widespread chaos. There were more and more scenes of raiding and looting in grocery store parking lots nationwide. Mobs of people ventured away from parking lots and started raiding homes. Much fighting and blood and death followed. Looters would be killed trying to enter homes and looters would kill to gain entry into homes. Fires were started in a mob's blind rage and there was no one to put it out. Rescue crews were either too busy trying to keep up with the many emergencies or had left to take care of their own families. News reports estimated that hundreds of thousands of people had died in the short few days.

Their power flickered throughout the days but remained mostly steady. No doubt due to all the fires. They were sure to affect the lines. Beth's home had some alternatives to the standard grid. They had the option to be powered by wind and solar. It would be a great reduction in capacity if they needed to use it solely, but it would be better than nothing at all. Their phone service remained mostly non-existent. Occasionally, someone's phone would pick up service for a few moments and a message would come through with a chime to notify them. By the time the phone was picked up, the service would be gone. They kept their phones charged out of habit at this point.

The moment Lea heard Will's Jeep return, she popped up out of the chair. She tip-toed as quickly and as quietly as she could out of the room. The sound of that Jeep had given her a boost of energy and hope. She threw the front door open and nearly hit her father who was reaching for the door handle. She apologized and hugged him and then hugged Will more tightly than her father. Alejandro noticed and lowered an eyebrow at Will. He tried to hold the gaze but couldn't help but laugh.

"That was quick," Lea said trying to catch her breath from the sprint through the house. "There was no trouble getting the antibiotics? Does it look bad anywhere?"

"Surprisingly, no," Will answered. "We even stopped by the grocery store again to see if we could get anything else. Not much there right now. It's a bit of a mess actually."

"It looks pretty much like the pictures you'd see in history class of the Soviet Union grocery stores," Alejandro added. "It's mostly empty shelves with a few things that no one wants scattered around. Picked clean."

"I went and talked to Mary and she told us that most food is now being diverted to those big camps that they talked about on the news," Will said.

Lea jumped in before Will could finish, "Are we going to have to go to one of those camps if we can't get food? I don't want to live in one of those."

"No way," Will said with a chuckle. "I have no desire whatsoever to be in one of those. I imagine sickness is going to spread like a wildfire in there. Let alone, the whole thing being way too weird. It's like we just had a coup in the government and now they want everyone to gather together at these fenced-in camps. Not for me," Will shook his head back and forth and paused for a moment. "Anyways, Mary said the empty store was temporary. It was done to initially stock all of the camps and she said they are expecting a delivery up to a week from now. I think they said on the news that the camps are meant for people from big cities."

"Yeah," Alejandro said. "They don't want tons of people moving to small towns that don't have the infrastructure to keep them there. They are supposed to go to the tent cities...if they don't all kill each other before they can get out," he paused for a moment. "Is your mom awake yet? The doctor said to start the antibiotics as soon as we can."

"Not yet. I was in there watching over her until I heard you guys get back," Lea said. She turned to Will, "Your mom was making breakfast. It might be ready by now."

They all made their way inside and Will and Alejandro leaned the rifles they brought with them to town against the wall near the front door. Alejandro went straight to the spare bedroom he and Juana were using. She was stirring and he anticipated she would be waking up any moment now. He took the bottle of pain medication from on top of the dresser and removed a pill. He pulled the new bottle of antibiotics out of his pocket and removed a pill and placed both of them next to her glass of water on the nightstand. He stood over her for a moment considering waking her and then decided against it.

Alejandro was carefully and quietly shutting the door as Lea approached from down the hall. He relayed in whispers that he wanted Juana to continue sleeping as long as she could. Lea let him know that food was already set aside for her for whenever she woke up and that breakfast was ready for the rest of them to eat.

*****

The coming days brought much improvement for Juana's recovery. The redness receded and she no longer had a fever. Her spirits were on the rise. The exhaustion no longer dominated her day, however, the group still wanted her to take it easy.

Alejandro and Will were contemplating what work could be done around the property to make it safer. They didn't anticipate much traffic around their location, however, they still wanted to take some precautions. They knew it would be difficult to keep a constant watch with only five people and they kept Juana out of their plans for the time being bringing their number of able bodies down to four.

"Do you think we need to keep watch day and night?" Alejandro asked Will and Beth. "We'll be working on things around here and will be starting a garden soon enough. We'll be outside a lot. If anyone is on watch at night then they'll be sleeping for a portion of the day. That's less work to be done gardening or hunting for food."

Alejandro, Lea, Will, and Beth stood outside the house. Juana had settled down on the couch in the living room for a nap. They went out to keep the house quiet for her. They were enjoying the sunny day with milder temperatures. The week before, when life as everyone knew it changed, the weather had been bitter cold. They were happy with the reprieve, however temporary.

"We might not need to keep watch all the time," Will answered. "I just worry about all the looting we see on the news. Maybe it's my imagination getting the best of me. I mean, I know the house can't be seen from the road, but I just wonder if that group that you ran into at the grocery store is sticking around this area. I hope they moved on. What if there's more like them from Fresno that come up here to loot?"

"The news said there's a CMA camp accepting people in the Fresno area," Lea chimed in. "Looters might have less opposition in Fresno if a lot of those people move to the camp. They might have free reign of thousands of homes in Fresno. Or, hopefully, the would-be looters go to the camp and have no reason to go out and do that. Sorry, is that wrong to say? Wanting them to stay in Fresno and loot there. I don't really want them to loot there. I just don't want them here."

Beth laughed. "We know what you mean, honey. I think we are all in agreement on that."

"Those are all good points, Lea," Will said. "I hope having a camp located there helps us out here. We'll just have to keep our eyes open. Luckily the house is set back from the road. There is quite a bit of work we should get done, especially if we are going to get a big garden going. I hope Mary is correct that the grocery store should be kept stocked. It emptied so quickly last week that I don't want to bank on them. We'll have to make a run to the store in the next couple of days to see if they have anything yet."

"What kinds of things need to get done?" Lea asked.

"For starters," Will said, "I want to put a roadblock up on the end of the drive. I think people are less likely to come up here to attempt to steal anything if they have to haul it all the way down the drive. I've read signs can be a big deterrent in situations like this."

"Signs?" the other three asked in unison. They all laughed at doing so.

"Yeah, signs that say, 'Trespassers will be shot on sight' and 'Beware of dog' or 'Beware of the angry bull'. I've read in some prepper blogs that when people see signs like those, they'd rather not deal with a fight. They are looking to take the easy route and not have any opposition."

Alejandro laughed. "I like it. The only problem would be if they are looking for a fresh cut of beef."

Will smiled at the joke. "Good point. If things get bad enough then we'll take down that sign."

"What else do you think we need to do?" Beth asked.

"Oh," Will began and paused. He scratched his head and looked past them in thought, "I'd like to check all the fencing along the road. We could also start breaking up the ground where we want the garden to go. There's a good chance we'll have some larger rocks to get out of the way."

"We get the most precipitation in the fall, winter, and spring," Alejandro said. "We might want to try to find a way to collect as much of it as possible. Maybe use tarps funneling to barrels? The summer months can get pretty dry and we'll want to water the garden during those hot dry months."

"Good idea. I didn't think of that," Will said. "We could tap into the downspouts from the gutters as well. We might be able to build something that directs the water straight to storage right at the garden. That way we don't have to collect and carry a lot of large barrels."

"Looks like we have our work cut out for us," Beth said with a chuckle. "What should we start with? Blocking the driveway?"

"That's as good as any," Will said.

"We still want to be able to get out," Beth said. "We should probably build a gate."

"We could do a gate," Will said. "I think between my stock of supplies and what we have around here, we shouldn't need to go into town to buy anything."

"Do you think we should be worried about anyone trying to ram through it?" Lea asked.

"That's something to keep in mind while we build it," Will answered. "Maybe we'll use some whole logs in the construction so no one will want to attempt to ram it," he said laughing. "In all seriousness, I bet we could make a spike strip as well. Lay it right on the inside of the gate and keep it camouflaged with branches or dirt or something."

Will looked around at the others, widening his eyes to see if they liked his idea at all. Alejandro was nodding his head in approval. He put his hand up to his chin and looked down as if he was thinking about the idea or planning how to begin the project. Will looked to Lea and his mother.

"What's a spike strip?" Lea asked.

"I was wondering the same thing," Beth said.

"Oh sorry," Will said, "I suppose I should explain it a little better. It's those strips that the police put across a road to stop a car. They are spikes of sharp metal that will pop all the tires. They have some that are just a slightly raised bump where the spikes stay down so others cars can keep using that route. When the car they want to stop comes up, they put the spikes up."

"Oh right. I know what you are talking about now." Lea said.

"Do you think you can make it so we can still drive over the spot?" Beth asked.

"I'm pretty sure I can. We'll have to put all the spikes on a bar that we'll attach a lever to one end. We'll lay them flat when we want to drive over. They'll have to be set into the ground a little bit so when we lay the spikes flat, they'll be below ground so we don't accidentally pop tires driving back onto the driveway towards the house. Going that way will be driving towards the spikes. I think our biggest challenge building it will be finding enough pieces of metal to turn into spikes."

"Will," Alejandro cut in and then paused for a moment, "do you think a spike strip will stop someone? Or a group? To be honest, I think a spike strip will only slow someone down. I bet it's groups out there stealing from people, not just a single person. If a group comes in and loses tires on one vehicle then it's only going to slow them down. They'll have more vehicles and people. I think we need something more than spikes."

"Well, what do you think we should do?" Will asked. "A moat?" He laughed at his own suggestion.

"Yes!" Alejandro answered excitedly. "That's exactly what I'm thinking. We dig out a section of that lower drive." He pointed down the driveway. "Then we build a drawbridge. We'll lower it and then open the gate to get out."

"Guys," Beth said, "can't someone just walk around the spike strip and lower it or around a hole in the driveway and lower our bridge?"

"I guess that's possible," Alejandro said. "The point is for it to be a deterrent."

"I'd just hate for us to do all this work when it might not be needed," Beth said. "I think a chained and locked gate will do the trick. If we see a lot of people coming through this area then maybe we'll reconsider. You can't even tell there's a house up here from the road. I also think if someone gets in through the gate and doesn't realize there's a hole in the driveway and their car drops in, we won't have any way to get it out and out of our way. We could have trouble getting out if we need to."

"We'll just make it deep enough for the car to go completely in the hole," Alejandro said with a big smile on his face. "We should at least do this gate first," his smile faded as his tone turned more serious. "No question in my mind that the gate should be done before anything else. Since we know there is looting, I think security becomes a top priority."

Will wondered to himself if Alejandro's heightened desire for security was a result of Juana being attacked. He didn't mind beefing up the security on the property. He didn't want any more trouble for them than they had already dealt with. It was just a thought in the back of his mind.

"I'll go see what materials we have to work with," Will said. "I know I have some wood already. However, if we are building it to prevent someone's truck blasting through it then I'm sure we'll want to cut down a few good sized trees. Something this heavy will probably need a wheel to help it move and to support the weight. I think I have something that will work. I'm hoping we won't have to go to the hardware store for anything. I'm guessing there is a good chance they might be low on supplies as well. You guys should head down there and check out the fencing along the road. Might as well make sure we don't need to do anything while we are going to be down there working."

Lea and Alejandro went in to check on Juana and let her know they'd be down by the road for a little while working. She was awake from her nap and she told them that she didn't need anything from them and that she was now perfectly capable of managing most things on her own. Lea didn't like her mother's stubbornness when it came to her recovery. Lea had become too stressed and too overwhelmed with her mother being out of commission for so long and for such a reason. She couldn't think of any time in her life that her mother had to deal with something like this.

They filled up several bottles they found in the kitchen with water and rejoined Beth who was waiting on the porch. They began the walk down the drive. The driveway went downhill through the trees before reaching the road. This made Alejandro grunt in dissatisfaction. He was realizing the climb he would be making back up the hill once they were done. He wished he had kept himself in better shape.

It didn't take them long to walk the fence line along the road. They found a few spots that needed repair. Fencing had either come loose from the wood or a log was rotted to the point of near collapse. Will arrived in his Jeep, the back open to accommodate a load of wood he gathered from the shed.

"How's the fence? Will asked as he got out of the Jeep.

Lea explained the few repairs needed on the fence. Will wasn't too surprised. He had always tried to keep up with repairs on the property. He usually kept himself busy working for other people so he could make some money.

He was pleased there wasn't much to do for that project.

"I don't think we need to take a trip to the store. I found a lot of heavy duty hardware in the shed. There's obviously plenty of wood," he motioned a thumb behind himself to the Jeep. "Of course, we still want some heavy duty logs that we'll need to cut down. I was thinking that the gate should open outwards. We'll have a log the gate will lock to and butted up next to that, set inside slightly, we'll post another log that will be a block. That way the gate won't open inwards." He was using his fingers to demonstrate what he was picturing.

"Yeah, that way it makes it even harder to ram open," Lea said with a smile.

"Mom, do you and Lea want to design the gate?" Will asked. "I brought down some paper and pencils. If you two do that then Alejandro," he paused, "...I mean Al," he said sarcastically as he looked over to Alejandro. "he and I can get started on bringing down a few trees."

Alejandro was shaking his head and chuckling. "See, I knew you'd get it down eventually. I hope we have a chainsaw and not one of those two-man blades to get these trees."

"Yes," Will said. "Oh man, I think we'd break our backs trying to work one of those big blades. I'm pretty sure there's one of those collecting dust in the far reaches of the shed. I've never used it, but I bet it's grueling work."

"That's fine with me," Beth finally answered. "Lea and I will draw out a design for the gate. We'll figure out final dimensions once the posts are set. I don't want you taking any of the trees around the driveway. Go over that way," she pointed off away from the driveway, "if you can get your Jeep over there. Are you going to drag the logs back over using your Jeep?"

"That would probably be the easiest way to get them back over here," Will said. "Hey, what do you think about getting the trees from across the road? That's all power line easement and they cut down trees every year anyway to make sure they don't get close to the lines. It's a lot closer too."

"That's fine with me. I don't think anyone will mind," Beth said.

They began the project right away. Will and Alejandro took the wood, tools, and other supplies out of the Jeep and then drove it across the street and began scoping out which trees they wanted to select, bringing the chainsaw along. Beth and Lea drew out a few designs based on Will's description. They brought the designs across the street for them all to choose one. After they all finally agreed on one, Lea took the post hole digger from the Jeep and began the back-breaking task of digging out the location the trunks were going to be placed. Beth started measuring out and marking the pieces of wood Will had brought.

Beth took notice that no vehicles had come down the road. It wasn't common for many to come by, but it reminded her of the others that lived further down the road away from town. All but one of the houses would be empty. There were four other properties with homes on them. Three were summer cabins used by families that lived the rest of the year in San Francisco and Los Angeles and would most likely still be empty this time of year. The other full-timer was a retired farmer, Lewis, that had been a good friend of her husbands. Lewis had stayed a good friend of Beth and Will over the years. He had a large farm in central California for many years before retiring and moving up the road from them. He had lost his wife to cancer soon after the move. He had a surprisingly positive attitude for being alone. He kept most of his property up by his house empty of trees and full of crops. The excess he didn't use himself or give away to a charity through his church, he'd sell at a farmer's market down in Fresno. Beth began to feel guilty they hadn't checked in on him. She decided they should check on him soon and walked across the street to talk to Will.

"Will," Beth said, "I think we should check in on Lewis today or tomorrow."

"Ohhh," Will said as his eyes widened and he shook his head. "I forgot about him. I feel bad."

"Me too," Beth said with a frown. "I've always hated that he's alone up here. Do you think we should see if he wants to join us here? He'd be a really good resource for our garden. He's got a lot of knowledge about the best things to grow and how to get good quality food out of them. He's always talking about that kind of stuff."

"I doubt he'll want to leave that place," Will said. "His wife is buried there. He's far away from everything too. He's the last place before the four-wheel drive trail begins. He's close enough to us that we can check on him often. We can always ask if he wants to join us, but I highly doubt he will."

"I know," Beth said with a sigh, "I still want the offer on the table."

"How about I go check on him in the morning?" Will asked. "Before we get back to working on this gate."

"I'll go with you," Beth said. "It's been a few weeks since I've seen him."

Chapter Seventeen

April 2037

Marcus followed Anthony and Kenneth into a makeshift room within a large, white, canvas tent. It was a much larger tent than the others surrounding it that sat centrally in a CMA operations camp. The room was made of glass partitioned walls to make a barrier for sound. It wasn't sound proof, but it did the job to keep the contents of the meetings held there only amongst the people that were invited. The rest of the tent had row after row of cubicles surrounding the central conference room. Administrative workers filled this tent. They supported the regional higher-ups that were now running this part of the country. There were no refugees at this camp. This was a CMA employee camp. Just as they had been prepped for, the majority of WWNL's operations were now based at this camp as well.

Marcus was almost amused by the proximity of this CMA camp to Thomas's ranch. He could drive there in fifteen minutes. Of course, he didn't drive there. Thomas and the rest of the ARF leadership no longer wanted to be seen with him. They had to keep their connection a secret. They were sure that the CMA was suspicious of the American Right's Foundation's intentions. They were all especially spooked to find out the CMA had one of their headquarters locations right in their backyard. They became paranoid to the point that they only allowed Marcus to contact them through a series of encryption and closed network devices.

Marcus would have to type out his message on a computer that had no internet capability. The computer was provided by the ARF and had an encryption program that converted his message to PGP, which meant 'Pretty Good Privacy' format, or so he was told. He remembered getting a headache while the technician at Thomas's ranch explained the process to him. He knew that both his computer and a computer at Thomas's ranch held the cipher to decode his message. He would load his encrypted message onto a thumb drive. He would have to get permission to leave the camp, which was a process in itself that annoyed Marcus, and go to a local cafe. They only allowed Marcus to leave camp once a week on his day off. He was allowed to do work related trips in the helicopter almost at his own will. He was baffled by how little sense it made.

Thomas's tech had set up an antenna at the cafe that transmitted directly to an antenna at the ranch. Marcus would have to sit in a specific seat in a back booth. There was a hidden USB port underneath the table to plug in the thumb drive. Once plugged in, the message would automatically download and transmit. Marcus could monitor the whole transaction from a small device connected right in the open. It was a smoke detector. A raging inferno could be right underneath it and it wouldn't make a peep. All of this smoke detectors guts were removed and replaced with a simple circuit board that communicated with the antenna on the roof. It would indicate what was happening through a series of lights. If the red light on the left were flashing, it meant that his message was being uploaded and transmitted. If a steady red light on the right side appeared, it meant the transfer was complete. If a green light appeared in the center of the device, it meant a message was available for Marcus. He usually left the thumb drive plugged in the entire time he sat in the cafe and incoming messages were loaded to the drive automatically. He could then take the drive back to his computer and it would decode the message. Marcus thought it was all way too much work and worrying, but he didn't mind the excuse to leave the camp. If anyone ever discovered the drive, they'd find some old pictures from Marcus's college days and text files that looked like they were corrupted with a virus.

Marcus chose his seat at the conference table next to Kenneth. He dreaded coming to these meetings. He used to be able to be free at work. Free on the news. He had had his own segment for years where he could basically say whatever he wanted. Now he was an actor. He had a part to play. He had to be in character anytime he was anywhere outside of his room. He even wondered about his privacy in his own room. He had wished for at least a hotel to live in but the CMA wanted all the personnel, especially Marcus, living at the camp. His 'room' was a Conex container. He would have felt infinitely more comfortable in a cheap motel. Their strong desire for him to live nearby is what made him suspicious of his privacy. Was his room bugged? Had CMA personnel been listening in on his personal calls? Did he now have to keep up the act all the time?

Keeping up with being the CMA's propaganda face was stressful and exhausting. Marcus's mind was on a higher alert than it had ever been. His brain was working overtime. Any moment he thought he could relax and take the mask off, a CMA employee would arrive and he would have to instantly snap back into the role they expected of him. This wasn't him. He wondered why he should be working so hard at pleasing them. They already knew his thoughts on much of what they did. He had broadcast it to the world for years.

"...and General Gray from the Southern region had reported the approximate death rate in his region has equalized with what other regions are reporting."

What had Marcus just heard? Marcus didn't even know who this man was. He looked possibly military. He wished he had been paying better attention now. Perhaps he could pull some of this information out of Kenneth later.

"Thank you for the report, General Bryce," Anthony said. "That brings me to Kenneth, this is for you to pass on to the WWNL crew," Anthony said, "the skeleton crew we've left behind at the WWNL building has now been relocated. They've had to evacuate several times in this last week because of fires on lower levels of the building. The levels of violence in the city only seem to be increasing so for the foreseeable future, this camp is work and home. The CMA, for the time being, won't be getting too involved in suppression of these problems. We want to focus manpower on the camps."

Marcus noticed that Kenneth didn't seem affected by the news. He was taking notes like it was any other boring meeting he had been to in his life.

"Where have they been relocated to? Here?" Kenneth asked while still scribbling some notes.

"Um," Anthony shuffled through some papers trying to find the answer. "I can't tell you for sure but I think they are at a WWNL affiliate in Boston or Philly. I'll find out for you."

"As long as we are broadcasting without interruption. That is all I care about," Kenneth said.

"We need to get Marcus out to Denver and Salt Lake," the lone woman in the room said.

Marcus leaned forward in is chair. "What is going on there?" he asked. "And I'm sorry, who are you?" Marcus asked the woman.

"My name is Mara. I'm the head of the Western region camps. People seem to be more independent out West and the camps aren't filling like we expected. We need you, someone that people recognize, know, and trust to help usher them in the right direction."

"Oh, of course," Marcus said. "Nice to meet you, by the way. What about other Western cities? Vegas? Los Angeles? San Francisco?"

"They each have their own problems," Mara answered. "I want to focus on Denver and Salt Lake for now. Los Angeles is going as expected. It's a nightmare. It's ready for the next step."

"Next step?" Marcus asked.

"We aren't talking about that now," Anthony said quickly. "We won't be discussing that now." His eyes shifted in between Mara and General Bryce. "We can have Marcus head out West right away. How about the day after tomorrow, Marcus?" Anthony was looking at his phone now, presumably checking a calendar.

"That sounds perfect," Marcus said with a smile painted on. He pretended to no longer care about what the 'next step' was.

Marcus wanted to pay closer attention to the rest of the meeting. It wasn't directly about him or his assignments so his mind seemed to wander. No, his mind wasn't just wandering randomly, it was trying to process all the things he had just heard. There was probably plenty more he was missing right now as he was contemplating all this new information. It was as if every corner he turned there was some new surprise. What was this next step? Why would L.A. being a nightmare cause it to be ready for whatever this next step was? What had he missed about death rates?

*****

Marcus moved forward two steps at a time, sliding an empty tray down the long mirrored, metal surface. He was in the WWNL mess tent and hoped they might surprise him with some new mouth-watering dish. He peered ahead and saw it was another stew, his hopes shrank. He noticed the cooks had little to no creativity. The vast majority of the meals outside of breakfast were stews. They'd mix together all the food items for the day in a giant pot of water and serve it for lunch and dinner. Perhaps he was a food snob, but he thought it was getting too repetitive. He wondered if the CMA mess tent served more creative fare.

He retrieved his bowl of stew along with a piece of bread. He laughed to himself thinking this was the bland government bread he thought of in the past. He glanced around the tables. He spotted Kenneth alone at a table reading through his notes as he ate. Marcus's mood brightened. He thought this should be easy to learn more about whatever these death rates were. He grabbed a bottle of water from an ice bucket located at the end of the food line and made his way to Kenneth.

"This seat open, boss?" Marcus asked.

"Please sit," Kenneth said through a mouthful of food as he motioned across the table from himself.

Marcus situated himself across from Kenneth and repositioned some of the items on his tray. Kenneth brought all his pages of notes together in one pile and smoothed out the edges to straighten them all. He picked them all up and tapped the bottom against the table to help straighten them and then set the pile aside.

"Say, Kenneth," Marcus said as he was bringing a spoonful of stew to his mouth, blowing on it, "what is meant by 'death rate'? I know I've probably missed some meetings while out covering a story, but I don't recall that being talked about before in any of the meetings I've been in."

Marcus hadn't planned on jumping right into the topic, but he just couldn't hold his tongue with the level of curiosity he had. He shoveled a few more spoonfuls into his mouth waiting for Kenneth to finish a bite to answer.

"Yeah, you probably missed the meeting this was initially discussed," Kenneth said. "It's the rate at which the overall population is dying. It includes people killing each other, sickness from not being able to get medical help, the usuals such as old age. I'm sure there are some other categories that I can't think of."

"You are talking about this like it's not a big deal," Marcus said. "Are the numbers much higher than they were before all this began?"

"Look for yourself," Kenneth said as he picked up his stack of papers. He flipped through a few before pulling a single sheet out and handing it to Marcus. "You really should pay better attention in these meetings," he said with a chuckle.

"What!?" Marcus blurted out after scanning the page. "These numbers show over a thousand percent gain! Am I reading this correctly?"

"Lower your voice," Kenneth said in a quieter yet commanding voice.

"Is the CMA doing anything?" Marcus asked, still not much quieter than before. "All this chaos began with the government's recklessness and then escalated with the CMA takeover. How come I didn't know all of this death was going on? I work for the news! Shouldn't I be reporting this? I mean, I knew there was some violence going on, but this?"

"Marcus, are you trying to get yourself canned?" Kenneth said in a near whisper, hunched forward over his tray. He looked around at the surrounding tables to see if anyone was now focused on them. "The contract you had with WWNL doesn't mean a thing anymore. It's worthless. Anthony told me that he talked to you. He said you were on board with the CMA way. I was surprised to hear it since I've known you for so long and know how you think. I know you don't agree with all of this. I just figured you wanted to end up on the good side of things. If you go spouting off things like you just said around the wrong people then they'll boot you. I'm sure of it. They've kept you in the dark on some things because of how you lean...politically. They'll bring you in fully, but you have to keep your mouth shut."

Kenneth sat back and adjusted his tie. He glanced around again to make sure their conversation was only between them. Marcus looked around too, worrying that Anthony was about to pop up from underneath a table. He remembered the threat he gave him at the camp the day he met him. Was this task of being an inside man for

Thomas and his group going to be too difficult for Marcus? Was he too vocal about his opinions? His life's work was talking for millions to hear, of course, he was too vocal.

"Yes. Anthony did talk to me," Marcus was now speaking quietly like Kenneth had. "I...didn't realize this was something they didn't want to be reported."

"Of course they don't want this reported. They want the CMA shown in good light. Ya know, how helpful they are being. They only have so many people. I don't even know how many would even be trained to handle this," he paused and looked up as if he were searching for a word, "civil war, I guess it is. People run out of food and supplies for a week and look what they do. I know it's crazy. I don't think the government or the CMA anticipated or wanted all these problems. They are dealing with it as it comes. There are just steps that need to be taken."

"I just," Marcus said shaking his head, "I don't know. Do they know how many have died so far?"

Kenneth leaned forward again, "A few million," he whispered. "I think it's probably more than that. Don't tell anyone else. And don't tell anyone I told you. I don't think we are supposed to talk about this outside of that meeting room."

Marcus didn't say anything. His eyes widened and he stared down at the table.

"Marcus, you're my friend," Kenneth said. "I've pushed hard for you to be a part of this. We've known each other for a long, long time. We've helped eachother out countless times as we've climbed the ladders in our careers. This is a major turning point in our country's history. People will read about this for hundreds of years. Those words in the history book will be written by you and me.

We have a chance to play a big part in this. You and me. It's what we always wanted." Kenneth had passion in his voice. He was speaking with animated, clenched fists. "The CMA is going to lead the recovery. They want you to be the face of the CMA. This is going to be a new and stronger country." He sternly pointed a finger at Marcus. "Don't screw this chance up."

Kenneth gathered his papers and took the sheet from in front of Marcus. He got up, grabbing his tray and hurried off. Marcus watched him leave. He was dumbstruck. Why were they keeping the fact that millions had died and were still dying in the dark? Was there any point in hiding that information? He hadn't even gotten the chance to ask what 'the next step' was. He needed to keep low now, he thought. This was the second warning. How many more would he be given before they got rid of him? He would keep low and still keep up the act, as stressful as it had been. No more slip-ups, not even in front of Kenneth. He needed to get to the cafe and get this latest information to Thomas.

He had kept Thomas in the loop over the past month and a half but still never gave him an answer about being a part of the American Rights Foundation's plans. This latest news just made him more suspicious of the CMA. More suspicious and more frightened. Kenneth was sure they were a part of the solution but Marcus wasn't buying it. There were many factors leading up to it, but this spike in death was directly caused by what the CMA was doing. Plus, they weren't doing anything to help stop it. The country had descended into chaos and then now it was digging even deeper. They talked about death casually in meetings. They were talking about millions of people dying as if they were telling co-workers the weekend's adventures by the water cooler. Marcus knew what he needed to tell Thomas. He knew exactly what he needed to do.

Chapter Eighteen

April 2037

"Do we have everything?" Lea asked looking down at the small, red, child's wagon.

"I think so," Will said. "I hope so. I don't want to have to walk back for anything. Lewis will have tools as well."

"Does everyone have their guns?" Beth added.

Everyone nodded.

"Well," Beth said, "we have tools, guns, and water. I say we better get going. Can't be lazy today."

They all patted pockets and searched around them to make sure all items had been accounted for. Will, Lea, Juana, and Beth were now off, with only little groaning, on the almost two-mile trek to Lewis's farm. They were to spend the day tending to the crops. Alejandro had left a couple of hours before dawn to meet Lewis and get an early start.

It had been two months since they decided to join together and hunker down at Beth's property outside of town. Just as they had thought, Lewis refused to leave his place and join them. However, he did join them in the efforts of farming. He had most definitely been a wealth of knowledge for them. The six of them had filled nearly every open piece of land on both properties with seed and starter plants. The labor was the most strenuous they had experienced in their entire lives, save Lewis, who would do much of this labor normally on his own every year. Their backs ached from days of stooping low to dig and plant. Their fingers stiffened, barely being able to move for several days.

A couple of trips into town to check on the status of available food at the grocery store revealed how lucky they had been. It appeared that the pandemonium they had experienced the day Juana was injured had only magnified exponentially. What Alejandro and Will thought would be a casual stroll into town turned out to be a nightmare. They had assumed, wrongfully, that the situation had probably settled after a couple of weeks. As they approached town, they weren't too surprised to see smoke rising from numerous points. It could easily be thought that the inconsistent electricity and gas problems persisted, which was exactly what Will had thought. Once in town, their jaws dropped in shock to see the charred remains of once familiar storefronts and houses. Very few of the rising pillars of black smoke represented cooking fires.

The next horror was when they noticed the bodies. There were bodies scattered here and there. In one parking lot, they noticed a small pile of bodies. Were these their friends? Maybe neighbors? The putrid stench made both Will and Alejandro gag and nearly retch. The only thing that made them able to bear it was the constant smell of smoke that thickened in waves. Even the smoke was a bit sickening after a few minutes of it wafting on their faces. It was as if they just happened upon a war zone. Where were the police? Where were the firefighters? There were people's homes still burning. Where was the news? They had kept up with the news when electricity allowed it, which was most of the time. The news made it look like things were improving. They constantly showed the CMA camps and busloads of peaceful people being brought to a camp. Was it possible that large cities settled down and their small town was an anomaly? Yes, they knew the CMA camps were set up to help the people fleeing the violence in big cities, but the news showed a completely different picture. The group had discussed their thoughts on the matter at length, in wonder of what was going to happen to their country. They guessed that the camps were going to stay in place for some time due to the fact that distribution and supply chains seemed to be rerouted to them. They figured this out on an earlier trip to the grocery store. It was still empty.

Now, as they approached the store again, they saw it was even worse on this trip. Had there been a delivery of food in the past week that they missed? It was probably best that they missed it. The scene was of more bodies and more smoke billowing out of the store. It was either that the store had gotten some food and people charged the few items causing an all out battle or people became upset of the ever-empty store and decided to destroy it and each other.

Will and Alejandro came to their senses, breaking themselves out of the shock they were experiencing, and decided to rush home quickly. They could feel the watching eyes, most likely curious of their gas filled vehicle and the places far away that tank of gas could take them from this war zone. They saw one woman drop whatever she was carrying and turn in an all-out sprint away from them. They had looked at each other in confusion. They didn't stop to find out. They rushed home and told the others. They collectively decided to stay in between the two properties and forget any trips to town for the time being. They reduced the use of any vehicles to emergency only. They had no way to get any more fuel. Will had been frustrated by the wasted drive and the wasted fuel.

They continued to watch the news nightly, as long as the power would allow it. They anticipated stories on what happened in Oakhurst, or perhaps to see similar scenes in larger cities. They were puzzled day after day when the news showed nothing of what they expected. They felt like they were in an isolated pit. They wondered how Oakhurst, a small town, turned into a war zone while everywhere else seemed to recover from the initial violence after the restructuring of the country took place. Needless to say, they made sure to always be armed. They imagined the only ones remaining in Oakhurst were those that would fight and kill and steal for what they wanted rather than work for it.

They gradually approached the drive to Lewis's property, pushing on in the uphill climb. They enjoyed early morning air, dew clinging to the spring blooms. Still along the road that bordered his property was a thick hide of trees. All the properties on the road were like this. Maybe it was originally planned that way for privacy reasons. Looking up the long drive, one would think it lead nowhere; that if you decided to take this route, you'd be turning around once you got to the first bend past the thick patch of trees. Lewis had no fence surrounding his property. He had wanted a tall deer fence to keep them and other animals from grazing on his crops but never did put one up.

They paused partway up the drive for a rest. They each silently dreaded the work to come that day. They were already winded, needing a break. The work hadn't even begun yet. They would be bending low, on hands and knees, pulling weeds and pruning. They would check for any problems with the plants, such as disease so that Lewis could quickly address the problem before it could spread too far. It was sure to take them a few days to finish this project. As if on cue, they all regathered their things and continued on.

As they passed the different blocked sections of strawberries, raspberries, potatoes, spinach, corn, and other plants they couldn't identify by sight they slowed, considering what needed to be done in each plot. They were surprised to see Alejandro and Lewis not working in the gardens, but skinning a deer. It was tied up to a low-hanging branch of a large oak near Lewis's house.

"Dad!" Lea blurted out in surprise of what she saw.

Alejandro and Lewis turned, they seemed to not realize the others had approached.

"Good morning everyone," Alejandro said with a large smile. "We got lucky this morning," he said holding an arm out to present the deer.

"Alejo, is this why you wanted to come out here so early? To hunt?" Juana said sarcastically, with a half smile on her face.

He laughed, "No, I really came to help Lewis with the plants. He had the rifle watching for the deer. Once we spotted this one coming in to feed on the plants he let me get it." His smile grew, "To be honest, I've been hoping this would happen."

Will chimed in, "You've been hoping to down a deer? Nice shot by the way. Well-placed."

"That's what I said," Lewis added.

"Yeah, I've been out early every morning," Alejandro said. "I see the deer around here and at our place. Since I'm normally working in the garden, I don't have the rifle handy, just a sidearm."

"You've been wanting to kill a deer?" Lea asked sounding somewhat sad in the question.

"Lea, there's a lot of good meat on this," Alejandro said. "We've got to have food. There's none in the store anymore. This is how it's done."

"I know I know," she said. "I just don't like seeing it like this."

"We should take you hunting then," Will said grinning. "It's a good skill to learn."

"Oh, Will no. I don't know," she said almost sounding as if she was considering it.

"Juana, do you think we can get some of your jerky made from this?" Alejandro asked.

She stepped forward and further examined the deer.

"I don't think we've ever made jerky from deer before but I figure it'll be similar," Juana said. "Lots of good meat on here it looks like."

"Oh, of course," Lewis said. "I've done jerky with deer many times. It makes for good jerky."

"Ohhh," Juana sounded out excitedly. "We'll have to do both recipes and have a taste testing."

"I see," Lewis said smiling. "You are quite the competitor, it would seem. You're on."

They all laughed at the exchange.

"A cook-off seems like a long lost thing of a distant past," Beth said. "Too weird. I'm looking forward to some jerky. We can make a good stew out this other meat too.

Maybe do it for lunch tomorrow?"

"I'll help," Juana said. "We should probably start mid-morning tomorrow."

With plans in mind and mouths watering for the stew they could hardly wait another day for, they began the grueling labor for the day. They each took their own plot next to each other and started working it back and forth, row by row. Alejandro and Lewis continued working on butchering the deer. The others were on their hands and knees, pulling weeds and pruning the plants as Lewis had instructed in the days before. If they noticed any insects or evidence of their recent dwelling on a plant, such as mostly eaten leaves, they were to show Lewis for his further analysis. He had a few different natural products to help rid his vegetables of the insects. He didn't want to banish all bugs since some were beneficial to the life of the garden, only the ones that would destroy the plants to the point they were a worthless food source for him. He had a few different mixtures he would make up with a variety of products such as garlic, vegetable oil, coffee grounds, and even habanero peppers.

They were at least lucky in the sense that is was still spring and the indiscriminate pounding heat of the sun was not yet on their backs and being radiated off the earth into their faces. The nights and mornings were still cool and the afternoons were a comfortable warm. However, their toiling combined with the afternoon warmth was sure to exhaust them and drench them in sweat. While they took a break for lunch, they looked to the sky in hope of seeing cloud cover for the afternoon's labors. Chances were good for this as most afternoons throughout the spring brought rain. They had set up rain collection at both Beth and Lewis's properties. Lewis said he was wanting to hold off on using it until the summer time when the rain was more scarce. They were gifted with only a short rain shower in the mid-afternoon, but they were still thankful for the reprieve. The sun had reappeared from behind the clouds only a short hour later.

At dinnertime, they wrapped up their work for the day. They collected and accounted for all the tools they had brought and decided to store them at Lewis's since they'd be back the next day. They gathered together on Lewis's porch to review which plot of plants had been covered that day. Lewis had a notepad with a rough sketch of his property with the layout of the garden. He checked off the areas as each person listed the sections they had worked. He placed the pencil above his ear and examined the drawing.

"Looks like we covered just under half," Lewis said. "That is with Alejandro and me working on the deer for most of the morning. I think we are slightly ahead of what I expected. Beth and Juana will start that deer stew tomorrow mid-morning." He looked around the gardens and thought for a moment. "I had anticipated three full days of this work. I think we'll have it done before noon on the third day if we continue at this pace. We could rest half a day and then have your gardens done the next. After that, we just keep an eye on it for a couple of weeks before we do this again. Make sure it all gets plenty of water. Keep looking for pests. I know I've told you this all before. I'm just repeating myself now."

"We certainly appreciate the education," Beth said.

"Yes, thank you," Juana said. "I didn't realize there was so much to know about farming."

"Yes, yes. Just like any other specialty," Lewis said. "I'm sure you know I could go on for hours and hours about farming." He smiled at the thought of it. "We should all get some dinner. I'm sure we are all hungry after working like we did today."

*****

After dinner, they began the two-mile walk back home, leaving Lewis alone as he had become accustomed to after many years. They could foresee themselves in their own beds. They imagined a deep sleep. Their aching and sore muscles and tender knees reminded them every step of their cozy, comfortable beds waiting for them. Waiting to draw them in and pull them closer. The sun was on its final descent below the trees and out of sight. It cast a unique and mesmerizing light; the type of light that made all objects have a new vibrancy and created new colors painted on the scattered clouds above. No doubt the continual smokey haze in the air contributed to the new combination of color and light. It was so brief that every occasion one could experience the sight it would cause wonder and awe. They stopped for a moment and stared up at the clouds, their faces still aglow with radiating heat from the day's work. They continued on once the captivating masterpiece that God revealed for them faded away. And that is how they thought of it. They thought of it as if God did present them with this gift, at this particular moment, only for them.

It was now low light and getting dark quickly. They approached the last quarter mile rounding a bend in the road. They came abeam the trees where they could now see the entrance to the driveway and the gate they had built. Alejandro saw them first. He shushed everyone and started herding everyone towards the trees. There was a truck facing their gate with its lights shining on it. A man was at the gate testing the lock and chains. The truck was a faded black that appeared to have some patchwork spray paint in spots along the step-side bed. A few patches of rust outlined the wheel wells. The truck obviously lifted higher than stock with larger wheels and tires.

"I know that truck," Alejandro whispered.

"That's someone you know?" Will asked. "Why are we hiding then?"

"No, I don't who it is," Alejandro answered. "I recognize the truck from the grocery store. It was with that group. The guy who attacked Juana." He looked over to his wife

Juana's face filled with worry and fear. Alejandro could tell she was reliving her attack in her head and creating new scenarios of what could come next. It must have been obvious to the others as well because Beth quickly put an arm around Juana and began rubbing her shoulder.

"I'm gonna go through these trees to get closer and see if I can hear anything better," Will said pointing to the trees along their property.

"No," Lea said almost too loudly.

"Why would you want to do that?" Beth asked.

"I want to know what they are planning," Will answered. "Maybe we can stop them. If they are from that group that was raiding cars at the store then I'm sure they've been the ones that were a part of destroying Oakhurst."

"What do you think we could do to them?" Lea asked.

"Take them out one at a time," Will said. "Now would be the time. There is only two of them."

"What do you mean take them out?" Lea asked with a rising panic in her voice. "Kill them?"

Will looked around at everyone before answering.

"Yes," he said matter of factly. "Look, there are no police. No military it seems. Our town is destroyed. Somebody has to stop them eventually. It looks like they have probably run out of places and things to steal in town and now they have moved out here." He pointed towards their house.

Everyone remained silent for a moment, considering what Will had said. Alejandro was the first to answer.

"I agree. Where will we go if they take the house? They won't just raid it and leave. They burned down the town. What if they do that here? I don't want to have to rely on those camps."

"Will is right," Beth said. "We need to do something." She sighed deeply. She was clearly thinking about the possible consequences of fighting these people.

The look of worry grew on Juana's face while Lea appeared to be coming to terms with their plans.

"Alright," Will said, "I'll get over there and stay in the trees. Don't worry, I won't do anything yet. I just want to hear if they are talking about plans. I'll only shoot if I need to right now."

Lea grabbed Will and hugged him tightly. "Be careful," she said into his ear.

Will wanted to tell her. He wanted to say that he loved her. He had wanted to tell her for the last couple of months. However, he didn't want it to seem like it was words of desperation. A situation like this, a powder keg of potential chaos and violence, was not the scene he pictured in his mind when he told her those words. For some reason, he still imagined it happening in the life before. Normal date nights. A meticulously planned romantic adventure. He didn't know why he still held on to this. He didn't foresee the world returning to the old normal anytime soon. He thought he could see in Lea's eyes that same desire. He wasn't sure if he was ready. Certainly not at this exact moment.

He stepped further into the trees and crept towards the two men at the truck. He could see they were both standing outside the truck now. He thought that one might have been talking into a handheld radio. He couldn't make out what they were saying this far away. He went slowly, bending down low and dropping to one knee every few steps. He constantly checked to make sure neither of them was looking his way when he moved at all. It was now dark enough that he was sure they wouldn't be able to see into the trees. He continued along steadily now. He could start to make out the words.

"...tell him we think we should use some gas to burn down this gate," one of them said into a handheld radio.

The radio beeped and the man held it up to his ear awaiting a response. The men waited only a few seconds before speaking again.

"This might be the jackpot," he said. "This place is secured really well. I bet there is a lot up the hill. We can't see it from the road."

A muffled response finally came. Will couldn't hear exactly what was said but he thought they said something along the line of waiting for more people. He hoped they meant the next day to at least give themselves more time. They could be desperate now. It could be why they were out at night. He wanted to get to the house to get some supplies so they could rush back to Lewis's. Hopefully, they wouldn't find that place too.

Will was so focused on trying to listen that he almost didn't notice the other truck approaching. Its lights were pointed in his general direction, however, he had his head tilted to the side as he tried to listen to as much as he could. He caught a flash of light in the corner of his eye as the arriving truck turned towards the gate and parked next to the other truck. Will abruptly turned his head and his heart skipped a beat. Were they already going to attempt to get inside right now? The added sound of the second truck made it nearly impossible for Will to hear any of the conversation going on now. Will decided to try to get a little bit closer. His mind was racing. Should he get up to the house and get his go-bag? He had prepared a list of items he wanted with him if they ever had to leave quickly and packed them in a bag. Of course, at the time he wanted it with him the most he was separated from it.

He was now lying down, crawling forward a couple of feet at a time. He was trying to stay in the grassy areas as best as he could to stay as quiet as possible. He wondered what the others were thinking now. They surely saw the second truck. He hoped if he tried for the house that they would conclude to head to Lewis's and not wait by the side of the road. He was only about twenty feet away now behind a few wild bushes that grew along the fence line. If he was going to get to the house he would have to back out and get further into the trees. If he jumped the fence this close to them they would most surely see him. He could make out the conversation again.

"Gerard decided to bring everyone up here," one of the men from the recently arrived truck said. "You better be right about this place."

"Are we burning down the gate?" one of the first asked ignoring the other man's comment.

"Yes, they'll bring some gas up with them. Did you search further down the road?"

"Not yet. The map doesn't show anything down there

except a Jeep trail. Maybe there'll be more big properties like this one."

"We'll head down and check it out. Wait here for everyone else. This will probably be a good camp for now. It's all hidden from everything."

The two men that just arrived returned to their truck. They backed up and drove around the other truck and headed down the road. Will was panicking now. He held it all inward. His heart was pounding and he could feel his pulse all throughout his body. He started to crawl back towards the trees to make his way back to the others. Someone needed to get to Lewis and he still wanted to get to his go-bag.

He wasn't being careful enough now. He heard it as if someone clapped their hands right next to his ear. He had crawled onto a stick and it snapped under his knee. It was like turning on a beacon and yelling loudly 'here I am, I surrender'. Both of the men, now leaning against the truck, pushed themselves away from the truck and grabbed rifles that Will had not noticed before. They aimed in his general direction. Will lay frozen, his head was turned back to keep an eye on the men. Would they seek out the source of the noise or brush it off as possibly an animal, maybe a raccoon? Maybe they would fire off a few rounds towards him. He was at a loss for a decision. Lewis was alone with armed men headed for him. He was alone with armed men nearly standing on top of him. How big was this group? He was beginning to consider that firing at these men might be his only chance for escape. He could only hope they would retreat for cover behind their truck before firing back at him.

Will slowly reached for his pistol. His hand reached his holster and he covered the button to try to conceal the noise. He opened it and started sliding the pistol out, again slowly to prevent any sounds. This whole situation with two guns pointing at him could have been avoided had he been careful in the first place. He had panicked. He never considered himself as one to panic. Their whole future was in question again. Where were they going to go? Was everything, all the work they had done in the last two months, all of his prepping, about to disappear in such a short amount of time. He was taking aim at the closest man. Both men were still aiming in his general direction. He was certain that only thirty seconds had passed since the stick snapped under him, yet it felt like hours. The radio crackled.

"How far up this road are you?" a garbled voice said.

The two men turned to look at each other and then looked at the radio perched up on the hood of the running truck.

"That sounded like Gerard," one said to the other. He picked up the radio, "A few miles. By the map, we are a couple of miles from the end of the road."

"Be there in five or so," the voice said.

Was this Will's lucky break? Had God just opened a door for him? They seemed to completely forget they were concerned about the snapping sound just twenty seconds earlier. He quickly started to move, this time being careful to avoid or move any sticks he saw in his path. He glanced back to see the two men resting their rifles against the truck and recommencing their lean upon it. He sighed in relief as he arrived deeper into the woods. He raised up from his crawling position and brushed himself off. He looked back again to gauge the distance between himself and the men waiting to burn down their gate. He figured he was far enough away to be able to run, so he did. He arrived back at where he left the others to see no one in sight.

“Will,” a loudly whispered voice said.

Will turned trying to find the source of the whisper. Lea, Juana, and his mother approached from the dark depths of the trees.

“What did you find out?” his mother asked as she hugged him. A sense of relief shone on her face. “We couldn’t see where you were.”

“They are going to burn the gate down,” Will said shaking his head. Lea approached quickly after Beth to hug him as well. “They are bringing more people. They were talking to others on a radio. Did you see the other truck? Where’s Alejandro?” He had too many questions and too much he wanted to go over.”

“We saw the other truck,” Lea answered. “Once it headed down the road Dad ran to go after Lewis.”

“Good,” Will said. “That’s why I rushed back here. I need to go up to the house and get a few things. Did Alejandro say if he was coming back to this spot? Or another meeting point?”

“What’s at the house?” Beth asked.

“I have a go-bag,” he answered. “I want to get that and some other supplies before we have to find somewhere else to live.”

“Somewhere else to live?” Juana said. She still had the look of horror on her face from earlier.

“It sounds like they have a lot of people on their way right now,” Will said. “They’ll be here any minute now. They also talked about this being their camp. I need to get up there now.” Will was backing up with urgency to get to the house. “What about Alejandro? Once he gets Lewis is he coming back here?”

“He didn’t say,” Beth said.

"Wait here then," Will said. "I'm assuming he'll come back to where he left you. Stay hidden. I'm going up the property line and will jump the fence higher up the hill. I'm going to leave out the back," he said pointing up towards the house, "I'll cross at the back corner of the property and make my way back along the property line again back here."

He didn't wait for any more questions or conversation. He took off running into the trees. Will wouldn't have seen it as he rushed away, but Beth, Lea, and Juana all turned at the same time to see a long line of vehicles coming up the road, their many headlights illuminating the trees. The convoy went as far back along the road as they could see from where they stood. All three started to back up further away from the road again. They knelt down near where they had hidden before. Juana was in tears. She folded her hands in front of herself and prayed. They watched as the first vehicle slowed and stopped by the other truck in front of their gate. Their gate they had spent over two days building to keep out people like this. All of their work was about to go up in flames if Will had heard correctly. They watched a man from the first vehicle get out and inspect the gate. He looked up along the driveway. A gas can was being held by another man by the gate but it was returned to a truck. A pair of bolt cutters was retrieved and brought to the gate.

Beth cursed. "Oh no," she said.

"What is it?" Lea asked.

"I was hoping they'd go with the plan to burn it," Beth said.

"Why?" Lea asked with a perplexed look on her face.

"It would take longer to get in," Beth said. "It would

give Will more time." She paused and then groaned. "Why would they burn it down? That is a stupid plan. Of course they wouldn't burn it down. They'd be sitting around forever for those logs to burn through."

Lea didn't say anything. Her face scrunched up in worry.

*****

Will's lungs burned as he sprinted up the hill. He was abeam the patch of trees that their driveway curved through when he decided to jump the fence. Once over, he continued along the fence. He was slowing once he got to where the land leveled off and their house was just beyond the clearing. It wasn't by choice, it was due to his lungs grasping for more and more oxygen. He made no effort to avoid the plants as he cut across the yard directly to the house and crossed the gardens. They wouldn't need to care for them anymore.

He reached the porch and leaned forward, placing his hands on his knees. It was all he could do to draw in as much oxygen as his lungs desired. He looked back down the driveway for the first time since sprinting up. He saw a glow illuminating the trees from a distance. He thought it was the gate being set aflame. He had a little bit of time before it burned enough for the trucks to drive through but still wanted to hurry. He didn't want to be anywhere near the house when they came up the hill. Drawing all the energy he could, he opened the door and rushed inside.

The go-bag was in the closet by the front door. He pulled it out and placed it on the floor in the middle of the room. He went back to the closet and grabbed an empty canvas bag that had been used for grocery shopping. He pulled all the boxes of ammunition from the shelf above down, placing them in the bag. He pulled two rifles that leaned against the back wall of the closet as well and placed everything on the floor by his go-bag. He ran back to his room and into his closet. He pulled out the tub of camping gear and carried it out to the living room and placed it next to the other items. Looking at all the things piled together, he wished he could use his Jeep. Maybe he could. He could load all the things and drive the Jeep across the back yard and to the back corner of the property. Beyond the back lawn, it was all trees again. There should be room in between the trees to get his Jeep through, he hoped. They had thinned the trees on their property to help prevent wildfires from burning through the area. The worst case scenario would be to hide the items there and come back with the others to get everything all at once. Perhaps he could break through the fence at some point up there and they'd have an easier way to travel.

He swung the go-bag on to his back and secured the front buckle across his chest. He took one of the rifles and put it on his shoulder. He picked up the tub of camping supplies and quickly went towards the back door. He wasn't sure how he had any energy to carry one of these items, let alone being weighed down by everything he decided to pick up at once. He went around to the side of the house where his Jeep was parked. He paused for a moment considering the noise it would make. He could hear vehicles running from down the hill, presumably the truck that was there before and at least another. He thought he would be safe since their loud exhaust would conceal any noise his Jeep made. He opened the back of the Jeep and loaded the tub, go-bag, and rifle. He ran back in to get the other rifle and the ammunition and glanced out the large window as he picked everything up. The trees were getting brighter. It definitely wasn't light from a fire. It wasn't flickering. Were they already through? It seemed way too quick. He rushed to the back door. He had wanted to get more things. He got half way to his Jeep when he remembered he hadn't carried his keys for at least a month. He turned and ran back in. He swiped the keys from the hook in the kitchen and rushed back out.

As Will approached the Jeep he saw headlights through the trees where the driveway curved. Not just one set, but several. He threw the bag of ammo and the rifle across onto the passenger seat and he jumped in. Some of the boxes of ammunitions spilled onto his lap. He put the key in and the engine turned and turned as it attempted to start. He could see the vehicles moving slowly, still in the trees. Will thought they must be making sure no one was about to ambush them. He wished he could.

"Come on," Will said out loud to himself.

Will turned the key again. The choking sound was all he heard again. The Jeep hadn't been used in over a month. It was another thing to add to the list of things he wished he would have done. This situation was eye-opening. All of his prepping and planning didn't mean much for this situation thrown at them. He wished he would have started his Jeep every few days. Wishes weren't getting him anything right now. In about thirty seconds he would have to bail and run. He could probably only get the go-bag and maybe one rifle and one box of ammo. He wouldn't have time to get anything else. He would be too slow if he tried to carry everything with the vehicles nearing the house.

The engine finally caught and he threw the transmission into reverse. He backed up steadily, making sure not to have too much noise until he was fully hidden by the house and turned around. As he shifted into drive and started moving forward he saw all the trees on the edge of the yard become illuminated. The vehicles must have reached the leveled out front yard. He would have to stay in the shadow of the house. He hoped they kept their vehicles running so they wouldn't hear his Jeep. He guessed they would since they were keeping all the lights on. He turned to what he thought would be the widest opening in the trees. He wished again, hoping for a more satisfying outcome compared to the last wish, that there would be a wide enough path all the way to the far corner of the property. There should be with the tree clearing they had done.

"Thank you, Jesus," he whispered as he reached the corner section of the fence.

He brought the Jeep forward until the front bumper was up against the fencing. He slowly continued ahead waiting for the fencing material to break away from the posts. The Jeep struggled slightly and finally broke through. He passed through the opening and drove straight ahead, away from their property for a few hundred yards. He would hide the Jeep before heading back on foot to everyone else. He considered the possibility of this group noticing tire tracks across the gardens in the backyard and following them to find the broken fence. From there, they might be able to find the Jeep. He decided he would have to take the risk. He would take the go-bag and continue on foot.

*****

"Shoot. Shoot. SHOOT," Beth said rapidly.

Beth, Lea, and Juana were all watching as the long procession of vehicles, cars and trucks now, turned onto their driveway and slowly started up the hill. About a dozen men walked along with the first couple of vehicles. They all had some type of military style rifle with long magazines protruding below them. They kept the rifles ready, sweeping both sides of the convoy. Several of the vehicles at the front had spotlights trained at the trees on either side. The three of them felt helpless as they watched all this unfold.

"Is that a semi-truck?" Juana asked, pointing down the road.

"Looks like a fuel carrier," Beth answered. "I bet that's how they can keep driving."

"And we can't," Lea added.

"Will, you better be out of there," Beth said openly with gritted teeth, staring at all the vehicles occupying her property.

The three were now all standing back up, feeling they were safely hidden in the trees. The noise of all the cars and trucks luring them into a sense of security where they could speak openly. The chances were so small that they would be seen. They didn't realize how brightened the forest had become from all the headlights and spotlights. There were no lights directly pointed at them, however, the light found its way. It would snake through the trees unexpectedly. Every time a vehicle made the turn from the road on to the driveway and brief flash of the headlights would illuminate where they stood. Someone would have to be in just the right location and know exactly where to look through the trees to see the three women.

*****

The truck that had gone further down the road towards Lewis's farm was returning to their comrades. The driver let off the gas as he approached his group. The passenger glanced up the hill into the trees just as another vehicle turned from the road to the driveway. He reached over to the driver, grabbed his shirt at the elbow area.

"STOP!" he yelled. "I see people in the trees. It doesn't look like they've seen us."

"Where?" the driver asked.

"Right up there," the passenger said pointing into the trees.

The driver turned off his headlights and they both exited the truck. They left the doors open, presumably not to alert the people they saw in the trees. The driver joined the other man and they both kept their eyes and weapons trained on the people in the woods as they quickly crept up the slight hill into the trees.

Beth, Lea, and Juana were too focused. All of their hearts were pounding, palms sweaty, eyebrows involuntarily lifted in worry as they waited and wondered if Will was in the clear. The constant engine and exhaust noise overpowering all other sounds.

"All three of you hands up," a voice said.

All three, startled by the voice, jumped in surprise. Juana, seeing the two men, started and suppressed a scream, holding a hand to her mouth. The blood drained from their faces as they all realized there were two men with guns trained on them. They couldn't make out their faces as they stood in the shadows of the trees. They could easily assume these were the two men from the other truck.

"We could always use more women," the driver said.

The other man laughed. "Use. That's for sure." He paused for a moment. "Say, look here. I call the young one. That's some nice tan skin."

"I'm sure Gerard might have other plans than you have," the driver said.

"Gerard doesn't have to know about them quite yet. He's busy anyways," the man pointed at the vehicles crawling up the hill.

Tears were now streaming down the faces of all three.

"Now don't cry about something so fun," the man said, still with his creepy smile. "Come on. What's your name? Come with me." He extended out his hand as if he were about to help Lea.

The three were in shock, frozen. The only thing moving was their eyes and the tears that fell from them.

Chapter Nineteen

April 2037

Marcus sat on the bed in his Conex container, laptop perched on his legs. He typed out a message for Thomas.

I'm in. 100%. Whatever your plan is. Millions around the country dead. CMA doing nothing about it. CMA purposely hiding this news from me and everyone. It sounds like they want people dead. Will find out more soon. Heading West this week on assignment.

Marcus clicked through the few options as he was instructed. He entered his password to run the encryption software. He copied and pasted the resulting gibberish onto the memory stick and then placed it in the breast pocket of his suit.

Marcus quickly walked in between the containers, turning left and right, weaving back and forth to head as direct as he could towards the camp exit. He concluded that he would just pretend it was his day off hoping they'd let him out of the camp so he could get to the cafe. He paused next to the last container before crossing the dirt road to reach the pedestrian exit. He was clearing his head before approaching the guard.

A nervous sweat broke out on his forehead. It wasn't that hot out so he couldn't blame it on any heat. It was actually a gorgeous spring day. His palms began to sweat too. He wondered how he could be so comfortable on t.v. in front of millions but nearly broke down when it came to hiding one little secret from the guard, a stranger. No time left now, he was only steps away from the guard.

"Howdy, sir," Marcus said to the guard.

The guard nodded his head and said, "Marcus." He reached into the small toll-booth sized guard shack and retrieved a clipboard. "Heading to the cafe again?" he asked as he looked down at the clipboard.

"Yes, sir," Marcus said. "I want to get a cup of their fine coffee before they ship me out of here for a few days."

The guard flipped through a couple of pages attached to the clipboard. "Hold on now. It looks like you were off base earlier this week. Is that right?"

Marcus raced through several options in his mind. None of them seemed to mesh well with his plan to stay off the radar for a little while. Lying could very well bring more attention to him.

"Oh," Marcus said. "Maybe I was. I've been so busy that I couldn't remember when the last time I was off. What day does that say I last went to the cafe? You know, I actually am not sure what day today is," he told the little white lie thinking it wouldn't hurt him.

"It says you went two days ago on Sunday. It's Tuesday. Sorry, Marcus. I'm not going to be able to let you off today. Rules are rules."

"My mistake," Marcus said with a slight chuckle. He hoped he was acting well enough. "I'll just grab a coffee from the mess tent. I just like the cafe's coffee so much better. Have you been over there? They just always seemed to have the freshest coffee. Maybe they buy whole beans and grind it themselves. Maybe I'm just too used to the coffee here." He laughed.

"Nope. Haven't been there," the guard said straight-faced. He wasn't joining Marcus in any of his laughter. "Maybe I'll make it in there the next time I'm out and I'll give the coffee a taste. I'll let you know what I think."

"Yes, thank you," Marcus said. "That'll let me know if it's all in my head." He smiled. The guard forced a smiled back. "I'll see you next week then."

"Bye, Marcus."

Sometimes Marcus wished people didn't recognize him so easily. He had no idea who the guard was. He had probably seen him before, but there always seemed to be a different one every time he left the camp. He wondered if his nervousness showed too much. If he was too awkward in the exchange the guard would easily be able to report who he was.

Marcus walked towards the mess tent as not to alert the guard. He would have to pretend he was on his way for the cup of coffee. Now he had to come up with a new plan. Maybe he would get a crappy cup of coffee from the mess tent. He was already heading in that direction anyways. He had to figure out some way to get to the cafe and thinking over a cup of coffee might do the trick. Then the thought crossed his mind. He had passed a few tents by now and was out of sight of the guard. He turned abruptly towards the center of the camp, making a B-line to the administrative tent.

He walked into the administrative tent. It technically was a work day for him and he should probably appear like he was working. There was a tent next door for the WWNL personnel but he still had business in this tent from time to time. He went to Anthony's office along the side of the tent. His door was open but the office was empty. He remembered seeing Anthony in some of the other offices some of the times he came in here to find him. He peeked his head into the open door next to Anthony's office. This office was empty as well. He moved on. The next office was empty as well. All of their doors were left open. He had never seen Anthony's or any of these other doors left open, ever, not even when their habitants were inside. He wondered if the had been called away in a hurry.

Marcus looked towards the center of the tent and saw there were plenty of people looking busy in the open desks that surrounded the center conference room. The conference room. He could see through the window into the room. From where he stood all the way across the tent he could tell there were people in the room. Anthony must be in there. He turned back to the open office. He saw some papers on the desk. He thought they had 'TOP SECRET' written across the top. He looked back around. Satisfied no one was watching him, he darted inside.

Once inside, he noticed a coffee maker with a full pot of coffee sitting on a table that wasn't visible from the open office door. He thought for a moment that he could use the excuse of stealing some coffee if he got caught. *So much for laying low*, he thought. He would have to be quick to not get caught. He looked down at the page.

TOP SECRET Level One Security Only. **STEP TWO** Procedures

He felt adrenaline rush through his veins. His heart began to pound. This must be the 'next step' Mara almost spilled in that meeting. The sense of panic that overwhelmed him caused him to quickly skim over the document.

...eradication of mobs and generally violent regions.

...acceptable non-violent civilian losses...

Non-nuclear option only

Avoidance of CMA assets and Level One Security interests is HIGH PRIORITY

...acceptable CMA asset losses...

Planned option: MC-150A 30,000-pound SAT-Guided Ordnance

Marcus couldn't believe what he was reading. The last half of the page was five columns of the smallest font size legible. It was a list of different cities. There were so many cities from all over the country. They were planning on bombing nearly every large city in the United States. They not only didn't care that millions had already died, they wanted all those people dead. They wanted millions and millions more dead. What could be the reason? Marcus was unable to comprehend it. His head began to spin. He felt dizzy. He looked down again, there was another page. He looked at the door. Now that he was in the office he couldn't see out the partially open door. He didn't hear anyone nearby. *Here goes*, he thought. He figured he could always play it off like he knew what the 'Next Step' was all along. Kenneth had said they were keeping him out of the loop so he could only hope it would work. He slid the top page aside.

Reestablishment plan named **STEP THREE**. Summary of plan follows:

Marcus skimmed down the list.

-Remaining population, assumably from camps, will conform to CMA plans and work schedules.

-New population centers, as defined in **STEP THREE** document, to be established.

-Utilities and services to be wholly owned assets of CMA.

-Laws and duties of government will be set in regulatory document, currently named 1000.1 (to be renamed),

-CMA founders, Level One Security, will set areas of governance, and will be the governing body.

-All non-conforming subjects will be either be reeducated or terminated, depending on law or decision of governing body.

-Time frame: currently set for Spring/Summer 2037.

Marcus thought he might be sick. He wasn't sure if he could read anymore. He reached into his pocket and brought out his personal phone. He opened up the camera and quickly snapped a picture. He quickly returned the phone to his pocket. Stepping back, he turned and leaned his forearms against the table, trying to slow his breathing.

"Mr. Braden, what are you doing in here?" a voice said.

Marcus nearly jumped. He stood up straight and turned to see General Bryce, the military commander for the Northeast Region. He was quite the intimidating man. Marcus thought anyone who reached the status of general would have to be. *Did he see me taking the picture of the document?*

"Oh General," Marcus said. "You startled me. I...uh...apologize for being in your office. I was looking for Anthony." He was trying to collect his thoughts.

"Well he clearly isn't in here, Mr. Braden," General Bryce said. He made a sweeping motion across his office with his arm after completing the statement.

"Yes, I know," Marcus said. "I came into your office to see if Anthony was in here. I've seen him in here before when looking for him. I assumed he could be since he wasn't in his own office." Marcus was worried he was rambling, which might make him look even more suspicious than he already did. "Anyway, I saw your coffee and was going to steal a cup. Is that alright with you? I was hoping that you, being a General, that you'd have more premium coffee than the mess tent." He smiled, hoping to lighten the mood in the room.

General Bryce narrowed his eyes at Marcus, studying him. "That would be fine. I can't finish a whole pot anyway. I'm a bit of a coffee snob. I take it you are too?"

"Oh yes," Marcus said. "I make it out to the cafe in town the once a week I'm allowed just so I can get some different coffee."

General Bryce stepped to his desk and saw the pages he

had left out. Marcus took a styrofoam cup and poured himself some coffee.

"Would you like me to pour you a cup?" Marcus asked.

"No, thank you, Mr. Braden," General Bryce said. "I'll get one after we are finished with our meeting in the conference room." He paused, looked down at the pages and then back to Marcus. "Anthony is busy in the meeting as well. What did you want to see him for?"

"I overheard about a supply issue," Marcus said. "I thought it would be some decent news as filler for when I'm gone. I was going to get permission from Anthony for a vehicle or the helicopter."

The General pushed the two pages back together and pursed his lips. Marcus thought he no longer looked like he was in any mood to chat about coffee. He was trying to conceal his growing fear.

"I'm sure it would be no problem," General Bryce said without looking at Marcus. He took the pages along with another folder from the top of his desk and stepped to the door and opened it wider, a clear signal for Marcus to leave. "I'll let Anthony know that you were looking for him and that you'll be leaving the base to cover a story."

"Thank you, sir," Marcus said and he stepped towards the door.

"Mr. Braden," the general said as Marcus passed him, "make sure I am in here before you come in next time."

The General, only slightly shorter than Marcus, stared directly at him. Marcus was drawing from every ounce of his being not to show any fear. General Bryce was trying to establish himself as greater and more powerful than Marcus.

"Of course, General," Marcus said. "I do sincerely apologize. I shouldn't have come in. I was tempted by the coffee," Marcus laughed, hoping humor would settle the General down.

General Bryce smiled. Marcus was fairly sure it was a fake smile, perhaps to conceal the anger he felt towards him. Marcus wasn't sure if the General figured out that he had read the document or took a picture of it.

"Feel free to stop by for a cup of coffee whenever," General Bryce added. "There are just too many high-security items in my office for people to be in here without me. I'm sure you understand. We wouldn't want you to get into trouble."

General Bryce was still smiling. Marcus thought the smile might actually be sincere. Maybe the General would let this go and not tell anyone that he had caught him in his office. Most importantly, he was beginning to become fairly certain the General didn't see him take pictures of top secret documents.

"Thank you, General," Marcus said. "I definitely will. Very good coffee, by the way," Marcus said holding up his now half-empty styrofoam cup.

General Bryce smiled and nodded. He stepped out of his office and closed the door behind himself. Marcus turned and walked towards the tent exit, not looking back. After exiting the administrative tent he breathed deeply and quickened his pace towards the WWNL tent. Now he would somehow have to gather a team that he could fool into letting him make a stop at the cafe.

Reaching his desk, he tossed the now empty styrofoam cup into his trashcan and dropped all his weight in his chair, letting out a long sigh. He sat for a moment trying to catch his breath and collect his thoughts. He wasn't out of breath from rushing from one tent to the next or from facing the General. He was out of breath due to all the information he had learned. Marcus unlocked his desk and started to gather the few things he always brought with him when he went out for a story. He looked around the tent to try to spot Blake.

Marcus placed his hand on his breast pocket, feeling for the memory stick. The memory stick was now full of incomplete information. Before gathering a team he needed to change the message. How were they going to stop full-scale annihilation? He supposed it didn't matter quite yet. He needed to pass this on immediately. A plan could be made from there. The network the ARF seemed to have would most certainly include a military portion. Marcus relocked the items in his desk and took off for his Conex container.

*****

Marcus was again sitting in his dimly lit Conex container with his laptop perched on his legs. He typed as fast as his fingers allowed him. He tried to get every bit of information he could remember. He knew there had to be some sort of way to send pictures but he wasn't the type to be able to figure it out without instruction. He added to the message that he had a picture of the document but didn't know how to send it. He completed the encryption process and placed the memory stick back in his breast pocket. Marcus raced off back to the WWNL tent.

He hated the WWNL tent set up. He never remembered where he could find anyone when he needed them. He went from area to area asking for Blake. He could freely walk the office area and halls of the WWNL building with his eyes closed. He was way out of place in the much smaller workspace of the WWNL tent. He figured the smaller space should have been easier. He saw Kenneth approaching him.

"Hey Marcus, what are you up to today?" Kenneth said.

Marcus, not wanting to be assigned something from Kenneth decided to tell him his faux story of supply chain issues in the region. "I overheard something about supply chain issues this morning. I figured I'd get Blake and go check it out. It'd be good filler for while I'm out of town for a few days. Viewers won't get the impression that Ava is running solo and I'm not around anymore. They might stop watching if they thought that." He smiled at his own light joke.

"Supply chain issues?" Kenneth asked, not paying any attention to his joke. "What kind of issues? I haven't heard anything about it."

"Not quite sure," Marcus said. "Just overheard something about it walking around camp this morning. I got cleared with General Bryce earlier to use a chopper or a vehicle to go investigate."

"Now I'm curious," Kenneth said. "Let's go get Blake. I'll come along with you. I don't have anything else important today."

No, Marcus thought. His heart sunk. When was the last time Kenneth tagged along on an on-site investigation? There wasn't even a solid story yet. Were they on to him? Had Kenneth been in the meeting with General Bryce? Did General Bryce tell him of their whole interaction? Was there no step in this uphill battle that didn't include a possible hidden land mine? Was this his battle in this war? Hit after hit after hit. Why was it up to him alone to endure all of this?

Chapter Twenty

"Everyone, drop your pistols," the man said motioning towards the three women with his rifle.

A shot rang out, piercing the air and piercing their ears. Each of the three women dropped to the ground and covered their heads with their arms. They all wondered why the man shot and who had been hit. What sort of evil drove this group? They were threatening rape and now they killed one of them? Only seconds had passed, the three women slowly looked up. The man who had wanted the three of them was on his knees, slumped against a tree. The lights from the vehicles allowed them to see the dark liquid seeping down his face.

The other man raised his rifle, only aiming towards a general direction into the trees and started firing. Beth, realizing what was happening, scrambled for her pistol. She fired several shots at the man. The bullets pelted his body. He let go of his rifle and stumbled back a few steps and dropped to the ground. They heard yells coming from the convoy of vehicles. They must have heard the shots.

Will came running out of the trees.

"Don't shoot," Will said. "It's me."

"Oh, thank God," Beth said as she lowered her pistol. "I thought he shot you."

"He came close," Will said. "I was pretty sure he couldn't see me. I was going to come around the side to get him next."

Lea was helping her mother up. Both of their faces were puffy from crying. Will put an arm around both of them in a wide hug.

"We need to get out of here," Will said. "They definitely heard the shots. I'm sure they saw the truck parked down there on the road too. We need to get to Lewis's. I didn't imagine there'd be so many of them," Will said as he looked over at their property. He sighed. "We probably can't stay at Lewis's either if they are going to be here. It's too close. There's no way we can fight a group that big."

"I know," Beth said solemnly.

"He's still alive," Lea said. She pointed to the man Beth shot.

They all went over to him. He had an arm across his chest, grasping his side. He was breathing heavily.

"Oh no," Beth said as she put a hand to her mouth.

"Beth, is that Tanner?" Juana asked.

Beth nodded her head.

"The Tanner that you work with?" Will asked. He stepped forward and lowered his head towards Tanner trying to get a better look in the dark.

"Yes," she answered.

Tanner was normally a clean-shaven man. Now he had an overgrown beard. He was in his mid-thirties and was always kind to everyone while Beth worked with him. The bad economy had come down hard on Tanner. He was a computer programmer that had been laid off and was forever trying to re-enter the field. The only job he could find in Oakhurst was at the gift shop with Beth. He couldn't afford to move to find work. Now in this new world, it appeared he joined the mob that pillaged his own hometown.

"We can't leave him for the others to talk to him," Will said. "We've already mentioned that we are going to Lewis's."

Beth knelt down to Tanner. She noticed he smelled foul. "Tanner, I'm so sorry," she said as her eyes welled up with tears. "I didn't realize it was you."

Tanner answered, barely audible, "No, Beth...I'm sorry." He was struggling to breathe.

"Mom," Will said, "Tanner probably brought this whole group up here. This is the group that attacked Juana. They weren't from around here. He joined them. We need to go. They are coming this way now."

"We can't just let him die," Beth said through tears. "He's my friend."

"Beth, we need to go," Lea said pleadingly.

Will aimed his pistol at Tanner. Beth noticed and backed away. Will fired. They were temporarily deafened by the shot. Tanner's heavy breathing had stopped. Lea's jaw dropped open in surprise at what Will had just done. Will looked around at everyone. Juana, having a deep disdain for this group, nodded approvingly at Will.

"We need to go," Will said.

Will picked up the weapons from the two men and

headed off into the woods. The others followed. Beth remained silent, tears still flowing down her face. Lea walked alongside Beth, keeping an arm around her shoulder.

The first words that anyone spoke came after about a mile of walking. The walk was much more difficult through the woods than that morning when they did the walk on the road. It was pitch dark now, with only slight streams of moonlight shining through the trees. The rocky terrain would rise and fall. There were constantly tripping over unseen rocks and fallen trees.

"Will," Beth called out. "Will...how could you kill him so easily?"

Will, still about ten paces ahead of the others, stopped. He stood facing the direction of Lewis's farm and waited for his mother to catch up. She stopped next to him. She could see his eyebrows furrowed in anger as he continued looking ahead. Juana and Lea stopped behind them, remaining silent.

"How could you kill him?" Beth asked again. The question and thought of her friend being dead caused her to begin crying again.

Will finally turned to his mother. "He brought them all here. He must have. Look what they were about to do to you and Juana and Lea. You haven't been to town. I have. There are bodies everywhere. They are killing anyone they want. There is no police. There's been no one stopping them. They've burnt down nearly the whole town." Will paused from his angry rant, processing his thoughts. "Look, Mom, I liked Tanner too. We have to think about us now. Because of him, we could have all been dead...tonight. It could've been worse. They could have wanted to keep you three. Who knows what they would be doing to you."

"We could have helped him," Beth said through her tears. "We could have brought him with us."

"Mom, are you mad that I finished him or are you mad that you shot him first?" Will asked the question before thinking it through.

Will knew the question would pierce his mother deeply. He knew she had to be upset because she had shot a good friend of hers. She shot him to the point that it was inevitable that he would succumb to the wounds. Will wondered if he shot Tanner because it needed to be done or if he subconsciously wanted to take that burden from his mother.

"He would have slowed us down too much," Will continued. "We couldn't have brought him with us and he knows where Lewis lives. We said we were going to Lewis's. If they had time to talk to him then they could have gotten to us tonight. They might still find Lewis's tonight. It had to be done. He brought this on himself."

Will was now cold in his tone. He didn't like being this way to his mother. He didn't like being this way in front of Lea. He knew it was a different world now. They had to bring their own justice. He wanted the others to understand what he understood.

"We need to keep moving," Will said. "We still don't know for sure if Alejandro was going to get Lewis and bring him back to where we were hiding or if they were going to stay there."

Beth was silent again. She began walking ahead of the others and Juana started to follow. Will looked at Lea with pleading eyes as they both still stood there. He figured Juana was on his side, but he needed Lea on his side more than anyone. He held out his hand to her, wanting her to take it. She began walking, ignoring his hand. He dropped his arm to his side as a feeling something like defeat came over him. He sighed deeply and followed behind.

As Will could tell they were nearing Lewis's, he decided to catch up to Lea to talk with her for the last section of the walk.

"Lea, what's wrong?" Will asked. "Why are you mad at me?"

"You just killed those two guys...like...it wasn't anything to you," Lea answered. "And then you were so harsh to your Mom. That was her friend."

"It wasn't nothing to me," he said. "It wasn't easy. I thought of Tanner as a friend as well." He looked ahead to keep track of Juana and his mother, their moving figures just visible due to the moonlight. "It's just this whole night," he said in a frustrated tone. "I've always been into planning and prepping and now that hardly did anything for us. All this work we've done to survive is going to be gone. Our town is gone. Who knows how many of our friends. I can only hope they made it to those camps. I was scared for you. I came back down the hill and heard what that guy was saying. I know what he was going to do. So do you."

"I don't know," Lea said. "This whole life, it's so different. It's not what I wanted. I know those men were bad. I don't know. I don't know what to say."

Will could tell she was struggling with this new way of life. He wasn't sure if he had noticed before. Maybe it wasn't until the reality of it landed at their gate.

"I know it's difficult, Lea," Will said. "I know having to kill someone or watching it isn't the life we would have chosen for ourselves before all of this happened. That is the world we live in now. I've read tons on this type of stuff from military experts and survival experts. When societies crumble, the system of justice is placed in the individual's hands. There's no police or courts. And where is the military? We just have to make sure we are making the right decisions. I think what happened earlier was clear cut. I know Tanner was a friend, but he was the aggressor."

"You still didn't have to be so harsh to your Mom," Lea said.

Will had hoped for some response to what he had said about justice being in their hands.

"Maybe I was being too defensive," he said. "I know she was upset that she had shot Tanner. I know she was upset that I shot him too. Like I said, there was just so much that happened tonight. We are losing all the work we've done. We are losing our home," he said and then paused. "What do you think about the stuff I said about justice being up to us?" He looked at her in the dark, trying to see if he could discern any reaction on her face.

"I don't know," Lea said. "Like I was saying, this way of life still seems foreign. I can't wrap my head around any of us having to kill anyone. It still seems weird to me that my Dad shot the guy that cut my Mom. Anyone that did these types of things before always seemed to be criminals."

"We are protecting ourselves from criminals now," Will said.

"I know," she said. "I don't know how to explain it." She paused for a moment. "You've been reading and preparing for something like this for a while. You had the food stored. You have survival gear. I've never read anything about this. I've never done any preparing. You've had plans and scenarios in your head for years. Every single thing about our lives now seems new and scary. I'm sure I've seen movies that demonstrate this type of situation, but I think of them as just movies. I don't watch them for education on the subject. They are entertainment."

"I guess I have to remember that," Will said. "I have to remember that for you and everyone else. I might be the only one out of our group that basically studied this type of stuff. Lewis knows tons about working the land which is great for survival in situations like these. But, my Mom is probably going to be similar in thought to what you just told me."

Their conversation ended as they approached the edge of Lewis's farm. Beth and Juana were waiting for Will and Lea, staying in the trees. Once they were all together, they all stood silent for a few moments, listening for any indication of vehicles or members of the intruding group.

Beth broke the silence. "I think we should approach Lewis's house from the back. Maybe only one of us."

"I'll go," Will immediately offered.

Beth and Will looked at each other, still remaining silent on the subject of Tanner. Beth nodded to Will.

"Alright," Will said, "you all stay here and stay down. Keep an eye on the direction we came from as well. I tried to as we were walking. Someone could have followed. I never saw any indication of it, though."

They all nodded to Will in acknowledgment. Will hunkered down low and took several steps into the planted field. He scanned around the house across the field and the whole surrounding tree line. He saw no movement. He dashed quickly about half way across the field, still bent low as he ran. He stopped again and knelt. He scanned the whole area again, searching for any new movement. He thought he had been doing a lot of ducking and crawling around this evening. He wished he had a way to signal Alejandro and Lewis. He didn't want them to be spooked by his arrival and for himself to get fired upon for the second time tonight.

He turned back to where he left the others. He couldn't see them anymore which meant they were hiding well like he wanted them too. He wished he had said more to his mother. He kept replaying his handling of the situation, the things he had said. He wished he could start again. He wished he had at least hugged Lea before dashing off on another mission tonight. He did one last sweeping scan of the area and moved again towards the rear of the house. He stopped about twenty feet back from Lewis's back porch. After looking from side to side, he considered taking a detour before approaching the house any further and try to get a better view of the front side of the house and possibly the drive heading down the hill.

He decided to do just that. It had been a long day and exhaustion was beginning to overtake him. He had to be as careful as possible. He turned to his right and ran, staying bent over still, until he was abeam the side of the house. He was surprised to see Lewis and Alejandro standing near Lewis's truck. It appeared Alejandro was keeping watch down the hill along the driveway while Lewis was loading items into the bed of the truck. A sense of safety came over Will and he stood and called out to them.

"Guys, it's Will," Will yelled as he waved an arm over his head.

"Will!" Alejandro yelled back. "Where are the others?"

"They are back across the field," Will answered while pointing in the general direction that he left the three. "What are you guys doing?"

"Lewis said the truck that we saw come down this way came all the way up here by his house," Alejandro said. "I'm sure they will bring more back. We are loading some stuff to hide out for a few days. We should get the others so we can get ready quicker."

"We might have a little bit of time," Will said. "Those two in the truck are dead. They never made it back to their group."

"What happened?" Alejandro asked while a surprised look formed on his face.

"The two guys in the truck spotted my Mom, Juana, and Lea and then came after them. There was some shooting and we are all okay," Will said, purposely leaving out all the details.

"Oh man," Alejandro said while placing his hands on his head. "I wish I would never have left them alone."

"You couldn't have known," Will said. "We are still going to have to get out of here. There must have been thirty more cars and trucks show up to our place. I'm sure they'll either search the area tonight or tomorrow for sure. Especially with losing two of their own."

"Thirty more?" Alejandro said in disbelief.

"Yeah," Will said, "and we couldn't tell how many people were in each vehicle. I know it's been a long day but we should get out of here soon. What do you think? Go further up the four wheeling road? I guess that's a stupid question. We can't go the other way. We'll just run into them."

"That's what Lewis and I were planning," Alejandro said. "Go up the trail to wait them out. Do you think they are going to stick around?"

"I overheard them talking about making our place a camp," Will answered. "I'm guessing they are staying a while. They might see all these fields of food and decide to stay to harvest it. Who knows?" He looked around at the moonlit planted field. The thought of all the work they had done going to waste still depressed him. "I'll go get the others so we can get out of here."

He ran straight to where he left the other three. This time, he made no effort to move quietly or stay low. As Will approached the tree-line he yelled out for them.

"Alright guys, it's safe. They're safe," Will said referring to Alejandro and Lewis.

He glanced back and forth along the trees waiting for them to pop out. After a brief moment, they all stepped out of the woods and began brushing themselves off.

"They are loading up Lewis's truck," Will said. "They think we should get out of here quickly too."

They all walked across the field and then around the house. They all gathered together at the bed of the truck. A light from the porch illuminated them and the truck.

"Well..." Lewis began, "I loaded some camping supplies. There's some food." He was clearly depressed and saddened by the abrupt turn of events. He sighed. "I really didn't want to leave my home." His eyes appeared to be filling with tears. He didn't look at anyone. He kept his eyes pointing towards the items in the bed. "That cooler there has a lot of that deer meat." He nodded his head in the direction of the cooler. "Anything else you all think we should get?"

"I have my pack here," Will said. "It has some survival gear to help get us through. A little bit of food as well. I had more stuff in the Jeep." He let out a forced laugh. "I forgot to tell you, I hid the Jeep up in the woods up beyond our property. I grabbed this bag and left all the other stuff I had. I'm glad I didn't try bringing the Jeep all the way back to the road. If I did..." He stopped, not wanting to bring up the shootout and death from before. "Anyway, the wheeling trail eventually cuts back higher up the mountain behind all of our land here. We might be able to sneak down at some point and try to bring it up. Or, at least get the stuff I packed in there."

"There's a lot of thick woods and rock outcroppings between here and the road," Lewis said. "It'd be a bear of a job."

"Yeah," Will said solemnly.

"If there's nothing else to get then let's get going," Beth said.

"I'll drive," Lewis said. "You all have been running around the woods for hours. You should try to sleep."

"One last thing," Will said. They all looked to him. "We need to check down the road before we drive the truck down the driveway."

"Good idea," Alejandro said. "I'll run down there. Someone should stand higher up to pass on to bring the truck down."

"I'll go with you," Will said.

"Ladies, you should get settled in the truck," Alejandro said.

"Once we are on our way, you all should go to sleep," Lewis said. "I'll take care of it from there."

Lewis and the three women sat quietly in the truck as Alejandro scouted their exit route. Will stood part way down the driveway waiting for Alejandro's signal. He couldn't see the truck from where he stood. He would have to turn back uphill and walk a bit to be able to signal the truck. He dreaded having to take a single step uphill.

Beth, Lea, and Juana were all situated in the back seat of the truck. The sudden halt of all the night's excitement, their bodies being overcome with fatigue, all being paired with the still and quiet of the night caused their eyes to become heavy. A cool breeze swept through the valley. The comforting air passed through the open windows of the truck. Lea lay against her mother's arm. She was already fast asleep. Beth and Juana lay against opposite doors, their eyelids shutting for longer and longer periods as sleep tried to take them. Lewis sat in the driver's seat. He leaned forward with both forearms resting on top of the steering wheel. He watched down the hill for Will, waiting to spot his figure somewhere on the dark, tree-lined driveway.

Lewis heard a distant yell. He moved his right hand to the key in the ignition. He didn't start the truck yet. He wanted to see Will giving them some sort of signal that they should come down the drive. He squinted and leaned forward a few inches with the hope it would help see into the dark. Now there was more yelling. It was from multiple people, none of which sounded like Will or Alejandro. Lewis's mind clued into what was happening. He whipped his head around to see figures in the distance across his backyard. The moonlight giving just enough to differentiate the multiple figures as they emerged from several locations out of the trees. They must have sent out these search parties to comb the woods.

Lewis immediately turned the key and the large diesel rumbled to life. He quickly shifted and slammed down the accelerator. The tires spun in the dirt before grabbing and jerking the truck forward. All the women were awake again, Lea in pure confusion from being yanked from a deep sleep. Lewis could hear shots being fired. Bullets were whizzing by his window. A couple hit the truck somewhere near the rear. It made a sound like someone had taken a baseball bat and slammed it against the bed of the truck.

It didn't matter now if this group was waiting for them at the road. There was no need to scout it out. They were either there or they weren't. The only option now was to try. They were without a doubt behind them, now claiming Lewis's land as their own. If they held the road as well, they had them no matter what. Lewis guided the barreling truck down the driveway, ready to slam on the brake pedal at any moment to pick up the other two.

Chapter Twenty-One

Marcus sat in the back of a Humvee next to Blake. He turned to his right to watch the cafe pass by. He thought for only a fleeting moment that he would suggest a quick stop for coffee or a bite to eat. He would have had to make the suggestion prior to reaching the town. He would have needed a better excuse beforehand as well. Perhaps something about asking locals if they knew of the supply chain issue. Of course they wouldn't have, it was a product of Marcus's imagination. The cafe was already behind them. It would look desperate at this point to try to get them to turn around. Marcus settled back in his seat. He placed a hand on the breast pocket of his suit jacket, feeling the memory stick. He would have to be sure to figure out a way to stop on the way back to the camp.

Marcus focused on the Humvee. He was sure that only months earlier this vehicle was used exclusively by the United States Military. The vehicle along with every part meticulously accounted for. He knew that every single item owned by the government had a stamp or sticker indicating the owning agency and the part number. He had done a story once before on the steps used by the government to keep track of everything it owned. Marcus remembered being impressed by how well the government accomplished this task. Now, how many of those items such as this Humvee were in the possession of this new government-created corporation? This vehicle now being driven by some random corporate employee who wore some strange-looking military-like uniform.

"So, you think this maintenance facility is how we figure out if anything is going on?" Kenneth asked.

"I'm sure of it," Marcus answered. "If there are any issues, the news will show up there."

Kenneth had called around before they left to see what he could find out about this 'supply issue'. His calls brought him no information. Marcus had hoped that was the case. He didn't want Kenneth to get a report of something minor, such as a slightly delayed truck, and then call off their excursion so they wouldn't waste time on a worthless story. He needed to get to the cafe.

They arrived at the maintenance facility a little over thirty minutes after leaving the camp. They found the man in charge. He was a rugged-looking, middle-aged man. He looked like he led a rough life that aged his body an extra ten years which would explain his haggard appearance. He became somewhat defensive after hearing the questions of the 'issue', most presumably because he thought they were there to blame and question him. Marcus assured him they were there only to gather information. He told him that they were doing a story on how the CMA moved goods around the region and country and thought it would be good to see how problems were handled as well. The man seemed to think for a moment.

"We had a truck break down last night," he said. "It

happens all the time, though. We sent out a tow this morning. The truck is here in the shop." He motioned further inside the garage. "The trailer, however, is back on the road. It's fairly common. Not something I'd expect to see in the news." He said it almost as a suggestion.

"Well, sir," Marcus said, "perhaps we will turn it into a story on the efficiency and expediency of your shop here." Marcus smiled widely. "Nothing wrong with a feel-good story." Marcus turned to Kenneth, "That must've been what I overheard people talking about this morning."

"What?" Kenneth asked in an annoyed manner. "A single truck going into the shop?

"What else were you going to do today?" Marcus asked with a wry smile.

"Whatever," Kenneth said. "I guess we can come of with something since we are out here. Like you said, a feel-good story."

"That's the ol' investigative reporter I remember," Marcus said in a sarcastic tone.

They filmed a few scenes around the facility. They interviewed the crotchety foreman. Marcus gave a wonderful speech for the camera about the shop as if he really knew something about the place. They loaded back into the Humvee and set off back for the camp. Marcus still hadn't come up with something decent to make them stop. His mind was racing now trying to think of a reason. As they approached the outskirts of the small town, Marcus considered an idea similar to what brought them all the way to the maintenance facility. He went for it.

"I was thinking Ken," Marcus began.

"That's never good," Kenneth interrupted. He shifted in the seat so he could see Marcus more easily.

"Funny," Marcus said with a straight face. Blake laughed. "Since we are out here, how about another filler piece. We could record a little bit about this town. It could be about how the presence of the CMA in the area has boosted business around here."

Kenneth raised an eyebrow. Marcus thought Kenneth might actually be going for the idea.

"Not a bad idea," Kenneth said. "Think we need another filler piece?"

"I don't know," Marcus said. "I assume I'll be gone for the better part of a week if I'm going out to Colorado and Utah. It'll take some time to put together a piece out there for that story." He paused to let the new lines sink in for Kenneth. "Plus, I could use a good cup of coffee."

"I think it's a good idea," Blake said. It surprised Marcus and Kenneth. Blake wasn't one to give his opinion on much of anything.

"Why not?" Kenneth said and then sat back into his seat as if he were signaling the conversation was over.

Marcus reached forward and patted the shoulder of the CMA driver.

"Stop near that little cafe in town," Marcus said. "We can go in there and a few of the other nearby places."

After they parked, Blake filmed a few shots of the buildings around the area, leaving out any of the closed down businesses with boarded windows. Marcus was so excited that he almost had an extra skip in his step. He needed to calm himself. He didn't want to make Ken suspicious of him.

"I was thinking we could get some words from the cafe owner," Blake said. It was another surprise to Marcus. He was starting to wonder if Blake was reading his mind.

"My thoughts exactly," Marcus said as he held the cafe's door open so Blake could get through with the camera.

Marcus looked at Blake curiously as he walked into the cafe and headed towards the back corner. It really was as if Blake knew Marcus's whole plan.

Blake motioned towards the back, near where Marcus's booth sat, "We should set up back there so we aren't in the way."

Marcus froze in horror as he turned the corner and his booth came into view. A man sat in the seat he needed. And it wasn't just any man.

"Anthony?" Marcus blurted out the question.

"Gentleman," Anthony said in acknowledgment. "What are you all doing in here?"

"Oh, hey Anthony," Kenneth said as rounded the corner behind Marcus and saw him sitting there.

"We are getting some footage of the town and we were going to do a story about how the CMA's presence in the area has boosted the local economy," Blake said, nonchalantly. Marcus was becoming more and more impressed by Blake with every sentence he spoke.

"Marcus," Anthony nodded his head to him, "that doesn't sound like a supply-chain issue."

"We finished that one up already," Marcus said. "Wasn't really any issue. We turned it into a story about the efficiency of the maintenance facility. We'll show you after editing."

Marcus was hoping he wasn't sweating nervously. How could Anthony be here? Not only that, how could he be in the exact seat that Marcus needed?

"Come here often?" Marcus asked Anthony.

"I've been here a couple of times," Anthony said.

"I like coming here for the coffee," Marcus said.

"Yes, I know. The General mentioned it," Anthony said.

So the General must have told more than Marcus's request to go out for the story. If he told Anthony that Marcus mentioned something trivial like going to the cafe in town for coffee, then he probably told him everything about their encounter. Marcus wondered what that included. What had the General seen and not given away that he knew?

"Why don't you all join me?" Anthony said, gesturing to the empty seats.

Marcus sat down and slid up against the wall, bringing himself directly across from Anthony. He could picture the empty memory port under the table. It was probably only inches from Anthony's knee. Marcus started to weigh the consequences of getting caught. Was it worth the risk? Was there another way? Perhaps while out in Colorado or Utah he could get to a phone that the CMA wouldn't think to listen to and call Thomas. Marcus saw a possible flaw in that plan as well. He was supposed to be doing stories on camps out there. He would probably be on those camps most of the time out there. At least with trying here at the cafe, if he could pull it off, the CMA couldn't monitor their system for sending messages. If they somehow retrieved the message, they didn't have the passkey to decipher it.

The conversation turned lighter. They ended up ordering food, an early dinner, in addition to the coffee. They all chatted about mostly meaningless subjects. Blake and Kenneth mostly seemed interested in talking about their gripes with living in the camp. Marcus contributed some to the subject. He, being a well-known face in the news, made quite good money and had become accustomed to a more lavish and convenient lifestyle. He was flexible, however, having lived quite poorly for many years trying to get started in the career in smaller markets.

Marcus managed to slip the memory stick from his breast pocket. He had waited for the opportune moment. Someone had made a joke which everyone laughed at. Anthony had thrown his head back as he laughed. Marcus noticed and quickly grabbed the stick. Now the memory stick sat next to his leg, up against the wall. Maybe he should drop something? A fork? He could shift lower in the booth to pick up the fork and place the stick in its' place.

He did so. He bumped the fork with an elbow. It tumbled across his lap and down to the floor, coming to rest by his shoe. Marcus grabbed the memory stick as he shifted himself in the seat to make it easier to reach under the table. He couldn't see the port. Anthony had a leg propped up on the other and his knee blocked it. Was this not meant to be? He came back up with the fork and placed it on his empty plate. What to do now?

"I better be on my way," Anthony said.

Was Marcus finally being given a reprieve? Blake, who was sitting next to Anthony, stood so he could get out. Anthony shook their hands. Blake took his seat, luckily not scooting all the way down the booth to block the port. As the focus was still on Anthony about to leave, Marcus quickly reached under the table and placed the memory stick in the port with ease. He was worried it would take him several tries. He shifted in the seat to place his back against the wall. This way he could more easily glance over casually to see the smoke detector on the wall. The red light on the left was flashing. His message was being transmitted. He wondered if they were going to be able to write and send a response before Kenneth would want them to get back to base.

"Well, shall we?" Kenneth said.

Could Kenneth have any worse timing? It seemed like everyone knew exactly what Marcus was trying to do and were setting up road block after road block.

"I was hoping to get one more top off on the coffee," Marcus said, trying to stall. "Can't get coffee like this at the camp."

"We've been here long enough today," Kenneth said. "Plus, you've had like four cups of coffee. Let's get back. Today's footage needs to be edited before you leave. If there are any voice-over corrections to do, I want you to do them today. You leave tomorrow, right?"

"Yes, in the morning," Marcus answered, hiding his disappointment.

As they all stood from the table, Marcus looked over to the smoke detector. There was a steady red light on the right side which meant his message had been sent. The center green light lit up as Marcus watched. They were sending a message back already. If they leave now, it could be a week before he could see their answer. Blake took off for the restroom. Kenneth put an arm on Marcus's shoulder and guided him out of the cafe.

"Look, Marcus," Kenneth said in almost a whisper, "I'm glad you didn't make a scene about what I told you. This really is a great opportunity for you and I. We are going to come out on top of a new America. We are going to be kings of the industry."

Marcus smiled and nodded at Ken. He didn't know what to say. They stood by the exit waiting for Blake.

"Whew," Blake said as he walked up to them. "I definitely had too much coffee too. I was about to burst."

"I should run back there too," Marcus said. "I did have four cups. I'll meet you at the Humvee."

Blake and Kenneth exited the cafe while Marcus rushed to the restroom. Once he was done, he quickly returned to the table. The table was still covered with their plates and cups meaning the waitress hadn't been there to clean up yet. He slid into the booth and reached under. He felt around and couldn't feel the memory stick. He eventually bent over and looked at where the port was. The stick wasn't there. It was gone.

Chapter Twenty-Two

Lewis's truck lights fell onto Will. He slammed the brakes and Will jumped into the passenger seat. Will didn't ask a single question yet. He knew the other group showed up and started shooting. There was no time for questions. They needed to get Alejandro and make their escape further up the mountain. They heard more shots fired. Will stuck his pistol out the window and fired a few wild shots up the hill. He hoped that would cause them to back off and stop shooting long enough for them to get out of sight.

They came upon Alejandro only a few moments later. He had already made it to the bottom of the driveway and was starting to rush back up. Will threw the passenger door open and scooted towards the middle of the bench seat. Alejandro hadn't completely shut the door before Lewis slammed the accelerator to the floor again. He turned left out of the driveway onto the main road. The truck's rear end skidded a few feet before catching again. A few more bullets whizzed down the hill. Some slammed into the side of the truck. Others ricocheted off the road. The side-view mirror exploded only a foot away from Lewis. A few bits of the glass from the mirror flew into Lewis's forearm. He gasped and clenched his teeth. He shook his arm trying to calm the sudden sting.

Lewis's property was basically at the end of the main road before reaching the 4x4 trail. He was forced to slow down to begin navigating the rough and steepening trail. Will and Alejandro glanced back as the truck slowed. They saw no lights. They saw no figures in the dark. Finally, someone spoke.

"You okay, Lewis?" Juana asked.

"I'll be fine," Lewis said. "Just a couple of small pieces of the mirror sticking out of my arm. It's not bleeding much. I've had worse."

"We'll still want to get it cleaned up soon," Juana said. "Maybe someone else should take over driving and we get you cleaned up."

"Looks like it'd be alright," Alejandro said. "I don't see anyone or anything back there. Anyone see anything?"

"No," Will said. "It looks clear"

No one else saw anyone or anything so Lewis stopped the truck. He quickly got out and shuffled to the back seat to have Beth help take care of his arm. Juana got out and moved forward next to Alejandro. Will scooted into the driver's seat and took over driving.

"Everyone else okay?" Will asked.

Everyone answered in the affirmative.

Will continued on for over an hour. Someone would look back about every minute it seemed. Eventually, everyone except Alejandro had fallen asleep. He was still looking back every once in a while. It was a slow-going crawl up the technical trail. Luckily, Will had done it many times in his Jeep to find some new camping spots. Although, he was still being quite a bit more careful with Lewis's truck.

"We've gone at least ten miles by now," Will said quietly to Alejandro. "I think there's no reason for that group to pursue us up here. There's nothing up here for them. I really don't think they'd go through the trouble for revenge."

"I hope not," Alejandro said. "What are you thinking? We should stop now?"

"Yeah. There is another trail that should be coming up in about a mile or so. It's a loop that cuts around and reconnects to this trail. If we go up there aways I think we'll be well hidden for the night. We can figure out more tomorrow."

"Sounds fine to me," Alejandro said."

About ten minutes later, Will turned off the main trail.

"I didn't even see the trail," Alejandro said. "I've been keeping my eyes trained on the roadside hoping to spot it."

Will chuckled. "Yeah, it's hard to see. Even harder at night. I've been four-wheeling up here ever since I bought my Jeep. That was in high school. Anyway, if that group comes up here looking for us I think they'd pass by unaware."

Will spent another ten minutes maneuvering the even rougher looping trail. He finally pulled over in a small clearing. He turned off the truck.

The immediate stunning silence and the overwhelming exhaustion hit him all at once. He looked back to see that everyone in the back seat was still asleep. Alejandro shifted slightly to get more comfortable. Will leaned the seat back a few inches. As sleep was quickly overtaking him, he wondered if someone should stay awake to keep watch. He could already hear Alejandro's slight snoring. He was the only one awake still. He couldn't fight the exhaustion anymore. He thought he might already be dreaming. Was he awake keeping watch? He didn't know. His mind would tell him whatever he wanted to hear in his deep dream state.

Chapter Twenty-Three

Marcus sat back in the seat. How could the memory stick be missing? He searched both seats and the floor. Still nothing. Did Kenneth or Anthony see him? Anthony was already on his way out of the cafe when Marcus had entered the memory stick into the port so it couldn't have been him. Kenneth? When would he have taken it? He was baffled. What if there was a message for him? Can't act like anything is wrong. Have to roll with the punches.

His best hope was for the staff at the cafe to find it. They were in on the whole clandestine activity since it was their business that was being used. He walked at a quickened pace out of the cafe. No more time to waste now. If he spent too much time then Kenneth might become suspicious. He joined Kenneth and Blake in the Humvee.

The conversation seemed normal on the short drive back to the camp. It made Marcus think that Kenneth had nothing to do with the missing memory stick. Or, maybe he was waiting to talk to Marcus when Blake was no longer around. At least all the information on the stick looked like gibberish other than his old pictures.

Kenneth parted ways with Blake and Marcus as they walked into the WWNL tent. Blake and Marcus made their way back to the editing station. They spent the next hour editing the footage. Marcus had to re-record a few of his voiceover parts. As they had just finished up the project and were about to send the stories over to Kenneth for review, Blake stopped Marcus.

"Marcus, by the way," Blake said quietly, "you should be more careful."

Blake held out his hand as if he wanted to shake Marcus's hand. Marcus was confused but went to shake his hand anyway. When their palms pressed together, Marcus felt something solid in Blake's hand. Blake passed the item to him. Marcus looked at his hand and saw that Blake had just passed him the memory stick. He quickly snapped his hand shut around the stick. His eyes widened at Blake.

"What?" Blake asked. "You thought you were the only one passing information to Thomas?" Blake winked an eye at Marcus.

"I...I didn't know," Marcus said.

"I hope you got something good to them. That was pretty risky to do that with Kenneth and Anthony sitting there."

"You saw me do it?" Marcus asked.

"Maybe it was only because I knew where to look," Blake said. He casually looked around to make sure no one was near enough to hear their conversation. "I'll keep an eye on things while you are gone. Although, you have always been in a better position to get some decent info for the cause."

The cause. Marcus had never thought of it in that way. He was slightly suspicious of Blake. He didn't want to say too much in case Blake was really working for the CMA. Well, working for the CMA in a different capacity other than through WWNL. He made a mental note to send a message about Blake to Thomas to verify if he was working for the ARF.

"Be more careful," Blake said. "Let's get these made up stories to Kenneth."

"I will," Marcus said. He chuckled. "Made up...I guess I was being a bit suspicious."

*****

Marcus sat on his bed in his container. He went through the process to decode the message. A loading bar appeared telling him the computer was working. He looked over next to him on the bed. He quickly packed everything he wanted while he was gone. The last thing he wanted to bring was the computer. He didn't want anyone coming into his container snooping around while he was gone and start looking through it. Even with not being able to read any of the information on it, someone could conclude a lot by seeing the Pretty Good Privacy software loaded on it.

The program chimed. He looked down as the message appeared.

We will pass this information on to military command. Other sources tell us something is happening soon. This appears to be it. Call on secure line from other locations if you receive any new info.

He had hoped for something more. He wasn't sure what. Maybe he hoped they already knew and had plans in place to stop it. It looked as if it were a surprise to them. He frowned at the thought.

Chapter Twenty-Four

Will stood in the thick trees. Nothing could be seen through them except more pine and oak all around. It was dark but much brighter than he remembered. The moonlight pierced through the canopy of leaves as if it were the sunlight. He heard a noise and turned around abruptly. Two men knelt before him. He could see their ankles were tied. Their hands were bound behind them. Old socks were stuffed in their mouths, only visible because they protruded out further into the beams of moonlight. That was about all he could see of their faces. The rest was hidden in shadows. They were kneeling shoulder to shoulder.

Where is everyone else? he thought.

He looked down to see a pistol in his hand. He heard a voice in his head.

Execute them, it said in an almost imperceptive whisper.

The voice made so much sense. It was as if he had no more control over himself. What that inner voice said is what had to be done. His arm lifted and straightened out before him. He was focusing on the gun. He readjusted his focus beyond the gun and saw the pistol was aimed directly at one of the men kneeling in from of him. He pulled the trigger. His arm quickly shifted to the next man and he pulled the trigger again.

He walked forward and looked down. The moonlight now illuminated their faces. Tanner lay in a growing pool of blood. His eyes were wide open, almost as if they were staring at Will. There was a bullet hole centered on his forehead, blood seeping out. He looked over and the other man was...himself?

Will gasped and jolted forward. His head hit the steering wheel. He felt sweat on his forehead as he rubbed the sore spot. It was daytime and he was still in Lewis's truck. He had been dreaming. He looked around and everyone was still asleep except for Lewis. He was outside of the truck and it appeared he was assessing the damage done to it from the shooting. Will opened the driver's door as quietly as he could and joined Lewis outside.

"How's the arm?" Will asked as he walked up to Lewis.

"I'll be alright," Lewis said. "Just a little scratch." He held up his arm which was now wrapped in some gauze. "You doin' alright, son? Looked like you were having some tough dreams."

Will rubbed his forehead again. "I think I was just dreaming about," he paused for a moment, "...the shooting last night."

"It was definitely a scary thing. Made my heart pound for sure," Lewis said.

Will had been talking about the shooting in the woods by his house and not the shooting while they were driving away in the truck. He didn't say anything. He wanted Lewis to keep assuming the wrong event.

"Doesn't look like anything important got hit," Lewis said as he motioned to the truck.

"Except for the mirror. That usually comes in handy," Will joked.

"Not much other traffic up here," Lewis said as a smile formed on his face.

The others must have been roused when Will had opened the truck door. They all piled out of the truck at the same time.

"G'morning," Lewis said to the group. He received yawns in reply. "Sorry, I don't think we packed any coffee for our camping trip."

"Ugh," Alejandro moaned. "I can't remember the last time I stayed up that late. What time is it?"

Lewis looked at his watch. "Almost eleven." He paused for a moment. "Listen, everyone, I think after we get something to eat, we need to discuss what we are going to do."

"What do you mean?" Beth asked. "Aren't we going to hide out up here?"

"Well, as I see it, we have a few options," Lewis said. "Do you want to eat first and then talk it over? I know I like to wake up a bit and have a full stomach before discussing important things. We can start to talk about it over our meal too. If you can't tell, I'm quite hungry."

They all laughed. They went through the food in the back of the truck. They decided on cooking up some of the deer meat. A few of them gathered some kindling and larger pieces of wood for a fire. Will built the fire up and took a fire grate from the back of the truck. They all munched on some of the canned fruits and veggies that Lewis brought while they waited for the deer steaks to cook.

They all gathered in the shade of the trees along the edge of the clearing. As they began to tear into the meat, Lewis brought up the subject again.

"So, as I was saying," Lewis began, "we have some different options. If we are going to hide out up here then we need to be by a water source. I know there are some smaller streams up here and a couple of lakes. There is always the chance we'll run into other people if we head to one of those lakes. In addition to water, we need to consider food for the long term. It might not seem like it, but finding food for six people is going to be a lot of work. The next option would be to get to a small town, not necessarily Oakhurst, and borrow some living space for a while. There is still time to do some planting somewhere." He paused for a moment. "The last option is to get to one of those camps."

"Oh man," Will said. "I bet there is sickness running rampant in those places. I've read about places like that in World War Two and other disaster situations. The number one killer in camps is sickness. I prefer to fend for ourselves up here."

"Could we plant somewhere up here?" Juana asked.

"It's possible," Lewis said. "However, we don't have any of the tools. That's why I mention going to a small town. We could scrounge for what we need and there should be some open space to do some planting. To be honest, I'm tempted by the camps. It's not normally like me to go depend on help like that, but I'm older now. What's needed in the other two options is not going to be an easy road."

"I don't think there is any easy road anymore," Lea said.

"How about this," Alejandro said. "We wait it out up here somewhere. Near water, of course. In a week or two, we go check out the two places. Our homes. I honestly can't imagine them deciding to stay there."

"Why not?" Will asked.

"There's the food you had stored and some at Lewis's," Alejandro said, excitedly. "After that, they'd have to continue the farming. They've been surviving by taking existing things only. Chances are they aren't going to all of a sudden decide to do the work needed. I bet they are going to move to another town or they'll go to the camps or after the camps."

"After the camps?" Beth asked. "You mean raid the camps?"

"Yeah," Alejandro said. "I think they'll either go to live there or raid one of them for the food and supplies."

"I hadn't thought of that," Lewis said. "I definitely like and prefer the idea of going back to my home."

"Is anyone opposed to staying up here for a while and then checking to see if we can get back home?" Will asked openly.

Everyone looked back and forth at one another. No one said anything in opposition to the plan.

"So, we set up camp near water," Will said. "If we continue another hour or so on the main trail, it'll put us pretty close to a lake. Other than that, the main trail parallels a small stream. My vote is to stay near the stream for now. If it looks like that group is going to stay on our land then we can decide to move to the lake or somewhere else."

"Fine by me," Lewis said.

"Fine with me too," Beth said.

"It's a plan then," Alejandro said as he clapped his hands together.

Lea smiled as she watched Will take charge. He turned

towards her and noticed and almost blushed. He smiled back at her. He still wished the world was different. He was coming to terms that he would have to express his feeling for her in this broken and chaotic world.

The group finished eating and then started to repack the items they had taken out of the truck. Lewis took a fuel can from the bed of the truck and emptied it into the tank. He had one other fuel can in the bed that was full and that would be the last of the diesel they had unless they could make it back to their properties. Lewis had a large tank that he had brought from his farm in the central valley.

Alejandro and Will walked back down the small trail towards the main four-wheel drive trail. They wanted to check and see if there was any sign that they were followed the night before. It took them about twenty minutes to reach the main trail. They saw no signs of any other tire tracks other than their own from their arrival in the night. They were relieved and headed back to the others. Once they arrived, they all packed themselves into the truck and began their search for a good camping hideout.

After about an hour of ultra-slow driving and stopping to walk into the woods to check on different clearings along the creek, they came across a creek-side location they all liked. Everyone but Lewis got out of the truck. Will and Alejandro helped guide Lewis into the trees so the truck would be near their spot and hopefully well hidden from the road. While they were getting the truck parked, the women were clearing rocks and sticks from a suitable flat area to set up the tents.

Once they set up the tents, they began chopping wood for a fire. Once a fire was going, Will decided to instruct everyone on how to use the different water purification methods he had brought with him.

He had a small straw-type filter. It could be attached to a bottle filled with stream water. Or, it could be attached to a pouch and be filtered into a bottle, which is how they would use it since there were several people. It would need to be backwashed using a small plunger for cleaning after every five gallons filtered through it. Will told them he wanted to boil water to do the cleaning. The other type of filter he had was a pump-style that would sit in the water. They could pump water from the stream through it directly into a bottle. The pump-style's ceramic filter also needed to be removed and cleaned after every five gallons or so. He instructed them on the use of water purification tablets he had. He wanted those to be used as a last resort. He was adamant about everyone making sure they always drank filtered water. He didn't want anyone to get sick. They had no idea if there was a doctor available to help them.

He went over some of the other survival equipment that he had as well. Most of it was backpacking gear, but he wanted to make sure everyone understood how to use all of it and knew what was available.

"Thanks for going over all this stuff, Will," Juana said. "Just one other important thing I think we need to cover."

"What's that?" Will asked.

"Where are we going to go to the bathroom?" Juana replied.

"Oh right," Will said. "We need to establish somewhere for the camp." He thought for a moment. "Well, definitely not by the stream. We could designate somewhere over in those trees." He pointed to a thick forest area. "What we could do is build a makeshift bridge out of logs and use a spot across the stream. That way we won't have...that by the camp."

Juana laughed. "Well, I can't wait for a bridge to be built."

Everyone now laughed.

"We'll use that spot in those trees over there for now until we can build it," Will said.

Juana grabbed a roll of toilet paper and headed into the trees.

"Be conservative with that paper," Will called out to her. "Once we use up what we brought you won't like what we'll have to do."

Juana waved without turning around to acknowledge that she had heard him. Alejandro and Lewis walked over to Will.

"We should probably make sure people are bringing some protection while doing their business," Alejandro said as he approached.

"I think everyone is still carrying guns," Will said. "We can remind everyone. Sometimes people can get complacent after being in one place for a while. That reminds me, I have some camping knives that people could carry too. A knife is always useful when out in the woods."

"Good idea," Lewis said. "What we came over to talk to you for is about home."

"Home?" Will asked with a raised eyebrow.

"Yes," Lewis said. "I know we just got up here, but we were thinking we should plan a trip back down the mountain to see if that group is still sticking around."

"We should probably wait for at least a couple of days to go by," Will said. "Give them some time to raid our houses and the other houses in the area." He paused.

"Again, I really hope they decide not to become farmers."

Lewis and Alejandro laughed.

"I was thinking a few days as well," Alejandro said. "The other thing about it that Lewis and I were talking about is that we think it should be a hike and not a drive."

Will nodded his head. "That would make more sense. Less noise. We don't waste the fuel. A whole lot more time." He frowned at the thought. "I guess I would be up for it. I could do the whole thing in a full day."

"I was thinking it would be better to go late," Alejandro said. "Show up in the dark. Check things out. Double-time it out of there once we see what we need to see."

"We?" Will asked. "I thought you were asking me to do it."

"We were hoping you would go. But, I think two should go. None of the women, in my opinion. So, I'll go too," Alejandro said.

"Hmm," Will said looking at Alejandro. "Are you sure you can keep up with me, old man?"

Will was visibly holding back a smile.

"Remember that I can take you down," Alejandro said as a smile grew on his face.

"Not after over twenty miles of hiking," Will said.

Alejandro lunged towards Will. His hand swiped down and brushed Will's shirt as he jumped out of the way. They were both laughing.

"See," Will called out as he ran around a tent, "you gotta catch me first."

*****

As the sun was setting that evening, everyone helped organize the camp with the remaining light of the day. They made sure to secure all of their food in the case a bear or other wildlife decided to visit. They built up their fire so they could have a nighttime hangout. The fire could help provide light before they went to bed so they could conserve batteries in the few flashlights that they brought. They had discussed using sunset as a bedtime, at Lewis's suggestion, to help conserve batteries and the work needed to cut so much firewood. They all liked the idea, but of course, no one was tired at sunset.

Everyone was getting cozy in their spots around the fire. Lea went into the woods to use the bathroom and Beth quickly took her spot next to Will. Lea and Will had been alone on one side of the fire. They hadn't gotten the alone time they did before the world changed and they both thought it could eventually wear down on their relationship. Will was surprised at his mother taking the seat since they hadn't really talked at all after the incident with Tanner.

"Hi Will," she said.

"Mom," he said while nodding his head.

"Listen, Will, I'm sorry," she said. "I know I blamed you for killing Tanner, but I know I shot him several times."

"Mom, it's okay. I know he was a friend of yours."

She interrupted him. "Let me finish," she said and paused, "please."

Will nodded to tell her to continue.

"I know he would have died of his wounds. I now know he needed to be finished off more quickly. I don't know what you heard when you came upon us, but the other man that you shot was talking about raping Lea."

"I know," he said quietly.

"Tanner had become a part of that. I hope I'm not just trying to justify it in my mind. I keep playing it over and over in my head. I do have sympathy for him still too. My feelings are so mixed. I'm glad he didn't have to suffer. I know he needed to die, but at the same time I'm sad that I lost a friend."

"I understand, Mom. I don't think things are going to be easy any time soon. Something like this is going to stick with us for a long time. I had nightmares about it already."

"Me too," she said.

"This new world...or life...or whatever it is, has come as a shock to everyone. I was talking about this with Lea. Until our society is hopefully reestablished, there are no police or military or judges or juries. That is our job now. We just have to always keep ourselves accountable to make sure we are making the right decisions."

Beth smiled. "Your father and I raised you right."

Will smiled too, but the thought of his father saddened him. He and his mother gave each other a big hug. Lea had returned sometime during their conversation and was standing to the side, smiling at them.

Everyone remained quiet for quite a while. They all stared into the fire, watching the flames jump into the air. The only sound to be heard was the crackling and popping of the fire.

Chapter Twenty-Five

Marcus shouldered his bag as he walked from his Conex container. He couldn't tell if it was too early or too late. All he knew is that it was still dark and he was way too tired to be awake. His feet shuffled against the dirt from time to time. As Marcus turned on to one of the larger walkways in the camp, he suddenly noticed all the people rushing around. Large, blinding, generator-powered light towers illuminated the corridor. He stopped and looked around. He wondered if this sort of thing happened often. He thought it could be part of the logistics of running a camp this size. It was like a grocery store having to stock shelves in the middle of the night.

"Marcus," a voice said.

Marcus looked around to find the source. As he turned he saw Blake approach him.

"Hey Blake," Marcus said. "Why are there so many people running around at this hour?"

"I had been wondering the same thing myself," Blake said. "What I've found so far is that a lot of the higher ups around here are heading out to Colorado...to Cheyenne Mountain."

"Cheyenne Mountain?" Marcus said, surprised. "The military installation?"

"Yeah," Blake replied. "I think the flight you are catching this morning is being rerouted to Colorado Springs."

"Hmm," Marcus said as he began to think over the rapidly changing events. "Well, I was supposed to be stopping in Denver. Colorado Springs isn't too far off."

Marcus had immediately thought that this 'next step' was about to take place. He wanted to warn Blake, but he still wasn't sure if Blake actually worked for Thomas or if he was working for Anthony and he was trying to find out what he knew. And what about Thomas? Surely the CMA knew about Thomas and the ARF. Would they choose his ranch as a bombing location?

"There are so many strange things that seem to happen with the CMA," Blake said as he shook his head. "Well, you better get to that flight. Keep me posted on whatever is happening if you can."

"Will do."

Blake walked off in a hurry. Marcus continued to the administrative tent to meet his ride to the nearby airfield. He arrived to a bustle of activity that was exponentially greater than what he'd already seen that morning. He somehow managed to push his way through the crowd of CMA uniformed personnel. Once in the tent, he found someone holding a clipboard, directing people. He queried the man and was told which number Humvee he would be riding in and where he could find it.

Once he found the Humvee and got settled in, he was surprised to be joined by other CMA people. They packed in tighter than sardines. Since their vehicle filled quickly, they headed off to the nearby airfield. This Humvee was going to return back to the camp to get another load of people. Most of Marcus's flights out of the area were always in helicopters that would depart and arrive directly at the camp. He had been to the small airfield a few times prior. He was surprised this time to see the vast number of larger jet aircraft along the small ramp. The tiny regional terminal building was dwarfed by the varying number of Gulfstreams, Globals, Falcons, and other large private jets.

Marcus found another clipboard-wielder and was guided to board a Global Express. He settled into his seat. It had to have been the nicest and most luxurious aircraft he had ever been on. He had the privilege of flying on some private jets, Lears and Citations, throughout his career. WWNL owned a few. None of them were like this. His seat had to be more comfortable than any recliner that had ever sat in his own living room. He saw a flight attendant move row to row placing coffee next to all the passengers. He quickly grabbed up the cup that was set on the table before him.

As Marcus sipped the silky smooth liquid, a hand set down on his shoulder. He jumped slightly.

"Mr. Braden," a voice said.

Marcus turned, "Oh, Anthony, you surprised me."

"Sorry," Anthony said. "I didn't realize you'd be joining us on this aircraft. It's typically reserved for senior CMA staff."

"Oh," Marcus began, "well...I was directed to get on here. Should I be on another flight?"

"No," Anthony said, "I'm sure you were told correctly. I'm glad you are here. I can update you on the changes to your trip now rather than when we arrive in Colorado

Springs."

"I go to Denver from there, right?"

"Wrong," Anthony said. "That is what has changed. Mara, from the meeting the other day, now wants you in California."

Marcus gulped. He hoped it hadn't shown. "She said there were a lot of problems there."

"Yes. And that's why we need you out there. You'll focus on getting people in camps so they can be helped. The humanitarian side of things."

As opposed to the military side of things, Marcus thought.

"Whatever I can do to help," Marcus said with a fake smile.

"Excellent," Anthony said. "You'll be hopping on a King Air once we get to Colorado Springs. It'll take you the rest of the way. Most of our jet aircraft have been designated for other purposes at the moment."

"Yeah, what's with all the jets here? And why Colorado Springs?" Marcus asked.

"Just some big meetings that the senior staff wants everyone at. Not to worry. The King Air is a very suitable and comfortable aircraft as well. Definitely not the size of this, but certainly does the job.

"Oh, I'm not worried about that," Marcus said. "I was just curious. I've never been on something like this."

Anthony nodded in acknowledgment. He handed Marcus an updated itinerary and then made his way to his own seat. Marcus shifted in the plush seat to watch out the window. Soon after their departure, the cabin was served a full breakfast of eggs and sausage and fruit. Marcus devoured his. Being up at these early hours seemed to make him hungrier than normal. Even after a few cups of coffee Marcus was able to nod off to sleep for the rest of the flight.

*****

Marcus was awoken by the touchdown and slight screech of the wheels meeting the pavement. He stretched in his seat and began gathering his things. He couldn't believe that he slept for the few hours it took to fly across the country. Once they stopped on the ramp everyone stood and collected their bags. Marcus stayed seated as he usually did until he was able to start walking down the aisle.

Marcus shouldered his bag as he stepped off the stairway and onto the ramp. He looked around hoping to see another uniformed CMA employee holding a clipboard. It had been useful earlier that morning in directing everyone where they should be. He was disappointed that he couldn't see anyone with that description. He started to walk towards what he hoped was a terminal building when he was stopped by Anthony.

"Your King Air flight looks like it's over there on the ramp," Anthony said jamming a thumb behind him.

"Thank you," Marcus said.

He turned around and headed towards the twin-turboprop. Marcus thought that Anthony didn't seem as friendly as he was when they were boarding the plane. No matter, he was happy that he wouldn't see him for probably a week or so.

Hopefully, I'm able to get out of California before any bombing starts, Marcus thought. *No bombing at all would be even better. I hope they'll need to fill those camps for the slave labor before they continue with their plan.*

Marcus wasn't sure if the King Air was normally flown by only one pilot, but his flight definitely only had one. He was also the only passenger. He supposed he wasn't important enough in the CMA to be invited to the big meeting happening at Cheyenne Mountain. He wondered if it was just a meeting or if they were fleeing to the safety of the underground complex.

Despite the coffee he had on the first flight and the soda he just drank on this one, Marcus felt a fatigue settling over him as he watched the endless mountains pass beneath. He glanced down at the empty can in his hand. He didn't recognize the off-brand. Maybe there wasn't any caffeine in it. Maybe it was the lack of conversation with the pilot and the constant droning of the propellers that was lulling him to sleep. He tried to stay awake by site-seeing out of the window. He knew it wouldn't work. The tiredness that beheld him that day was just way too strong. He wasn't sure when he fell asleep. He knew that it had happened quickly.

Chapter Twenty-Six

Marcus awoke confused. His vision was blurry. He squinted his eyes trying to focus. He felt drowsy. He only ever felt this way if he had taken Benadryl or cold medicine. How long had he slept? Why was it so loud? He could hear the propellers as if were inside the plane. The sound of rushing air was so loud and intense that he couldn't hear himself think. He rubbed his eyes with both hands and blinked a few times. The blurriness was fading. His eyes settled on the doorway. Rather, where the door should have been. Adrenaline shot through his system at the sight of the open doorway. The hormone quickly began to clear the drowsiness from Marcus's system.

Marcus unbuckled and stood. The seat in front of him must have been blocking some of the rushing wind because when he stood his hair started to whip around wildly. His tie flapped annoyingly all around randomly. Marcus tucked it into his shirt in between two of the buttons. He yelled out to the pilot. Had something happened to him during the flight? He held on to the seats as he stepped slowly up the aisle. He shifted his head from the right to the left trying to see if the pilot were laying to one side or the other. He couldn't see him at all. He reached the back of the cockpit seats. No pilot. Marcus's heart skipped a beat when he noticed the yoke tied in place with what looked like rock-climbing rope.

Scenarios started racing through Marcus's head. This clearly looked like they were getting rid of him. The pilot must have parachuted out of the plane. The opening door was probably what woke him. The drowsiness? Did they drug him? He looked back at the can laying on his seat. The strange soda. Chances were that he drank twelve ounces of Benadryl or something similar. He turned back to the cockpit. Everything looked normal to him for the time being, but he was no pilot. The left seat had the tied up yoke so he sat in the right seat. He tried the yoke in that seat. It was stiff as if it were also tied.

Makes sense, he thought. *Why would the two yokes control different things*?

He shifted in the seat and leaned lower to start working on untying the rope. An alarm sounded which seemed to trigger a few more alarms. He looked at the instrument panel. A flashing red 'FUEL' light made him widen his eyes. The other flashing light said 'ENGINE'. He quickly looked out of the window off his right. He could tell the propeller wasn't being powered. It was still turning, windmilling due to the speed. He looked back to the panel to the gauge that said 'AIRSPEED'. It needle was slowly coming back. He could feel the aircraft begin a slight turn even with the yoke tied tightly. The one working engine must be powering it in that direction. Marcus searched his pockets, hoping he had his pocket knife on him. He had awoken so early that morning that he was probably too tired to remember to grab it. That, or subconsciously his brain knew he'd be boarding an airplane and he usually couldn't take his knife anyway. He cursed not being able to produce it from his pockets.

He got up and began to look for anything that could cut the rope. He opened a small cooler that was buckled into one of the seats hoping to find a glass bottle. It was empty. He slammed the lid and continued looking around. More alarms began to sound. He could hear the left engine begin to slow. He could see the propeller windmilling on that side too. He felt the aircraft's nose dip. He immediately thought of the aluminum can sitting in his seat. He rushed to it, holding on to each seat he passed. He took the can back to the cockpit. He set it on the floor in between the seats and crushed it with his foot. He hoped the action would start a break in the metal. He picked it up and saw what he had wished for. There was a one-inch break in the aluminum. He pulled the can apart a few inches and twisted the top and bottom in opposite direction to expose more of the straight edge.

Marcus glanced up and could see the windscreen filling with the wilderness below. He could feel the aircraft accelerate towards the ground. He guessed that he maybe had only one minute before slamming into the earth. A fleeting thought that he should have looked for a parachute crossed his mind. It was too late now. If there wasn't one then he'd be dead. Getting the rope cut was his last chance.

He started hacking at the vertical piece of rope that was securing the controls to somewhere below the pilot's seat. He gripped the mangled can so tightly that blood started to seep out of a growing slice in his hand. He gritted his teeth from the pain. A small portion of the rope remained. Marcus grabbed the rope at the cut and yanked. It broke free. He tried the yoke and had gained some motion but was disappointed that he hadn't noticed the second rope that helped secure the controls. He cursed and started hacking at the other rope that was secured to somewhere forward and under the instrument panel.

He was surprised when the King Air started to level off. Had the engine started back up? The 'AIRSPEED' alarm and light began to flash. It must have picked up enough speed to gain some lift but now the airspeed needle dropped quickly and then the aircraft began another dive. He had paused at the attempt to cut the second rope when the aircraft had slowed the descent. Now that he was barreling towards the ground again he leaned forward and kept slicing. Sweat rolled down his forehead and into his eyes. He frantically wiped it away with his forearm. Half of the rope had been cut through. He grabbed it and pulled. Nothing. He didn't have the leverage he had had with the first rope and he hadn't cut through enough either. He jammed the end of the can into the halfway cut rope and started grinding it back and forth as quickly as he could. Fibers of the rope fell to the floor and blood was now dripping from his hand. He looked out through the windscreen and figured he had about a thousand feet remaining. What time did that give him? Seconds?

Instead of grabbing the rope this time, he placed both hands on the yoke. With all of his strength, he turned the yoke to the right in an attempt to break the remaining threads of the rope. It worked, but with the unintended consequence of turning the aircraft abruptly to the right. Marcus didn't realize it, but the turn caused him to drop even quicker with no power to maintain lift. He straightened the aircraft's wings back to level, however, the nose was still pointed downwards. Something in his mind told him he should buckle in so he did quickly.

He was above the crest of a tree covered mountain. He heard a thwacking sound as the top of a tall pine tree struck the wing. He could feel it reverberate through the aircraft and through the controls. The plane continued the descent into a valley. Marcus wasn't sure if he was really doing anything that would help him. He thought maybe if he could try to settle the plane down at the lowest part of the valley then he would be safe. He turned the yoke slightly to angle the aircraft for a better position. He wanted to be more aligned with the elongated valley. He could see some clearings down below.

Marcus could feel the aircraft descending. He swore there were trees higher than he was. He was right. The thwacking and clunking began again as the King Air met with the tops of the trees. Marcus's mind couldn't keep up with the chaos that unfolded.

This is the end, he thought.

The last thing he thought he saw before he covered himself with his arms was the aircraft rolling end over end as it slammed into the trees.

Chapter Twenty-Seven

"Did you see that?" Lea yelled out to the others.

"Yeah," Will said. "It sounded like it crashed right over there." He pointed towards the woods. "We should see if anyone needs help."

"Come on," Alejandro yelled.

Alejandro rushed into the woods before anyone else had moved. Seeing him enter the trees, the others started to run towards the crash site as well.

"I won't be able to keep up," Lewis yelled. "I'll hold down the fort."

Beth yelled back to him in acknowledgment. She was last to run towards the woods and she was trying to keep up with the others.

Alejandro stopped to scan the area. He was breathing heavily from the sprint. His eyes fell on the tail of an airplane about another hundred yards ahead. Will and Lea caught up to him. He looked back and saw Juana and Beth not too far in trail.

"I can see the tail of it over there," Alejandro said while pointing at the aircraft.

Beth and Juana joined them and they slowed their pace. They were all getting tired from sprinting. They slowed even further from their jogging pace to a walk for the last ten yards, now all nearly out of breath. The plane hung above the ground about six feet. It was upright. The mangled wings wedged into the surrounding trees.

"It doesn't look promising," Alejandro said in between gasps of air.

"We still have to check," Juana said to her husband.

"I know," he replied. "I wasn't saying that we shouldn't."

As they stepped forward, a metal on metal groan emitted from the airplane. They stopped and took a few steps back, sensing some sort of danger. The groaning got louder and the plane suddenly dropped the last six feet to the ground. Silence immediately followed along with a rolling cloud of dust emanating in all directions away from the plane.

"I'm glad we weren't trying to climb up in it right then," Alejandro said after a few moments.

"We should be fine now...I hope," Will said. "I bet the door is on the other side.

They walked around the plane and found the opening in the side. The door having been sheared off in the crash. Will walking up to the opening and stuck his head in. He looked left to all the passenger seats.

"I don't see anyone back here," Will said over his shoulder.

He lifted his right leg up to the floor and placed his hands on the inside of the opening. As he started to pull himself into the airplane, Alejandro called out to him.

"Just be careful! We don't know if this thing is going to light on fire or maybe explode."

Will chuckled. "I think things usually only explode in the movies."

"You never know," Alejandro said sarcastically.

"I'm trying to remember...I don't remember hearing the engines running when the plane passed by us," Will said.

"I don't think they were," Lea said in agreement.

"Maybe it ran out of fuel," Beth added.

Will nodded and turned around back inside the plane. Now that he was inside he was sure there were no passengers. He turned to the right and could see a shoulder. He stepped forward up to the pilot's seats. There was a man slumped forward and against the side of the plane in the left seat. The right seat was empty. Will took the man by the shoulders and straightened him back up in the seat.

"Hello?" Will said to the man as he shook his shoulder.

No response. He figured that he was dead. He grabbed the man by his wrist to check for a pulse. He felt one and it felt normal to him.

"Hey guys," he yelled while still focusing on the man, "there's someone in here and they are alive. Come help me."

Will felt the plane rock from side to side as the others climbed in. Alejandro arrived at his side.

"Wow," Alejandro said, "he doesn't look too beat up for having just crashed an airplane."

"Hopefully nothing major is broken," Will said.

Will unbuckled the seatbelt around the man's waist. Will stepped further into the cockpit by the right seat.

"Grab his under his shoulders and lift and I'll get his legs," Will said.

"Oh, of course," Alejandro said, "make me take the heavier end."

Alejandro wrapped his arms underneath the man's armpits and lifted. As soon as he did, Will stepped in and wrapped his arms around the man's legs at his thighs. They were both grunting and the brought the man into the cabin. They set him down in the aisle. The three woman had stayed out of the way and searched the several rows of seats while Will and Alejandro pulled the man out.

"Oh my gosh!" Lea said as she saw the man.

"What!?" Beth said in surprise.

"What is it?" Juana asked.

Everyone was looking in between the man and Lea.

"That's Marcus Braden," Lea said. "From the news!"

"What?" Will said in disbelief.

"Look at him," Lea said. "It's him!" She pointed down at him.

Will tilted his head slightly. "Maybe...I don't know."

"It's him. I'm sure of it," Lea said.

"Either way," Beth said, "he needs some help...whoever he is," she said sounding frustrated.

Beth knelt down next to the man and felt his wrist.

"His pulse seems normal," Beth said.

"That's what I thought too," Will said. "Not that I'm an expert."

Beth lifted each of the man's arms checking them and his sides for any bleeding. She opened his suit jacket to do the same over his mid-section. She then moved along his legs. She pushed down lightly on the front, back, and sides of his legs to see if any blood would dampen the black suit pants.

“It doesn’t seem like there is any blood,” she said. “It also doesn’t feel like any of his limbs are broken. I could be wrong, though. I’m guessing he was knocked unconscious in the crash. Worst case scenario is that his neck or spine is broken. I’m not sure how we will be able to tell until he is awake.”

“I’m not sure either,” Will said. “I also don’t have a clue what we’d be able to do for him if it is.”

They all looked down at the man. No one spoke for a few moments.

“Should we try to wake him up here?” Juana asked. “I’ve heard you aren’t supposed to move someone who has a broken neck.”

“True,” Beth said. “But what other choice do we have? Ya know what I mean?”

Juana gave her a confused look.

“I mean that we can’t get an ambulance up here. I don’t think there are any ambulances even operating in the area anymore. If his neck or spine is broken, are we just going to leave him here on the floor of this plane? We’ve already moved him once.”

“Oh, okay,” Juana said, “I see what you are saying.”

“I tried waking him when I found him,” Will said. “He didn’t respond at all.”

“Well, I think we should take him back to our camp,” Alejandro said. “Lay him on something more comfortable. Maybe splash some cold creek water on his face to see if he wakes up.”

Will grunted. He was thinking about the distance they

needed to carry the man.

“We’ll need some support on him from everyone to get him that far,” Will said. “He’s fairly heavy.”

“What about making a stretcher?” Alejandro asked.

“Hmm...good idea,” Will said. “I didn’t think of that. There should be plenty of materials from this plane that we could make one real quick.”

They all searched around outside and inside the aircraft to try to find something to build a stretcher. They all re-convened by the opening to the aircraft after a few minutes of walking around. Lea and Beth stood in the opening having had stayed in the aircraft to check inside.

“There’s a section of the tail that has broken off,” Juana said. “It looks like a control panel or something. I think it’s big enough for him to lay on. We would just need to find something to tie him secure.”

“There’s some rope in here we found,” Lea said pointing a thumb to Beth. “What’s weird about it is that it’s tied to the controls. It looks like he must have cut it away to control the plane.”

“Whoa, what!?” Will said

“Yeah,” Beth said, “it’s really weird. I think someone was trying to kill him.”

Will climbed up into the plane and looked into the cockpit.

“Wow, I didn’t even notice this before when we were pulling him out,” he said holding a piece of the rope. “There’s some blood here on the floor too. I think you are right, Mom. Someone was trying to kill him.”

“Why would someone want Marcus Braden dead?” Lea asked.

“If it’s Marcus Braden,” Will said.

"It is! I swear!" Lea countered loudly.

Will laughed and shook his head. "We better get to work on the stretcher," he said.

Alejandro and Will picked up the horizontal piece of the tail that was laying on the ground. They lucked out that it waited to fall off until the aircraft made its final drop from the trees to the ground. The flat tailpiece had some weight of its own, but the two figured that with everyone helping to hold the weight that they would be okay with the man secured to it. They placed it on the ground near the opening in the aircraft's side. Will inspected where the piece had broken from the rest of the tail. He reached in and yanked out the snapped cabling. He hoped to lighten it as much as he could.

"We might be able to use some of this cable as well to secure him if we don't have enough rope," Will said holding up the wad of cable he had extracted.

"We won't need it," Beth said. "We found the rest of the rope that had been used to tie up the controls."

Will saw the rope his mother pointed to and shook his head. He was still baffled by the strangeness of the situation that had been dropped in their lap. Will climbed back into the airplane to help bring the man out. Alejandro stood on the ground by the opening waiting to take the man. Will and Beth scooted the man carefully across the aircraft floor until his head was right by the opening. Alejandro reached in and grabbed the man by his shoulders.

"Alright," Alejandro said, "jump out and be ready to grab his legs. I'm gonna start pulling him out."

Will stepped around the man and jumped out next to Alejandro. As the man began to slide out, Will wrapped his arms around his legs again.

"Got him," Will said.

They lowered him onto the flat tailpiece.

"Now all we need to do is secure him down," Alejandro said. "Don't want him sliding off," he said with a smile.

Beth brought the rope over. They gauged the length they had and determined it was enough to cut in half to make two ropes. One would be secured at the man's chest and the second would go around his legs. Once they had wrapped the rope around him and tied it snuggly, they determined where everyone would stand. Alejandro and Will decided they would take the two corners nearest the man's head. They figured that part of his body would be heaviest. Beth and Juana would lift abeam his waist across from each other and Lea would lift on the end by his legs.

"Don't anyone hesitate to say they need a break," Will said. "It would be better off to have to rest several times than to drop him. He could get more injured if that happens."

They did a countdown to hoist him up equally. They held the position for a few moments to make sure everyone had a good grip on the tailpiece. The started shuffling along. They rested every few minutes and made it back to their clearing after about ten minutes of walking. Lewis spotted them as they breached the tree line. He rushed over to them after noticing the body on the makeshift stretcher.

"Let me take over for someone," Lewis said. "You all look tired."

He replaced Beth, who he thought looked the most exhausted from the trek.

"Thanks," Beth said as she backed away.

"How far away was the crash?" Lewis asked. "You all

were gone for quite a while."

"It's not too far in," Will said between grunts. "It was just that we had to come up with a stretcher. He's unconscious. Hasn't been awake at all since we found him."

"Oh my," Lewis exclaimed as he examined the man. "He looks like Marcus Braden, that newscaster."

Will let out a laugh, "Alright, alright," he said looking back at Lea, "I guess there's a slight chance I'm wrong."

Lewis raised an eyebrow in confusion. He looked back and forth between Will and Lea.

"There must've been some discussion on this already."

"Yes," Lea said. "I'm positive that he is Marcus Braden. Will won't accept it."

"Hey!" Will said. "I just said that I could be wrong."

He looked back at Lea again. She narrowed her eyes and scrunched up her face at him.

Chapter Twenty-Eight

Marcus opened his eyes a few millimeters. His head throbbed. Why? A thick haze hung over him. He remembered being groggy before. When was that? His vision was blurred and his eyes were barely open but he could still see some blue sky. He started to take in more information in between the waves of pain in his head. He was hearing muffled voices. He was also moving. His brain was too confused at the moment to process the information it was receiving.

He shut his eyes again and tried to think through the events that led him to where he was now. He had been on a flight. He slept for most of it. He had woken up and...nothing. He felt deep inside that there was something important he should be remembering but just couldn't get to it.

He felt like he was moving; was he still on the airplane? Was he caught in between dream world and the real world?

Wait, he thought. *Why could I see blue sky*?

Scenes began to flash through his thoughts. It was as if he were watching a movie. He saw himself on the airplane. He was flying. This amused him. Did he have a subconscious desire to be a pilot? The scenes continued. He was awfully close to the ground. He was...crashing?

All at once Marcus realized this wasn't the dream world. This was a memory. He remembered it clearly now. His last memory of the tumbling aircraft came into focus. He was in a crashing plane right now. His eyes flew wide open. He tried to sit up. He was being held back by something. He looked down and saw he was bound by ropes. He couldn't even move his arms. He hadn't noticed his surroundings yet. He started to panic and thrash. The voices around him became clear.

"Whoa, whoa! Keep him steady."

"It's alright man! We are helping you."

"We have to set him down. I'm losing my grip."

Marcus looked around at his captors. He was definitely no longer on the King Air. He remembered the tumbling final moments. Why was he no longer on the plane? Was he dead?

"What is this? Where am I?" Marcus asked with fear covering his face.

"You were in a plane crash," a woman told him. She was kneeling down next to him. "Do you remember that?"

Marcus nodded his head.

"Does anywhere hurt? Do you think anything is broken?" she asked.

"Why am I tied up?" Marcus asked, ignoring the woman's questions.

"We made a stretcher for you," a young man said. "We carried you back to our camp. We didn't want you to fall off." He bent down and started untying the ropes.

"Are you hurt?" the woman asked again.

Marcus considered the question for a moment. "My head is killing me." He shifted around as the ropes loosened. He winced. "I may have broken a rib or two it seems," he said through a contorted expression.

"We could probably wrap your chest with something to keep your ribs from moving," the young man said. "These ropes may work if they are comfortable enough. By the way, what's your name?"

"Marcus. Marcus Braden. You may have seen me before on the news."

The young man smiled. "Yeah, that's who I thought you were."

A young woman that stood next to the man smacked him in the arm.

*****

He was so thirsty. Marcus drank and drank and drank. There was still a lingering drowsiness. For now, he was wrapped around the chest with the rope. He noticed it was the same rope that had secured the yoke in the airplane. The rope prevented bolts of pain in his chest. It wasn't the most comfortable brace. The group told him they would come up with something better. They had examined his chest and come to the conclusion that he had two to three cracked ribs. They all seemed to remain in place. Marcus figured he was lucky that none of them separated. His hand had been wrapped with a bandage as well. He was lucky that was the extent of his injuries.

Marcus liked this group. He learned each of their names

fairly quickly while they patched him up. They were all very helpful to him. They seemed to have a cohesion with each other that he didn't experience any longer in his career life. They had lit a fire and said they were going to cook him some food. They all gathered around a fire on stumps and tree trunks.

"I think they drugged me," Marcus said.

"Who drugged you?" Will asked with a look of surprise on his face.

"The CMA," Marcus said. "Central Management Authority. It's now my employer. Well...I guess 'was' is the more appropriate word."

"Why would they want you dead?" Will asked. "I've been wanting to ask you about it. It looks like someone was trying to kill you by what we saw on the inside of the plane."

"Yeah, I figured that out too," Marcus said. He forced out a single laugh. "A little bit too late. When I boarded the plane earlier today I had a soda. I almost immediately fell asleep. There was no fighting it. I woke up to an open door and crazy wind and no pilot. The controls were all tied up and the fuel had just run out. I don't know what woke me up. Maybe it was God. I felt groggy and confused. That's why I think they drugged me with that soda. I still feel a little bit of the grogginess wearing off. I had to cut the rope away from the controls with a can. After that, I did what I could to keep the aircraft from doing a nose dive straight into the ground. I guess it worked."

"I bet it was a smooth landing," Alejandro joked.

"Yeah...I settled it into those soft, fluffy trees," Marcus joked back.

Everyone laughed.

"So," Will said, "that brings it back to the same question; why do they want you dead?"

"How long have you all been living out here in the forest?" Marcus asked.

"We just got here," Will said. "Why?"

"So you know about the CMA camps all over the place?" Marcus asked.

"Yeah. We've decided to avoid them. I have a bad feeling about them. Historically, camps like that are a good way to pick up some nasty sickness."

Marcus nodded. "I suppose they are. However, that is not the main reason you want to avoid them at this point in our history."

"Why?" Alejandro said as he leaned forward, now more interested in the conversation.

"Because they are going to be slave labor when this whole transition of the country is done," Marcus said.

"What!?" Will exclaimed. "Slaves?"

"That's not the worst of it," Marcus said. "The goal is to annihilate pretty much everyone else that didn't go to the camps. I've seen a list of bombing sites. It looked like every major population center in the United States."

No one spoke. Everyone was now in shock from the conversation. Jaws dropped open. Eyes were stuck open wide.

Marcus broke the silence. "I found those things out and I guess they didn't trust me. Rightfully so. I was spying for a group that is planning on fighting them...somehow." He paused. "If you all just got up here, where were you before?"

"Uh," Will began. He was still processing the information. "Uh, we were down the mountain a little closer to Oakhurst."

"Oakhurst? Where's that?" Marcus asked. "And why'd you leave there?"

"Oakhurst is near Yosemite," Will said. "We-"

Marcus cut him off, "Yosemite?" he said with a surprised tone. "I'm in California?"

"Where did you think you were?" Will asked.

"I guess I had no idea," Marcus answered. "I was headed from Colorado to Los Angeles. I assumed I wasn't that far from Colorado Springs. I didn't know how long I was out from the drugs. Anyway, I interrupted you. Why'd you leave?"

"No worries," Will said. "We were actually at our homes. My mom and I live outside of town on some property and Lewis is just down the road from us. We've all been holding out there. A large group came in and sent us on the run. We had been in town a couple of times since all this started and that group went through the whole town. They destroyed it. Raided everything they could find and then burned it down. There's a good chance when we go to check out our homes that they will be a pile of charred ruins too."

"Well that makes sense," Marcus said.

"What does?" Will asked.

"I had also found out just this week that millions and millions of people have already died," Marcus said grimly. "Disease, rioting, you name it. The CMA doesn't care because they want most of the people dead anyway. They are just telling people that they are fixing everything."

"Wow," Alejandro said.

"We had wondered why no one showed up to the town. Not even the news," Will said.

"They aren't going to allow something like that to be on the news," Marcus said. "They started censoring what I'm allowed to say the day after they took over the country. I had to go along because I was spying for the ARF." Marcus paused for a moment. He realized he hadn't told them about the ARF in full. "The ARF is the American Rights Foundation. I think they have some patriotic military forces that have joined with them. Anyway, I had no idea so many people had died. I had no idea that cities all over the place are destroyed. They kept it all from me. They probably assumed that I would say something about it on the news. I've been running around covering stories about CMA operations and how much they are helping people and other worthless stories. The whole country is crumbling around us and we are broadcasting rainbows and butterflies. Anyone watching probably thought I was an idiot."

"We were wondering if it was just our town or if it was more widespread," Alejandro said.

"With that amount of people dead it sounds like it's widespread," Will said and then turned back to Marcus. "You probably don't have to worry about anyone thinking you are an idiot."

"Why is that?" Marcus asked.

Will forced out a laugh. "I bet the only people watching are the people in the camps."

Marcus thought about that and laughed as well. "I bet you are right." Marcus paused for a moment and shook his head. "Those poor souls. They'll be slaves to a new government."

The news of annihilation ate at Will. He didn't want the conversation to move on to anything else.

"So, this bombing," Will began, "when is it going to

start? Are they just nuking the all the big cities? Do you think we'll be safe here?"

"Whoa, whoa whoa," Marcus said. "One at a time."

"Sorry," Will said.

"It's supposed to happen in the spring or summer," Marcus said. "The document I read didn't have any specific date. The reason I was in Colorado Springs, though, was because all the important people in the CMA were going to Cheyenne Mountain. It's a military base that's inside of a mountain. I was told it was for some big meeting. I have my worries that they are hiding out there while the bombing starts."

"Oh," was all Will said in return.

"It won't be nuclear bombs," Marcus said. "The document specified that. It makes sense. If they want to use the people in the camps to rebuild things how they want then they wouldn't nuke the country. It wouldn't be habitable for them either."

"So, what about people like us? People hiding out in the wilderness?" Alejandro asked.

"No idea," Marcus said. "My best guess is that they'd eventually try to find everyone they could. The document talked about 'reeducation'. I assume that means that people like you all that avoided the camps and probably people in the camps that don't want to go along with their plans will be indoctrinated. If it didn't work...they'd be killed. They don't want a rebellion on their hands. If you think about it, they must have been waiting for the country to be in the situation it was in."

"What do you mean?" Will asked.

"Huge division in beliefs across the country," Marcus said. "People wouldn't just protest, they would riot. Every single issue would polarize people in some way. The economy has been bad for years. States were broken apart. I don't think they could keep track anymore of newly created states...or regions. There were plenty of areas here in California that claimed to no longer be a part of the state or even the country. See, it's all prime for what the CMA is doing. They started off by presenting everything as a solution. Once that step is complete, they remove what they don't need and hit reset. Boom. Now there is a more manageable amount of people and the Central Management Authority is the new government and they control every aspect of everything."

Marcus had become a bit too animated and held his chest at his cracked ribs for a moment.

"There has to be something we can do," Will said with a growing look of panic in his eyes. "We can't just let them kill all these people. It's almost as if everyone is making it too easy for them."

"Maybe they are," Marcus said. "I'm sure people ran to those camps. How could they have known?"

"What about that other group you said?" Will asked. "They might have military on their side. Are they doing something?"

"The ARF. I hope so," Marcus said. "I was only told so much from them. They didn't want me to know too much if I was found out. I assume they have something planned."

"What if they don't?" Will asked urgently.

"Don't what? Have a plan?"

"Yeah!" Will said. "We have to do something. We can't just let them kill off nearly an entire country. There are hundreds of millions of people here."

Will's urgency made Marcus shift in his seat. At this point, he had written it off. Here he was, stuck in the woods after being in a plane crash. He had given up on the possibility of being apart of the fight anymore. Now there was a gung-ho young man sitting by him with such a great fire within him. He could tell Will would do anything he possibly could to stop this from happening.

"I do know they had plans to eventually announce the CMA's plans on the news," Marcus said. "They were going to hijack the broadcast and I was going to tell everyone."

"That's it!?" Will asked.

"Will, give the guy a break," Alejandro said. "He just survived a plane crash."

"I'm not giving him a hard time," Will said. "If the ARF is the opposition, shouldn't they come up with some kind of action to counter the plans of the CMA?"

"I agree," Marcus said. "When I passed the information about the bombings on to them they already had some idea about it. I'm sure I wasn't their only spy. Now that they have the details that I gave them, I'm guessing they can finalize their plans."

"But you don't know if they have a military?" Will asked.

"Um...I don't know for sure. I don't remember if he told me that," Marcus said.

"He?" Will asked.

"Oh, Thomas Allen. Thomas is who I was always in contact with from the ARF." Marcus said. "I think he is the overall leader of the ARF."

The conversation started to wind down and move to other subjects. Marcus could tell that Will was still frustrated and anxious to do something. He could see him across the fire, now sitting with Lea. It was obvious to Marcus that Will was still talking about the news he had given the group. He could see Will shaking his head as he and Lea whispered to each other. He thought that Will was quite passionate about people and his country. Marcus turned from them and stared into the fire. He was going into his mind now, deep in thought.

What could they do?

Chapter Twenty-Nine

The cool early morning air hung low over the mountain. The glow from the low sun pierced through the tent. The growing light began to rouse Marcus. He sat up. The chilly air hit him instantly and he reached for his shirt and put it on. He sat for a moment. He was still processing all the events of the last few days. He still didn't understand how they found him out. He thought it may have been the General, but why wouldn't he have called him out then and there? That was the best scenario he could come up with and there was no point in dwelling on it much more. There was no way for him to figure it out from where he was. What did it matter? The CMA thought he was dead.

Despite dreaming of close call spy work and crashing planes, Marcus still rested well. It had probably been the best sleep he could remember getting in a long time. He was sure his brain had longed for a reprieve last night, especially after the events that happened during the day. The moment his head laid down his brain had shut off.

Marcus finally got up and stretched. He finished dressing and stepped out of the tent. He felt odd wearing a suit out in the middle of the wilderness. He couldn't see anyone else around the clearing so he assumed everyone else was still sleeping. He stayed quiet and went to sit by the fire pit. A small amount of smoke continuously rose from the remaining hot coals.

He got back up and picked through the wood pile that sat near the fire pit. He took some smaller kindling sized pieces and placed them around the hot coals. He gathered some dry grass that had been set aside for starting fires and placed it directly on top of the coals. With a small stick he found as a fire poker, he moved some of the coals around to better expose the grass to the heat. More smoke began to billow up. Marcus blew into the coals. A small flame appeared and quickly spread through the dry grass. He pushed some of the kindling pieces closer and they started to light up and crackle. He grabbed a couple of larger logs and placed them onto the small fire and took a seat again by the fire. He had been living downtown Manhattan city life for such a long time that he couldn't remember the last time he built up a fire like that. His high-rise condo lacked a fireplace.

Marcus remained by his lonesome for about fifteen minutes before Lewis emerged from his tent. He gave a quick wave and walked directly to the bed of his truck. He opened a cooler and pulled out a few items and brought them over to the fire.

"You already got a fire going," Lewis said. "Thank you."

"Not a problem," Marcus said. "I'm just glad I remembered what to do. It has been years since I've been camping and started a fire."

Lewis laughed and then began cooking some of the deer meat in the fire. They both sat in the quiet while the deer meat cooked.

"What do you think about Will?" Lewis asked, breaking the silence.

"You mean about wanting to do something to stop the CMA?"

Lewis nodded. "He's a passionate young man. Always been very smart."

"Well," Marcus began and then paused, "I was thinking about it last night after his and my conversation. I'm sure there is something that we could do. And he's right. We don't really know if the ARF had some kind of plan."

"Do you have a plan?" Lewis asked.

"The best I can come up with is to stop them in Cheyenne Mountain," Marcus said.

"Whatever the plan is, I'm in," Will said.

Lewis and Marcus jumped. They hadn't realized Will was standing behind them.

"Whoa!" Marcus said. "When did you get there?"

Will laughed. "Sorry. Just been here a minute. I was up fairly early and went walking around the area. I didn't expect anyone would be up when I got back to the camp."

"What do you mean you are in?" Marcus asked.

"We need to stop them from killing millions more people," Will said. "They brought the country to a grinding halt. You said millions and millions have already died from what they did. Now they are going to kill millions more. We have to stop them. Whatever it takes. They already tried to kill you. We can't just sit around in the woods waiting for them to come looking for us."

Marcus pursed his lips and nodded. A smile formed on his face. Will raised an eyebrow in confusion.

"What is it?" Will asked.

"They think I'm dead," Marcus said.

"Yeah?"

"I have a plan," Marcus said, still with a goofy smile on his face.

*****

The rest of the group had awoken and joined Marcus, Will, and Lewis by the fire. Marcus had started to tell Will and Lewis his plan and had to start over as the others arrived. He had to pause many times to ask them questions about the area and their town and if he was going to be able to use a vehicle. Will told him that his Jeep was hidden in the woods near their house. He also warned him about the group that moved onto their property.

"Do you think we could get the Jeep back to the main road?" Marcus asked.

"I'm sure we could find a way," Will said. "I don't think a single tank of gas will get us to Colorado Springs."

"We don't need it to get us to Colorado Springs," Marcus said. "We only need to get to one of the camps outside of Fresno."

Everyone looked confused.

"Why to the camp?" Will asked.

"I'll be able to get us some better transportation there," Marcus said.

"Won't they be surprised you are alive?" Beth asked.

"I have a plan for that too," Marcus said with another large smile forming on his face.

*****

"Why do you need to go?" Lea asked.

Will could tell her anxiety was building again. Will had taken her aside after saying his goodbyes to everyone else. He and Marcus had decided they should leave right away. Tears were forming in her eyes.

"They need to be stopped," Will said. "If they get to go through with their plan, they will eventually be up here in the mountains looking for people. If that happens, there won't be much we can do to stop them. If we stop them now, before they can kill millions more people, we'll have a chance. They'll be cut off at the head."

"Can't Marcus do this?" Lea asked. "It's his plan."

"He will be doing it," Will said. "He needs my help. He's still injured. I can't just stand back. Not after knowing what they are planning on doing. If they find us up here we will have to be their slaves too. Otherwise, if we don't go along with their plans, their ideology, they will probably kill us."

"I want to go with you then."

"No!" Will said too loudly. He immediately regretted his seemingly harsh reaction. "I just don't want anything happening to you," he said more calmly and quietly. "You need to stay here with your parents, my mom, and Lewis. We can't bring too many of us."

"I don't want anything happening to you!"

"I don't either. I will be careful," Will said.

Lea lowered her head. She stared at the ground as tears flowed from her eyes. Will thought that this might be a good time to tell her that he loved her. It would still seem like an act of desperation. He was about to fight an uphill battle. It would probably be the riskiest and most dangerous thing he would do in his lifetime. He needed to comfort her in some way. He took hold of her and held her tightly. They stood there embracing each other for a few minutes. Lea pushed back slightly and looked up at Will.

"Will, I need to tell you something. I-"

"Don't say anything," Will interrupted her. "Not yet." He knew what she was going to say. He didn't want it to be an act of desperation on her part either. "Save it. I will be back. And I will have something to tell you as well."

He pulled her in again and hugged her tightly. He let go and turned away. He could hear her sobbing. He walked over to his mother. He had said his goodbyes to her earlier but he needed to give her one last hug. After doing so, he shouldered his pack and joined Marcus at the edge of the clearing.

He and Marcus now made the over ten-mile hike down the mountain to retrieve Will's Jeep. As they walked, Will described the layout where his Jeep had been left behind. He told Marcus how he thought they'd be able to get it out of there undetected by the new inhabitants of their property. He was planning on passing the Jeep by and remaining in the woods all the way down to the road to make sure they'd be able to drive down it. He thought there might be a chance that the group would put up a roadblock. After verifying they could use the road, he'd return to the Jeep and then drive it further up the mountain to pick up the four wheeling trail. They'd waste a lot of time, but driving it down near the property could easily attract the group's attention. Once reaching the main road, they'd have to race by the property as fast as they could.

Will had figured on a couple of hours to make the downhill trek to the Jeep. He was even cutting some time by leading them through the trees when they would reach some of the switchbacks that wound up parts of the mountain. He was beginning to worry about Marcus. On some of the rougher areas where they would be walking over rocky terrain, he could see Marcus wince and clutch the side of his chest. He had wondered if the cracked ribs would become a problem.

"Once we reach the trail again we'll continue on it from here on out," Will said. "I can tell the rocky areas are hurting you." He pointed towards Marcus's chest.

"It hurts a little bit," Marcus said, "but I'll be alright. We need to keep going and save as much time as we can."

Will thought that Marcus was probably just saying that it didn't hurt much because of the urgency of the situation. He went with what Marcus said anyway. However, he tried leading them by the easiest path he could find.

After a little over two hours and only taking two breaks, they reached the last part of the trail that was above the property. They stood on the road as Will tried to gauge where they stood in reference to where he left the Jeep. They walked down the road another half of a mile before they turned into the trees and down the mountain. As they walked down, Will tried to find a suitable route they could bring the Jeep up.

They came across the area Will had cut through with his Jeep. He could see some of the broken branches and the crushed forest floor. Will had thought that he gauged it correctly, but it had been a hectic night. Some of his memories of that evening had blurred together. He paused briefly and pointed an ear down towards his home. He could hear people in the distance. He frowned. He had hoped this trip would reveal the group had moved on already.

They turned and followed the path his Jeep had created.

After a couple hundred yards Will became confused by the tracks. He could see tracks on either side of the path. He couldn't find anymore that led away from the property. His eyes widened and he rushed back and forth examining the tracks.

"Shoot!" He nearly yelled it too loud.

"What is it?" Marcus asked.

"That group found my Jeep."

Chapter Thirty

"They found it out here in the middle of nowhere?" Marcus asked.

"Yeah, I guess so," Will said with a sigh. "If they went searching for us that night then I wouldn't be surprised if they searched the whole property too. It wouldn't have been hard to find where I busted through the fence."

"Does Lewis have any other vehicles on his property?" Marcus asked.

"I think he has a tractor and a riding lawn-mower," Will said. "I think they could walk up to us if we tried to drive by on those."

Marcus and Will both laughed.

"Man!" Will said in a frustrated tone. "They had tons of vehicles with them already. Why'd they need mine?"

All of a sudden, Will and Marcus both looked at each other.

"Tons of vehicles you say?" Marcus asked, raising an eyebrow.

Will smiled wide. “Yep. Let’s go check it out.”

They took off at a quick pace towards the break in the fence. They slowed as the fence came into view. Will was surprised to see that the invading group had attempted to put the fencing back up. It was angled upwards and tied to a tree with a section of rope. He wasn’t sure why they put the effort into it at all since they were still able to slip through the opening. They stayed in the trees along the fence line as the crept down the property.

They stopped and crouched down once they came abeam the house. Will was disgusted by the scene before him. Their crops were trampled all over the place. Tents had been put up in what appeared to be random locations. Areas that were once grass had been crushed too many times by footsteps and tire tracks that it was now mostly dirt. He could understand that with having a couple dozen people that some areas would get trampled, but did they not care about the food? They had tents on their vegetable plots. Vehicles were driven into and parked on planted areas. Will shook his head.

Marcus noticed Will’s disappointed. “They’ve really done a number on this place, huh?”

“Looks like it,” Will answered. “We had done tons of work here. Planted tons of food. I wonder if they’ve done anything like this to Lewis’s property.”

“Sorry, Will,” Marcus said in an effort to comfort him. “I see some Jeeps parked over there. Any of them yours?”

“I don’t see mine,” Will said. “At this point, it doesn’t matter if we get my Jeep or any other truck. I left the keys in the Jeep and I didn’t have a full tank of gas. We need any of those vehicles that have a lot of gas and the keys sitting in it.”

“If any of them have keys in there at all,” Marcus said.

They both scanned over the vehicles in view. They discussed the advantages and disadvantages of different placement of where trucks were parked. They didn't want to get too close to the tents or the house. There were men walking around the property that they needed to avoid. This was no time to get into a firefight with a group this size. The odds weren't in their favor. Plus, they didn't know what they would have to deal with once they took a vehicle.

The two argued over staying together or searching the vehicles separately. Marcus wanted to search separately so they could cover more vehicles. Will wanted to stick together so when they found a truck to take, they could jump in and go right away. Will was adamant about staying together so Marcus eventually gave in.

They stayed low and slowly made their way to a group of trucks parked together. They stopped behind every bush and tree they came upon to reassess the situation. The three trucks had been pulled up the driveway and turned right and parked in the rocky terrain. They sat parked downhill from the house in what would be considered the front yard. They aimed for the truck furthest downhill. They figured it would be the easiest out of all the vehicles they could see to escape quickly. They reached the truck and crouched by the front passenger side. They tried to keep any view of their legs blocked by the tires.

Will had Marcus stay crouched by the tire while he crawled around the front end of the truck to check for keys. While on the ground, he scanned from under the other parked trucks to check for any of the men walking around near the house. He couldn't see any so he started to stand as he reached the driver's door. He tried the door and was relieved to find it unlocked. He stayed bent low as he slowly opened the door. He continually looked back behind him. He leaned his chest down on the bench seat to keep his head out of view while he searched for keys. He was disappointed they weren't in the ignition.

He heard a tapping sound and jumped when he saw a head in the passenger window. He calmed when he realized it was Marcus. Will raised an eyebrow and gave a puzzled look at him. Marcus pointed a finger towards the house and mouthed something. Will lifted his head so he could see through the window. He saw a group of six or so guys walking from the house towards the trucks they were searching. As they were about half way he could start to hear their voices. He quickly glanced back at Marcus with wide eyes. As he did, he noticed the keys out of the corner of his eye tucked above the visor. He motioned for Marcus to get in. He reached up and pulled the visor down and the keys dropped to the floor.

"Gerard wants us to do some recon on that next small town we went through a few weeks back. The one towards Fresno. Some of the others traded some bullets with some locals there. There was plenty more for us to get in that town."

The group of guys had stopped behind the truck next to them. Will and Marcus could clearly hear them discuss their plans. The top of Marcus's head was still visible in the passenger window. Will motioned again for him to get in. He had inserted the key into the ignition and was waiting for Marcus to get in to start it. Marcus held up three fingers and then pointed to the ignition and then the door. Will understood that on a count of three he was to start the truck and Marcus would jump in.

Marcus held up the three fingers again. Will put his hand on the key. Two fingers. One. Marcus tried the door but it was locked. Will had turned the key on cue. Marcus's eyes shot to Will. Will realized the mistake and quickly reached over and unlocked the door. As Marcus entered the truck Will looked through the rear window. The group of men were startled and confused by the truck's engine roaring to life.

The men walked up behind the truck expecting to see someone from their own group. They saw two wide-eyed faces looking back at them that they didn't recognize. Will slammed down the accelerator. The spinning rear tires sprayed dirt and rock over the group of men as they were drawing guns. The debris caused the men to duck and cover their faces with their arms. The action gave Will and Marcus just enough time to begin their escape.

The truck bounced over the rough terrain as Will angled towards the level dirt driveway. A barrage of bullets was sent their way. They could hear the thunks and tings as bullets struck the truck. Will saw a branch a few feet to his left instantly snap out of the corner of his eye. He knew it was bullet striking it.

As the truck skidded onto the main road, Will yelled over the roaring engine. "Are you okay? Did you get hit?" He could see Marcus holding his chest. He hoped it was just the cracked ribs and not a bullet wound.

"I'm fine. No bullet holes in me," Marcus answered.

Will sped down the road as fast as he could. Marcus readjusted in his seat and buckled in as they accelerated faster. Will noticed Marcus buckling in and he did the same. Before reaching the town, Will began to slow down.

"Hold on," he said.

"What are you doing?" Marcus asked.

"I know a shortcut," Will said. "Well, it's not exactly a shortcut. It's just not the most direct way to get to the highway to Fresno. If they follow us, I think this will help us lose them."

Marcus grasped the handle on the door expecting another skidding turn. At the last moment, Will had decided against it. He slowed way down to make the turn and then sped up again. After the turn, he explained to Marcus that he didn't want the fresh skid marks left on the pavement acting as a giant arrow pointing to them.

Marcus looked back up the road and never saw any passing vehicles. It looked like they were in the clear for now.

Chapter Thirty-One

"What do you think we should do?" Lea asked her father.

"What can we do?" Alejandro answered.

"There were gunshots. We need to go make sure they are okay," Lea said with an increasing sense of urgency in her voice.

Alejandro sighed. "I'll make the hike down there. I definitely don't want you going."

"But I need to know Will is okay," Lea said.

"Once I can see what I can find out, then I am coming right back here," Alejandro said.

Alejandro dreaded what he had just volunteered for. He immediately played out several scenarios in his head after hearing the gunshots. One, which was the worst case scenario, both Marcus and Will were killed by the group that took their home. If that was the case, he didn't want his daughter taken by the group or seeing Will's dead body. He also did not want to come across Will's dead body. Two, Will and Marcus made it away with some injuries. Three, which was his hope and the best-case scenario, they followed through with the original plan of bringing the Jeep higher up the mountain to join the four-wheeling trail. The gunshots were from their dash by the property. Either way, there were gunshots and that could never be good.

Alejandro figured leaving now would put him at the property when there was still daylight. He had mixed feelings about it. He wanted the cover of night, but at the same time, he wanted the light so he could see as much as possible. He warned the others that he might spend the night somewhere on the mountain and head back in the morning. He didn't know the terrain as well as Will and didn't want to get lost in the dark. Alejandro packed a small bag with some food and a few survival items for the potential overnight stay and headed down the mountain.

Alejandro considered the gunfire could lead to the group deciding to search up the mountain for them so he concluded it would be best to parallel the trail at least ten feet in the trees on his way down. He hadn't been in that great of shape prior to the country spinning into chaos, but now that they had been doing much manual labor, Alejandro was energized by the trek. He made good time down the mountain and was even able to see ahead on some of the switchbacks and cut down on the distance he had to travel.

He made it to the portion of the trail that was above Beth and Will's property. He even got lucky and came across their footprints on the side of the trail where they entered the woods again. He was fairly positive it was their footprints because one set looked like they belong to the dress shoes Marcus was wearing. He entered the trees and cut over to his right. He knew he should eventually run into the fence that marked the property line.

He reached the fence where he thought he must be lower down the mountain from where Will said he broke through the fence with his Jeep. His tracking skills were non-existent so he had immediately lost the footprint trail upon entering the woods. He tossed his bag over and then managed to climb the fence and drop over to the other side.

Now that he was on the property, he crept slowly ahead. He stopped every few steps to listen. He could see the edge of the tree line ahead and decided to watch the property from here. He didn't want to get too close to the tree line and risk being seen. He pulled a small pair of binoculars that Lewis lent him and started scanning the area.

"Ruined a lot of my gardening work," he muttered under his breath.

Alejandro pulled the binoculars from his eyes and scanned the area without. He replaced them and quickly scanned around again. There was only one truck. He could tell that there had been many vehicles before. He saw the signs all over the yard and in the garden areas. There were tire tracks that beat the ground into a muddy mess and flattened areas that had to have been tents. Had they left? Maybe the gunfire they heard was another group threatening this one. The lone truck bugged him. It did look fairly beaten up and old. Perhaps they left it behind on purpose.

After fifteen minutes or so of reconnaissance at this location, Alejandro decided to move all the way around to the other side of the property to see what was on the other side of Beth's house. He made his way all the way back to the fence where he had entered the property and followed it all the way around. He had to remind himself several times to slow down so he wouldn't make so much noise. Once he arrived at a new spot he was satisfied with, he spent another fifteen minutes doing the same.

There was nothing out of the ordinary on this side of the house. He was happy to see no sign of Will or Marcus. Maybe the gunfire wasn't related to their arrival down here earlier in the day. Alejandro held on to that hope. He decided he would go to the opposite corner where Will would have broken through the fence and try to find the Jeep tracks. He could also head down to the main road to search for any clues with the little light of day that was left.

He was happy he didn't find the Jeep. He also didn't find anything at the road. On a whim, he double-timed it over to Lewis's property. The thought had crossed his mind that the group had possibly moved over there. He was glad to find almost no evidence of them living there. It appeared they had searched the house food and probably took everything that Lewis had stored. It was now dark and Alejandro started to hike back up the mountain. He would return in another day or so to make sure they didn't return. He would spend the night at least a mile beyond Beth's property, still worried about the lone truck. If the group did pack up and leave completely, it may be a confidence booster for everyone that they could return home.

*****

The next morning Alejandro awoke early to hike the almost ten miles up the mountain in the still-cool morning. He had felt good about what shape he was in the day before but going uphill told him a different story. His lungs were on fire. He definitely would have to wait an extra day or so before doing all this again to check if the property had remained clear.

He arrived as they were cooking lunch on the fire. He reported his findings and it did indeed boost everyone's mood.

"I'm still worried about what that gunfire was," Lea said. "It happened about the time they should have gotten down the mountain."

"It could have been anything, Lea," Juana chimed in.

"I wouldn't be surprised if those people fired on them as they drove down the road by the property," Alejandro said. "I went to the road and couldn't find any sign of trouble. Maybe someone was hunting in the area."

Lea nodded and remained quiet and in thought.

"After I can recover a little bit from the hike up this morning, I'll go down again to see if it's all still clear."

Chapter Thirty-Two

"That certainly wasn't a good start," Marcus said.

"Yeah," Will said. "Definitely not how I expected that to go."

The two had been driving for a little over thirty minutes. Their nerves had finally just begun to settle. Marcus stopped watching the road behind them and shifted on the bench seat to get comfortable. The loud rumbling exhaust on the ancient big block engine made Will cringe. Anyone would be able to hear the trucks for miles ahead of their arrival. He continually worried about any other similar groups that might stop passers-by and lighten their load of all their belongings, or perhaps even their life.

It seemed eerie that the only other vehicles they saw so far were ones abandoned on the side of the road. Had that many people either died or went to the camps to cause the area to be this empty? The thought made Will's blood boil. He pushed the thought away. He didn't want to be fuming the whole time. He also didn't want to drop into one of his dark, depressing moods.

As they could start to see the white canvas in the distance that was typical of refugee camps, Will began to wonder what Marcus's plan was. He had said that he had one, but he definitely hadn't told him yet.

"So, Marcus," Will began, "you never did say what the plan to get into this camp and get transportation was."

"We are going to walk right in like we own the place," Marcus said.

Will waited for more of the plan. He eventually raised an eyebrow when one didn't seem to be coming.

"That...that's it?" Will asked.

"Basically," Marcus said. "I've had a successful career talking my way into things and places I don't really belong. You have to do that to make it in the media. If you are a young investigative reporter and you let another network get the exclusive interview or break some big story before you, that very well could be the end of your career. Just follow my lead. Leave the talking to me."

Will suddenly lost some of his confidence in Marcus. He wondered if the plan to get into Cheyenne Mountain was as solid as he thought. They turned onto the dirt road that led up to the entrance of the camp. Will couldn't believe the size of the camp. It was massive. Looking to his left and right, it stretched to the horizon all around him.

"Are all of these camps around the country this huge?" Will asked.

"All the ones I've seen are," Marcus said.

Will shook his head. "I guess they would need this many people to rebuild the entire country after the destruction they caused."

Marcus didn't comment any further. He reached out his

hand and tapped it on Will's arm. "Remember, let me do the talking."

They had reached the entrance and two CMA security guards stepped up to the truck.

"Are you two here to seek refuge..." the guard had paused. He had just noticed Marcus. "Are you...are you Marcus Braden?"

"Yes," Marcus said. "What seems to be the problem?"

"It's all over the news that you are dead. Died in a plane crash in the Nevada desert," the guard said. He still had a surprised and confused look on his face.

"Yep, that's what happened," Marcus said jokingly. "In all seriousness, as far as you know, the story you've heard is what happened." Marcus's face turned serious quickly.

"I...think I understand," the guard said.

"No, I don't want you to think you understand. I need you to understand," Marcus said. He dipped his chin and kept his gaze steady on the guard just outside his open window. "If you have trouble understanding, I'll make sure Mara hears about this. If you know her at all, you know that she is very keen on re-education." Marcus didn't know if that was true or not. He had only briefly talked with Mara during the last big meeting he was in. "Now, if there's nothing else you two need, Mara has an assignment for me to complete."

"Where's your camera?" the other security guard said. He stood outside Will's open window. He had remained quiet up until then. He appeared quite serious. He also appeared to be eyeing the pistol on Will's side.

Before Marcus could come up with an excuse, Will decided to give it a go. "Not all tasks that we complete have to do with what shows up on t.v., if you catch my drift."

The guard looked back and forth between Will and Marcus. Will had had a boost of confidence when he decided to give the storytelling a try, but now the piercing silence and the steady look on the guard's face was causing that confidence to drain.

"Look, sir," Will said, "you've seen on the news that he is dead." He jabbed his thumb in Marcus's direction. "There's a lot that goes on behind the scenes that not every single person knows about. Mara has us on a tight schedule and we need to get going."

The guard nodded. "I was just making small talk. I've never talked to a dead man before." A slight grin formed on his face. "You can proceed."

Will smiled back. "Thank you, sir."

As they pulled away, Will could see in his mirror that the guard still looked a little suspicious of them.

"What was that?" Marcus asked. He kept facing forward to not alarm the two guards. They were still watching them drive into the camp.

"I thought it seemed legitimate," Will said. "It seemed like you needed a little help."

Marcus finally turned towards Will as they were a good distance from the gate. He dipped his chin and raised a single eyebrow at Will.

"You think I needed help?" Marcus asked.

Will laughed. "We are in, aren't we?"

Marcus responded, "Stick with the plan."

Will still chuckled for another minute. After he regained his composure he asked, "So, where am I driving to?"

"Glad you could rejoin me," Marcus said with a hint of sarcasm. "It looked like the aviation area of the camp was on the opposite side." He pointed straight ahead. "Just keep on this pathway all the way across."

After a few more minutes of driving, they arrived on the opposite side of the camp. Marcus had been right. This side of the camp was littered with helicopters and fixed-wing aircraft as well. Marcus noticed that this camp had the luxury of having a runway on site. It wasn't a runway in the usual meaning of the word. They had simply flattened out the farm fields to accommodate the smaller fixed-wing airplanes that were parked all over.

Marcus explained this portion of the plan to Will. They were going to be borrowing one of these aircraft and flying to Colorado Springs.

"Are you a pilot?" Will asked.

"Just became one this week," Marcus said. "Didn't you see my landing?"

Now it was Will's turn for the piercing stare at Marcus. Marcus explained that they'd be borrowing a pilot. He would do this all the time at the camp he was at in the northeast. They would have to keep up the story of his death being faked and that they had much more important and secretive work to do for the CMA. Marcus also warned Will that they should keep quiet during the flight. They didn't want to slip up by discussing any of their plans and have the pilot pass the information on ahead of their arrival.

They pulled up near a tent that sat apart from the rest of the tents in the camp. It was surrounded by helicopters so they assumed it was acting as the hub for aviation in the camp. Marcus pulled a credentials badge out of his pocket and wrapped the lanyard around his neck.

"Don't know why I didn't think of this for when we tried to enter the camp," Marcus said.

They walked around to the tent's entrance. As they entered, they felt a wave of cool air. There was a swamp cooler on the opposite side of the tent blasting cool air all the way across the tent. The inside of this tent was nothing like any of the tents Marcus had been in at the camp he lived at. It was mostly empty. A few workbenches lined the edge. It smelled of oil and grease and burning electricity. This had to be what was acting as the maintenance hanger.

They spotted a man to their left in the corner of the tent. He had his legs propped up on a desk and he looked to be reading a magazine. For a brief moment as they walked over to the man, Marcus wondered if this might be the pilot that pointed him westward in the King Air and then jumped. They approached him and Marcus cleared his throat. The man laid the magazine down on his chest and looked over at the two men that had just approached him. He noticed Marcus's credential badge first and stood fairly quickly. He then shifted his gaze to Marcus's face. It took the man a moment to register who he was seeing and then his eyes widened and he took a step back. Marcus was relieved that it didn't appear to be the same pilot.

"Yes, yes, yes," Marcus said, "you've seen the news that I'm dead. Big surprise, I'm here. And, I'm not dead. What's your name, son?"

"Uh...Jay," he said in an unsure tone.

"Is that a question?" Marcus asked.

"No...my name is Jay." he said more confidently.

"Jay," Marcus said, "there is something you need to understand. As far as anyone is concerned, including yourself, you never saw me or him." He pointed to Will. "Do you understand?"

Jay nodded.

"Are you a pilot?" Marcus asked.

"Yes, sir," Jay said. "For both rotor and fixed-wing. Pretty much everything we have here at the camp."

"Good," Marcus said. "Mara has an important task for my friend and I. We need your assistance. Why don't you go get an airplane ready? You'll be taking us to Colorado Springs."

"Yes, sir," Jay said. He ran behind the desk and grabbed a bag. He took a pen from the desktop and was about to write on a clipboard.

"Oh, no," Marcus said waving his hands from side to side. "This is a level one security operation. No records on documents from your security level."

Jay had a growing look of concern on his face but he continued to go along with whatever Marcus was telling him. He placed the pen down and nodded. He took the bag and started for the exit.

"I'll get the plane pre-flighted," Jay said. "You can come with me now and wait in the plane or wait for me to be done. It shouldn't take too long."

"We can come with you now," Marcus said.

Marcus had the slight worry that this young guy might try to call someone above Marcus's head to verify that he should be doing this flight. They walked around the tent and when Marcus saw the airplane his stomach sank. It was a King Air, identical to the one he flew into the ground.

"Figures," he muttered to himself under his breath.

Marcus did his best to hide his growing anxiety but he was pretty sure that Will could pick up on it. Marcus and Will got settled in their seats while Jay walked around the aircraft. Marcus kept an eye on him as best as he could through the small, round windows.

Jay reentered the aircraft and closed up the door. He picked up a small cooler that had been sitting on the floor.

"There are some drinks in here. They should still be cold." He pointed to a bag that also sat on the floor. "There are some snacks in there. Give me about ten minutes to do the flight planning and we should be on our way." He grabbed a tablet computer out of the bag on his shoulder and went to sit in the pilot's seat.

Marcus eyed the cooler. He wondered if it had any more off-brand soda cans.

Jay turned after a minute. "Mr. Braden, sir?"

"Yes?" Marcus said.

"I just wanted to double-check," Jay said. "Am I filing a flight plan for this flight? The CMA likes it that way for all flights."

"This isn't all flights," Marcus said. "No flight plan."

"I'll still have to talk to air traffic control in some of the areas we'll be flying."

"That's fine," Marcus said. "Just remember, I'm not here and neither is he."

Jay nodded and returned to his flight planning. After a few minutes more, Jay turned back again."

"Strap in tight," Jay said. "Looks like it's a bumpy day over the Rockies."

The announcement made Marcus slump in his seat and let out a deep sigh.

Chapter Thirty-Three

Marcus and Will unbuckled as the plane came to a stop on the ramp. Sweat lined Marcus's forehead. He stood and put on his suit jacket. He wanted to cover any sweat stains that might be present on his shirt after the turbulent flight. Turbulence and flying didn't normally bother him, but after having crashed in the same type airplane he was riding in again, his thoughts on flying were beginning to change.

Marcus looked to Will. He was yawning. He slept the entire flight. Marcus shook his head. He hoped he wasn't getting this young guy into more than they could handle. Marcus stopped at the cockpit as they were about to exit.

"You've done good Jay," Marcus said. "Now get this plane back to your camp. Remember, don't say a peep about us. If anyone asks, you were doing a special level one security job for Mara. You know Mara, right?"

Jay nodded his head. "Fuel truck just started loading me up for the trip home."

"Good," Marcus said.

Marcus leaned forward to shake Jay's hand and must have lost his balance and toppled down in between the two pilot seats. Will was right behind him and helped him up. Jay helped as best as he could from his confined seating area by allowing Marcus to hold on to his arm.

"Whoops," Marcus said. "I'm alright, guys. Thanks for the help."

He extended his hand again and Jay took it. Marcus and Will stepped onto the ramp. Jay closed the door up behind them. They walked around the plane and towards a small terminal building.

"You okay?" Will asked. "That had to have been killer on your ribs."

"Not to worry, my young student," Marcus said. "I'm getting quite a bit better at this spy game." He pulled a phone from his pocket. He quickly glanced back to ensure that the King Air was taxiing back out. The fuel truck had just pulled away and the propellers were starting to rotate.

"Looks like a phone," Will said. "It probably doesn't work. We lost all service the day the CMA pulled the country into the gutter."

"This is no ordinary phone," Marcus said with a sly grin. "This is a CMA satellite phone. All of their phones still work."

"If you've had that this whole time, why didn't you use it?" Will asked with a puzzled look on his face.

"My fall in there was controlled," Marcus said. "I saw Jay check the time on this thing about every twenty minutes for the entire flight. I could tell it was a CMA phone. They made me start carrying one like the day after they took over everything. I knew I had to snatch it from him. Luckily he had dropped it on the floor while landing.

He'll probably assume it slid back somewhere and will have to look for it once he gets back home."

"Sneaky sneaky," Will said as a smile grew on his face. "But, who are you going to call? Isn't it just CMA phones that work?"

"Thomas from the ARF must have had a sat phone as well," Marcus said. "Before we had to start using more clandestine methods of communicating, we still used phones. In fact, my personal phone had still worked. I wonder if they shut down communications by location rather than a blanket across the whole country. Anyway, I need to try to get a hold of Thomas and also one other person."

"Who?" Will asked.

"My brother," Marcus said.

*****

"General here," the gravelly voice answered. He sounded annoyed.

"Now don't go promoting yourself Private Ray," Marcus said.

"Talking Head!? Is that you!?" Ray said.

"Yes, sir," Marcus said.

Will had leaned in as close as he could to Marcus to try to hear the conversation over the phone. *Private? Talking Head? Were these code words?*

"How is that possible?" Ray said. "The news played a memorial for you."

"Wow," Marcus said. "That would've been interesting to see. Listen, Private, keep up the nicknames. I'm on a CMA phone."

"You called me on a CMA phone? What the-"

Marcus cut him off. "Just keep to the nicknames. I'm pretty sure they won't care about this number. Also, I think the CMA is way too busy right now. I think they are about to ramp up something terrible."

"Yeah, I've heard," Ray said grimly.

"I'm curious what you've heard from the military perspective," Marcus said.

"What do you mean?" Ray said. "I've heard everything you told the dog unit."

"The dog unit?" Marcus asked.

"Yeah," Ray said. "You know, 'arf?'" He sounded it out like a dog's bark rather than saying the three letters Marcus always referred to it as, ARF.

"You're working with Thomas?" Marcus was perplexed.

"Yeah," Ray said, "didn't he ever tell you? I was the one that suggested he contact you. Man, you are pretty dumb for a giant talking head." He laughed.

"Ha ha," Marcus said slowly in a sarcastic tone. "He never told me. Anyway, I've got a plan and I need your help. Do you have a way to move around the country?"

"Affirmative, Head," Ray said.

"Good," Marcus said. "Do you remember the place that Dad took us camping and hiking when we were teenagers?"

"Affirmative," Ray said. "I'm already here."

It turned out that another contact at Marcus's home camp had passed on to the ARF where all the big-wigs of the CMA were headed. Marcus knew it had to be Blake. Marcus made arrangements with his brother to get picked up.

Once Will and Marcus stepped into the small terminal

where the private planes would park, Marcus immediately went to the small shopping area. He grabbed a hat and sunglasses to help disguise himself. He noted in a mirror as he adjusted the hat that he was looking quite scruffy. This was probably the longest he had gone without shaving since he was a pubescent-thirteen-year old. His line of work was all about appearance.

"I think you'll be able to pass," Will said. "You kinda look like a homeless person."

"Hey!" Marcus said. "Pretty harsh."

Will laughed to indicate he was kidding with him. "Nice choice of a hat, by the way."

Marcus looked in the mirror again. He had grabbed the items without caring what they said. He hadn't realized that the small terminal also doubled as a school for beginning pilots. The face of the hat read, 'MAY YOUR LANDINGS ALWAYS EQUAL YOUR TAKEOFFS.'

Marcus shook his head. "Just perfect."

Chapter Thirty-Four

Marcus and Will exited the car and a cool mountain breeze hit their faces. They had been surprised by their surroundings as they arrived. It was a slightly upscale neighborhood. It was gorgeous. It was hilly and green and full of established trees. All the yards were beautifully landscaped with large decorative rock and well-trimmed bushes. Deep red mulches contrasted the gray river rock. And it was all surprisingly close to the entrance of Cheyenne Mountain. If it weren't for the thicket of trees, they'd probably be able to see the entrance into the mountain. It was most likely that it could be seen from some of the second-floor rooms of the large homes in the neighborhood.

The car that picked them up hadn't been what they expected either. There was nothing military about it at all. It looked like an average family sedan. The man that drove them had no signs of being in the military. His hair wasn't short like the typical military standard. It was a bit overgrown and might be considered shaggy. He had a few days of growth on his face. His clothes were average;

khaki pants and a sports t-shirt. He also didn't speak. His head was like a bobble-head doll. He constantly checked mirrors and looked directly out the side windows. He made seemingly unnecessary lane changes which actually had a purpose. He was trying to detect any surveillance activity following them.

As they approached the massive custom home, Ray burst out of the front door. He and Marcus rushed up to each other and grabbed one another for a tight squeeze. They spoke a few words to each other that weren't loud enough for any of the others that had gathered around. They pulled away and kept their right hands locked in a perpetual handshake. Tears were beginning to form in Ray's eyes. They both had wide smiles stuck on their faces. Ray cleared his throat in an effort to prevent the tears from beginning to fall.

"You look like hell," Ray said.

"Thanks," Marcus replied. "You too."

Everyone laughed.

Ray turned from Marcus. "This must be Will," Ray said.

"I am," Will said. "And you are...Private Ray?"

Ray's face became grim. He shot a glance at Marcus that could have burned through a solid concrete wall. Marcus let out a mischievous laugh. Ray turned back to Will.

"It's General. General Braden to pretty much everyone. Marcus is the only one that can call me Ray."

"Oh...," Will began, "I'm sorry, General Braden. My only reference was from Marcus."

"Clearly," General Braden said. He shot another glance at Marcus.

General Braden brought Marcus and Will into the house. The inside of the home was filled with extravagant woodwork. There were hardwood floors, wood trim, and what appeared to be hand-carved crown molding. It was an elegant western look. Will thought something like this must cost a small fortune.

"I see you admiring all the woodwork, young man," a man with a southern accent said as he approached Will. "Once upon a time, the economy was much more...lucrative for everyone. It was during that time I had this home built." The man looked up to the high vaulted ceiling in the room Will and the others had just entered. "I'm Matt Madison," he said extending a hand to Will. "Originally from Savannah. I decided like the great adventurers of old to head west and try my hand at a fortune out here. I had a slight advantage being that my wife and I were already inheritors of her Stainbrook family fortune, but don't tell anyone. Either way, I was a big construction name in Georgia and continued that success here. It's not as easy in today's world. I'm guessing pretty much impossible now that most industries are controlled by a government corporation. Also known as a militaristic, communist, tyrannical nightmare."

General Braden approached, "Will, don't mind him. He's probably the most vocal and passionate person you'll meet in our cause. Perhaps more than Thomas Allen, our leader. Mr. Madison has been most gracious to allow us to use his home. We are lucky that is about half a mile away from the enemy. He's been a part of the cause for years, both in advertising the cause on his own and helping to support it financially. When he found out that Cheyenne Mountain was where all the enemy went into hiding he called immediately to get us out to his house."

"Thomas!" Marcus called out, surprising everyone.

"Marcus," Thomas said as he stood up from a couch in the large room, "good to see you are alive."

The two shook hands. "This is quite the surprise," Marcus said. "Will and I thought we were coming out here to fight them alone. I had hoped you all had a plan."

"Well," Thomas said, "once we got word from Blake that all the important people from the CMA were heading to Cheyenne Mountain, we started heading this way. We unfortunately only have about five to ten percent of our people here with hardly any of our military equipment here yet."

"Oh," Marcus said in a disappointed manner.

"I know, I know," Thomas said. "You had become our greatest information asset. We were getting some information here and there from a few of our other insiders, but you were right there in the thick of it. Anything we found out from others was always minuscule to what you would pass on to us. It's difficult to plan a war based off of some of that information. The CMA definitely had a well planned out course of action."

"It seems so," Marcus said. "What can we do? I'm beginning to worry that we can't wait for the rest of your people."

They all settled down onto the couches. Marcus filled them all in on his harrowing story of the plane crash and Will and his group finding him. They were all shocked after hearing the story that he was even alive to be here. Marcus clutched his chest and told them that he didn't escape completely uninjured.

Thomas moved on and explained the ARF's plans. Their plan was, unfortunately, to wait for at least seventy-five percent of their forces and assets to arrive before moving against the CMA. Even then, they worried that they could be easily surrounded. The bulk of the manpower of the CMA was still spread around the country in camps and could be called to the area much quicker than the ARF had abilities to do.

"You see," General Braden said to Marcus and Will, "we are already risking a lot, from a military perspective, by bringing everyone here. We can only hope that most of their personnel aren't in it because they believe in this cause of total control over everyone's lives, It's practically a system of slavery they have in the works. I think the men they have are in it for the money and security. The economy has been worthless for at least a decade. Everyone is desperate to make sure they can feed themselves and their families."

"Well, why don't you leave it up to Will and I then?" Marcus asked.

Will's head snapped to Marcus. "Why would we do that now that we know they are here?"

"Because we have a fairly solid plan and we can't afford to wait," Marcus said.

"Fairly solid?" General Braden asked. "What plan do you have?"

Marcus took the next few minutes to explain his plan. The others slowly inched forward in their seats as they listened. They all finally sat back in their seats after he finished.

"You think you can pull all that off?" Thomas asked.

"We thought we could do it before," Will said.

Everyone turned and looked at Will.

"Of course, there are the few things we need help with," Marcus said. "I'd also like to get cleaned up and shave. I think he needs it too." Marcus lifted his eyebrows and nodded his head towards Will.

"Hey!" Will said and then laughed.

Marcus turned back to the others, "You know, we were able to get onto a camp and manage to have them fly us out here," Marcus paused for a moment, "all to fight them. In addition, it was all after I was supposed to have died in a fiery plane crash and the news had announced it nationwide."

The General, Thomas, and Matt all looked at each other. Thomas took a deep breath.

"This seems quite risky," Thomas said. "I'm not sure if I'm comfortable with this."

"Can we afford to wait?" Marcus asked. "Do you know why all their top people went into hiding in one of the safest places to be in the U.S.? They are deep inside of a mountain now. A mountain that can keep them safe from a bomb hitting it. I can't remember every place on that list, but I'd say Colorado Springs has a pretty good sized population. They also have a camp not too far from here. I'd bet it's on the list otherwise they wouldn't be hiding inside of a mountain."

Thomas began to continually nod his head. "I see what you mean." He sighed.

"This needs to be done and it needs to be done now," Marcus said.

"There are all kinds of military bases in the area," Matt said. "I bet we can find what you need fairly quickly. Some the people we already have in the area are military from these bases. General, do you think we can gather what they need quickly?"

"The CMA has taken over a lot of the assets in the area," General Braden said. "If we can get in contact with our insiders right now, we might be able to move on what we need tonight. Marcus, there's a chance that you and Will could get going on your plan tomorrow. No guarantee. It might take an extra day."

"I hope it doesn't," Marcus said. "I really do believe that I am right. I wouldn't be surprised if they've already started bombing areas. One lady was ready to bomb L.A. a few days ago."

"Get the word out then," Thomas said. "This plan is better than waiting around for the country to be blown to bits."

Their meeting concluded. General Braden left to start getting in contact with the military personnel in the area to start working on getting the items that Marcus and Will needed. Matt showed Will to a room he could stay in and get cleaned up. As Marcus was about to find where his room would be, Thomas stopped him. He held him by his arm.

"Marcus," Thomas said, "you do understand that this will be very dangerous for you, don't you?"

"Of course," Marcus answered. "No different than what you had me doing before."

"Yes, but now you have a young man with you who seems gung-ho," Thomas said. "What did you tell him to come along with you like this?"

"I told him everything I've told you," Marcus said. "Thomas, this guy has a passion for his country and his family. Even his friends. He knows that he is fighting to maintain freedom for his family, his girlfriend, for friends, and for millions around the country that he doesn't know. They haven't had it easy out in the woods. He's dealt with danger. I think this young man knows what it takes to complete this and what risks he is taking."

Thomas nodded his head. "Just so you are sure. I can understand sending trained soldiers to fight, but it's just much more difficult to send someone without the training."

"You do know I wasn't some sort of trained spy before you tasked me with the job?" Marcus asked with a smile.

"Point taken," Thomas said. He sniffed in Marcus's direction. "I would suggest getting cleaned up before you do anything else...anything at all." Thomas laughed at his own joke. "Whew!"

Chapter Thirty-Five

The military arm of the ARF, unfortunately, could not procure all that Marcus and Will needed to start the next day. They were, however, impressed with what they did get in only one night. The delay gave them a little more time to plan things out more efficiently. Matt took Will to another house in the neighborhood where they took Will's picture and came up with forged credentials that looked like a perfect match to Marcus's.

Once Will and Matt returned, Thomas took Will and Marcus aside to tell them about another contact.

"Once inside, you need to try to find a man named Jackson," Thomas said. "I don't know exactly where he'll be. He's been doing similar work to what you were doing for us, Marcus. He has been with some of the top members of the CMA for years. He hasn't been able to pass much information to us, though. His job is something like a butler...I think. To the best of our knowledge, he never gets to hear any of the important meetings. The most he has been able to tell us is that these people are on the move.

There is a slight chance that the CMA is on to him due to the fact he hasn't given us much information. We think he is rarely allowed to be alone."

"He's been with the CMA for years? They've been around for years?" Will asked, surprised.

"It hasn't always been called the CMA," Thomas said. "In fact, we believe Central Management Authority is the first name its ever had. They've existed in some form for possibly a couple of decades. They played the long game on this one. That is why they were so easily able to take over the government and the whole country. They've been planning that long. Jackson has passed us names of possible leaders and members for the last nine or ten years. I really hope they aren't on to him. He has always had the hardest time of all of our information gatherers to get word back to us. He works in circles of very rich and powerful people who have always been on top of their own personal security."

"So, these people who are doing all the destruction to the country are already rich and powerful and they want more money and power?" Will asked.

"You've hit the nail on the head, son," Thomas said. "For whatever reason, what they've had isn't enough. The information Marcus passed to us, where it sounds like they are going to enslave anyone they don't kill off, just baffles us. We always thought they had just wanted a completely different style of government. It appears that was our mistake to assume as such. The world has a history of this sort of thing, though."

"What do you mean?" Will asked.

"The power-hungry stopping at nothing to rise to the top," Thomas said, matter-of-factly. "Their deep down desire to be god-like. World history tells us that it should always be expected. The United States of America's founders knew it. They built us a pretty good system of protections. We call them checks and balances. Someone rises to the top and millions upon millions throughout history have died...killed so they can try to maintain that power...that absolute control."

Will could see emotions rising up in Thomas as he spoke.

"Assuming we can stop them, what will happen next?" Will asked.

Thomas's emotions subsided a little and he shifted in his chair. "Very good question. I wouldn't be surprised if this country broke up into smaller countries. It was already happening. People coming together and breaking away into new counties or claiming to no longer be a part of their state. There is such great polarization. We will just have to stand for what we believe and try to convince people that what our founders put together was pretty darn good. What has happened over the last decade and since the CMA took the reigns should be a helper for our cause...hopefully. It's sometimes hard to believe what people have bought into the last few decades...as far as politics go."

Will nodded. He wanted to say more and ask more, but he wasn't sure what to think about it all. He had considered some of these things on a smaller scale. He had thought of how law and order and justice should be handled in his small town. How were they going to reorganize an entire country? Were there going to be enough people still alive with the knowledge of how local and state and federal governments ran?

"I'm glad there are people like you thinking about this kind of thing," Will said. "I get a headache thinking about how this will be solved."

"You better get over that," Thomas said. "It is going to have to be people like you that get things back in order in your cities and counties and states. The ARF and groups like it can't do everything in every locality. Anyway, I've rambled too much. You got me. I like to talk. Obviously, I'm quite passionate about this subject. If you can find Jackson, he should be able to help you. Most importantly, we'd like you to get Jackson out of there with you. He's worked hard for our cause for so many years that we'd all hate to see him be a casualty for it. We understand that in war there are casualties, but we definitely want to minimize them."

"How do we find him?" Marcus asked.

Thomas laughed for a few seconds and then sighed. "Look for the guy that has the name tag that says 'Jackson.'"

"What? You don't have anything more than a name?" Marcus asked.

"Not exactly," Thomas said. "Our contact with him has always been electronic. I can't tell you what he looks like. I hope that Jackson is his real name."

"That doesn't sound too promising," Will said.

"I understand," Thomas said shaking his head. "Do what you can. We are trying to get a hold of him so he can help you while you are in. It's not like we are picking up the phone. Marcus, you know how difficult it can be to pass information with conditions like this."

"Ugh," Marcus groaned. "You don't even know the stories of how stressful and difficult it was to get information to you. Based on the fact that they attempted to kill me in a plane crash, I wonder if they knew I was passing information somehow."

"They could have," Thomas said. "I guess it doesn't

matter now. That makes me wonder, are you sure you are going to be able to move around that facility once inside?"

"Obviously, I've never been inside," Marcus said. "However, I think the hardest part will be getting in. As long as people think you belong, you can get away with a lot, even in a place like that. You wouldn't believe some of the places I've worked my way into throughout my career in the media business. I've done stories on military bases where I was unescorted and didn't have any official permission to do so. I've been in some high-tech corporate labs where they don't even allow workers to bring their families. And," he paused for emphasis, "I brought a camera."

"I like your confidence," Thomas said.

"Me too," Marcus said back with a smile.

The three sat back in their chairs to relax. Will couldn't help but admire the exquisite items that were everywhere in Matt's home. They were sitting in expensive leather chairs. There were large, real paintings all over the walls. One covered nearly the whole wall. Will's experience with art was usually reprints of a piece. Another entire wall was a bookcase. Will had repaired a nice bookcase for someone in his town and the few pieces of hardwood it required were more expensive than he thought they'd be. He couldn't imagine the cost of a bookcase that was an entire wall.

Thomas had just started to offer Will and Marcus a drink when General Braden flew through the door. He stomped in the room with Matt in trail.

"Thomas!" General Braden said as if he had been searching for him for hours. "The bombings have started!"

Chapter Thirty-Six

"What!?" Thomas, Marcus, and Will all said together. All three stood up at the same time as well.

"Where?" Thomas asked.

"West coast," the General said. "It appears they are obliterating California."

"What do you mean?" Will asked frantically. "All of it?"

"Well, certainly not their precious camps," General Braden said. "Our sources say they are sticking to the cities right along the coast for now. I'm sure they have all their strategic points. We also received word as we were heading out the door to find you that more bombers were in the air. Departed off the east coast."

Marcus turned to Will, "I'm sure they are safe up in the mountains. There's hardly anyone up there." He turned back to the others, "We need to act now. They've probably killed millions in California alone with bombing there."

"We don't have everything you need yet," General Braden said to his brother. "It could be a suicide mission."

"I think we have enough to stop them from sending out commands to bomb," Marcus said. "It won't be pretty in that mountain. Plus, I'm willing to do what is necessary to stop them."

"Marcus!" Ray said, "you can't be thinking about doing this. We don't have the capability to remotely detonate yet!"

"I'm well aware of the situation, Ray," Marcus said. "We have enough explosives to bring it down from the inside." He turned to Will, "Are you still in?"

"I'm in," Will said with a nod of his head. "We need to move now."

Will hadn't planned on rushing into the plan. He hadn't fully mentally prepared for what he was about to do. In his mind, he had pushed it back for one more day. They had hoped to have remote detonation capability for the explosives they were going to place on the inside of the mountain by the next morning. Will imagined the next morning he would wake up and just be ready to jump into the stressful situation. Now that it was here, right here, his stomach sunk and he was losing confidence in himself. He didn't have time to lose confidence. It now appeared that the entire country depended on him and Marcus. He knew they must do this. It could be the difference between life and death for his family up in the mountains.

"You don't," Ray said. "You don't have enough explosives to do what you think. I have a guy that will explain a better plan to you. Go get ready."

Marcus and Will rushed to their rooms. They needed to play a part now. Marcus had instructed him a little on the acting required, full time, in order to get where they needed to be. As they rushed to their rooms, Marcus reminded them that they shouldn't act like they are upset about the bombings beginning. Will thought he must be visibly fuming about the situation and he took a mental note to push back all the thoughts of his mother and Lea in California. He and Marcus were supposed to be two loyal CMA employees that were arriving as called.

They both dressed in their fresh, clean clothes. Will placed on his disguise which consisted of a 'WWNL' hat and a pair of glasses. He wasn't sure why it had been decided that he wear glasses but he still placed them on his face. Marcus didn't have a disguise at this point. He put on a nice borrowed suit. He combed his hair. He had already shaven that morning. He adjusted his tie in the mirror and went out in the hallway to wait for Will. Will walked out of the room a minute later looking like a new, eager, young employee that was to shadow the great Marcus Braden.

"You'll pass," Marcus told him.

He liked the glasses and hat. He especially was fond of the badge that Will had around his neck. It reminded him of every cameraman that Marcus ever worked with.

The two reconvened with the others in the great room. There was now several bags sitting on the floor. They looked like the typical camera equipment that would be carried on any usual job for Marcus. Will and Marcus knew that the bags weren't filled with any camera equipment. They were filled with plastic explosives. An unfamiliar face that stood next to the General gave them a crash course on the procedure for placement. They originally were supposed to be getting a little bit more advanced training at some point during the day.

The man looked like he spent most of his life in the military. He was maybe in his fifties. He still had closely cropped hair as if he was still required to do so. He wore a skin-tight shirt that he tucked into his pants. It was clear he still kept in shape from his toned muscles. His voice was constantly hoarse. It was probably from a lifetime of yelling commands at lower ranked soldiers.

The man drew a makeshift map for Marcus and Will. He told them that the plastic explosives had to be placed in exact locations for maximum damage. He explained to them that inside the mountain there were multiple layers of protection. There was the outer blast door, but there were also several inner blast doors. A nuclear bomb could detonate inside the main blast door and theoretically, people could still be safe inside if they were beyond another closed blast door. He further explained that with the meticulous placement of the explosive, they would not be trying to cave in the mountain. Marcus and Will were puzzled by this. The man told them the only way to penetrate all the security measures outside of a nuclear explosion going off inside the mountain with all the blast doors open, was his plan he was explaining to them now. Marcus and Will listened intently. They wrote a few reminder notes down on the map page. Marcus tucked the hand-drawn map into his inner suit jacket pocket after the man finished explaining.

Marcus considered the amount of detonation line they were looking at in the open bag on the floor. He knew the chances of survival for whoever was at the end of the line about to push the button were slim at best. After connecting all the charges together and trying to string the line far away from the explosive, he might be a hundred feet from the blast. Still inside the mountain. He pushed this thought far back into the pit of his mind.

Chapter Thirty-Seven

Will and Marcus walked up the long and wide concrete path that led to Cheyenne Mountain's entrance. Two guards stood behind a concrete blockade. Any cars approaching trying to breach through security would have to slow to weave around the concrete blocks. As Marcus and Will got within twenty feet, both guards lifted their rifles and took aim. They stopped. Marcus put up his hands. He could see they were wearing all black garb. A white and blue CMA armband was attached to their right arms.

"Hello fellas," Marcus said and took another few steps forward. "I'm Marcus Braden, I'm in charge of public relations for the CMA. I have other duties as well."

One of the guards, once he recognized who he was aiming his gun at, lowered his rifle. He had the typical response that Marcus was getting used to. His jaw dropped open.

"It's been all over the news that you died in a plane crash," the guard said.

The other guard noticed out of the corner of his eye that his partner was no longer holding his weapon at ready and he quickly glanced over at Marcus. He had been focused on the younger man that approached them. Upon recognition, he did a double-take between the other guard and Marcus and then he lowered his rifle as well. Marcus and Will still stood in place.

"Yes, I'm sure everyone has seen that news by now," Marcus said. "My future role with the CMA required that I be...reinvented."

The two guards looked at each other in confusion.

"As far as you two should be concerned, you never saw Marcus Braden," Marcus said. "That man did die in a plane crash." Marcus dropped his hands from the air. He grabbed his CMA badge and held it up towards the guards. "All you know about us two is that we are two CMA employees that have been called in. You checked our badges and let us through."

"Whoa," one of the guards said to the other, finally breaking their awestruck silence. "I bet the news guy does spy work."

Marcus's heart sunk. How could they have figured him out so quickly? Had the word been spread around the entire CMA staff that Marcus had been working for their enemy?

"Yeah," the other said in agreement and laughed. He turned to Marcus, "What do they have you doing? James Bond type-stuff?"

Marcus smiled. Now he realized that these two guards thought he was a spy for the CMA. "Just a simple newsman is all." He kept the smile on his face as he answered. He wanted the guards to continue to think he had very important work to do for the CMA.

"Riiiight," the guard said. "Come on forward, gentlemen." The guard appeared serious again as he waved them in. "Let's check your credentials and then you can get on inside. There have been other arrivals this morning so I'm guessing you all have a meeting."

Marcus nodded. He didn't want to get into much back and forth conversation. He had hoped asserting his dominance as they arrived would do the trick. It seemed to. The guards gave their badges nothing more than a quick glance and let them go. They were surprised that the main blast door was wide open. He assumed that it stayed closed pretty much all the time and then there'd be other doors for people to use.

They followed the instructions given by the man that drew the map so they could make it to the exact location deep inside the mountain. Marcus wished he had gotten the man's name. They were in such a rush to get here. That man may very well have saved their plan from immediate disaster. They had hoped to cave the mountain in with the explosives. Now inside, they could see the thickness of the inner walls and the several blast door inside would make that impossible with the meager amount of explosive material they brought with them. He noted that all the inner blast doors were open as well. This was good for their plan.

Marcus quickly threw on a hat and put on a pair of awkwardly large glasses. Now that they were inside it was more likely that they could run into someone who knew that he wasn't supposed to be there. He wasn't even supposed to be alive. They went winding through the halls and ended up making a few wrong turns. They tried to be casual about their lack of knowledge of their whereabouts, especially when they were around other CMA employees walking around. A couple of times they had to ask for where a specific door was. Marcus would drop back and act curious about something in the hall while Will did the talking.

They finally made it to the location after about five minutes or so of wandering. It was exactly as the man had described. It looked like a very small exposed section of what must be an extremely large, steel tank. There had to be much more of the tank beyond what they could see. They figured this must be in the engineering portion of the complex. There were a few scribbled labels on the map. It was drawn so quickly that is was difficult to understand parts of it. Large, steel pipes ran from the tank and were directed to what they guessed were pumps. There were a few of the pumps that sat in front of the steel tank. The lighting in the area was low, but they were happy about the lack of illumination on them because they were about to place plastic explosives over the entire exposed area of the tank.

They immediately went to work placing the clay-like material on piping and on the corners of the exposed area of the tank. They tried to keep it hidden on the back sides of the pipes and behind the pumps. Once they placed all that they had brought with them, Will turned and watched for anyone that might come by while Marcus placed the small metal tube detonators into the explosives. He then strung parallel wire to each detonator tube.

"Well, that was a bit easier than I expected," Marcus said as he looked around after finishing with the detonator tubes.

"Yeah, except it's going to be a little awkward running this wiring around these halls," Will said. He bent down and looked in the bags. "There isn't a whole lot of this wire left. There's the remaining from the spool you have and then just one more spool."

"Will," Marcus said, "we'll get it as far as we can and then you need to get out. Get out as fast as you can."

"Marcus, what are you saying?" Will asked. "We both need to make it out. We also still need to find Jackson."

Marcus took a deep breath. He had forgotten that Thomas wanted them to find Jackson.

"How are we supposed to do that?" Marcus asked. "This place is huge."

Will looked over at the tank and piping where they had placed the explosives and thought for a moment. "We could leave all this here while we go see if we can find him."

"I hate to say this Will, but I think his chances are slim," Marcus said. "We have no idea what he looks like. We don't even know if we are calling him by his real name." Marcus held his hands up by his sides. "Will, I'll blow this and then hopefully I can run out of here too. I imagine some people that are near the entrance will be able to get out. I just hope that Jackson will be one of them."

Will sighed. "He doesn't even know that this is coming."

"Listen, Will," Marcus said, "The business that Jackson is in...the business that I was doing for the ARF, is a risk. It's all volunteer. He knows that he is risking his life. I don't want this to be the end for the guy, but this needs to get done soon. If we cut them off at the head, they shouldn't be sending out any more bombers. Who knows what has been lost now on the east coast? Who knows where else they were planning on bombing today."

Will dropped his shoulders. "Alright," he said in a defeated manner. He picked up the camera bag that held the last spool of wire.

"This isn't on you, Will," Marcus said. "Is that the problem?"

"I'm tired of the death," Will said. He now looked angry. "It seems like most people in the country are dead. We went into our town and there were bodies all over the place. I've had to kill. One of them was someone I knew." He shook his head.

"This should be a step in the right direction to end all of that," Marcus said. "You know this needs to be done. Think of your family. Think of that girl of yours. Lea. What happens next after they kill off everyone in the cities?"

"I know, I know," Will said in a frustrated tone. He didn't want Marcus to say any more about what could happen to Lea.

"You are a strong man, Will," Marcus said. "Much more than many others. I saw how you were up there in the mountains. I know I wasn't there long with you all, but what I saw was a leader. Look, you are even here now."

Flashes of dead bodies lining the streets of Oakhurst started to pass through Will's mind. The putrid mix of smells; decaying flesh and thick noxious smoke. He pictured the man he shot in the woods. He fell, probably dying immediately. He saw himself holding a gun to Tanner's head. Tanner's eyes looking into Will's moments before he pulled the trigger. His mind moved to the bombings taking place today. How many people were still holding up in those cities? How many people who had the same mindset as him and his family? People who didn't trust what the CMA was doing, rightfully so. Then, his thoughts went to Lea. They went to his mother and Lea's family. To Lewis. What would happen to them if he and Marcus didn't succeed today? Were these haunting deaths just something he was going to have to bear? He would have to bear them on his conscience so that others would stop dying. He realized this was a war and horrible things happen in war. How could he have been so naive to think that they could hide out in the woods and never have to deal with anything difficult?

"Thanks," Will said. "I know that it needs to be done. It's just not easy. Just a moment of weakness for me, I guess. No one goes through life expecting to live in these conditions and have to...kill people."

"Very true," Marcus said and then paused for a moment. He bent down and picked up the bag that held the detonation control unit. He took a deep breath. "Are you ready?"

"Ready," Will said.

Chapter Thirty-Eight

Will regained himself from his temporary moment of vulnerability and then walked ahead of Marcus to check around the next corner. He waved Marcus on. Since they were in the engineering section of the complex, they came across some maintenance related items that lined the halls. They found a few yellow 'Danger' signs that are usually put up around chemical or water spills. They put the signs at the beginning and end of long hallways over the wire in a hope that if anyone came across it, they would think it was for some maintenance purpose and be none the wiser. They also found a roll of 'CAUTION' tape. They planned to use it at each major door they passed through to prevent anyone from finding the explosives before they could detonate them.

The remaining wire from the first spool brought them well clear of the engineering section. Marcus was relieved and beginning to think his chances were better than he originally calculated. Marcus and Will knelt to the floor to connect the next spool to the end of the wire. He picked at the plastic lining with his fingernail. He pricked his finger a few times with some of the stray fibers of copper that were already exposed.

"Marcus, is that you?" a female's voice said.

Marcus shot up straight and whipped around.

"Ava?" Marcus said in surprise.

"You are supposed to be...I mean...I reported that you had died in a plane crash," Ava said.

"That's what I keep hearing," Marcus said.

Will set his bag down on the floor next to Marcus's. Both bags sitting together now concealed the spool of wire they had just begun working on from Ava's view.

"I'm glad you are alive," Ava said. She extended her arms and walked towards him.

Marcus gave her a hug as she arrived. Something about the way Ava was acting just wasn't sitting right with him. He also wondered why she was here and not back at the camp. He was sure that everyone from WWNL would probably still be there. There wouldn't be any plans to drop bombs on a CMA camp.

Marcus stepped back. "Why are you here, Ava?"

"What do you mean?" she asked.

"As far as I knew, it was only the top CMA staff that came here for an important meeting," Marcus said.

She seemed dumbstruck.

"Well...why are you here?" Ava asked.

Marcus was quicker on his feet than she was. "I have other duties with the CMA that you wouldn't know about."

Ava burst out in laughter. It almost started to sound maniacal after she continued for so long. Marcus was puzzled. He turned to Will. He and Will both shrugged their shoulders at the same time. Ava eventually calmed back down.

"Oh Marcus," she said, "there is so much that goes right over your head that you miss."

Marcus tried to be persistent. "You can talk to Anthony. He'll confirm it."

"You are a very good liar," Ava said. "You just don't know who you are lying to."

Marcus narrowed his eyes towards Ava. He studied her. He looked into her eyes. Did she have a much larger role in the CMA than he knew about? She did seem to be absent quite a bit once they moved to the CMA camp. Marcus did plenty of the newscasts without her. He was never really given a concrete reason why she wasn't around.

Marcus drew in a deep breath. "Who am I lying to, Ava?"

As Ava opened her mouth to answer, a group of four armed security guards quickly rounded the corner. Their guns were drawn and aimed right at Will and Marcus. Ava stepped backward and up against the wall. She gave Marcus a closed mouth smile and held up a small black device. Marcus looked back at Ava. It must have been some sort of communication device that worked inside the mountain.

"It means nothing to you at this point," Ava said as the guards seized Marcus and Will.

*****

Marcus and Will sat side by side on the one bench against the wall in a cold, gray jail cell. The only other items in the cell were a small, metal sink that was attached to the wall next to a toilet. The sink looked dirty and rusty and had an annoying continuous drip. The bench they sat on was solid wood. It was probably meant as a bed as well and there was absolutely no padding on it. They both hadn't spoken much since being captured. Marcus was racking his brain trying to figure how Ava played into all of this. Had she just been in the right place at the right time to get some sort of position with the CMA? Marcus wondered if he had never spoken about the reasons behind the poor state of the country on national news if he would have some position like Ava did. Who was he kidding? He had no desire to have any position in the CMA. He would feel like he sold his soul if he tried to climb their ladder of power.

Will was defeated and depressed. He sat with his head lowered into hands. Would he ever get to see Lea again? He didn't think so. He thought back to their last conversation before he trekked off down the mountain with Marcus. Why didn't he just tell her then that he loved her? What was he waiting for? He knew the country wasn't going to instantly return to what it had been before. He shook his head and continued to stare down at the floor.

They both wondered if leaving them here alone for a long time was a part of a psychological mind game. Both Marcus and Will had heard that was sometimes used in police interrogations. A suspect would think too much with all the time they had and then talk more easily after someone finally arrived.

Will finally broke the silence in between them.

"Well," Will said as he raised his head up, "how many cities do you think they've bombed by now?"

"I was wondering the same thing," Marcus said.

"Dozens I'm sure...at a minimum."

"I sure hope the Oakhurst area is spared," Will said. "I think the worst part of all this is when I think of what it will do to my mom and Lea...me never coming home. I can't stand to think of what they will go through. I just hope they will all be able to take care of themselves and survive."

"And to think, Marcus, you had the chance to be on the correct side of all this," a man's voice said.

Will and Marcus were startled. They turned from each other and saw two dark figures standing outside of their prison cell.

"I recognize that voice," Marcus said. "Who's there?" His voice was filled with anger.

Marcus stood from the bench and rushed to the bars. The two figures stood across from him against the opposite wall. They were still concealed in shadows. They appeared to have their arms linked together at their elbows. Marcus squinted into the darkness. They stepped forward out of the shadows.

It took Marcus a few moments to register who he was looking at.

"You!?" Marcus said as he took a step back from the bars.

Marek Dominski, the billionaire businessman, was standing in front of him with Ava hanging on his arm. Marek was someone Marcus considered more than just some acquaintance. He had interviewed Marek many times over the years. He was considered a hero because his success in business was one of the only things that had prevented the poor economy from completely crashing to rock-bottom. *Ava...of course, her boyfriend in the financial district.*

"Marcus," Dominski said. "this is definitely an interesting surprise."

"Why are you doing all of this?" Marcus asked.

"I assume you are referring to the bombings," Dominski said. "Of course that would be your question. You see Marcus, this world we live in, this current civilization is broken. If you look to the past, there were civilizations that lasted for thousands of years. It all has to do with organized control."

Marcus interrupted him, "You are killing millions of people."

Marek looked at Marcus in the cell for a moment before continuing. "Sometimes sacrifices need to be made when you start thinking in the long-term, Marcus," Dominski said. A smug grin formed on his face. "Now, more importantly, why are you two here?"

Chapter Thirty-Nine

Lewis guided his truck through the last section of trees and turned onto the trail. The day before, Alejandro had mustered the energy for the twenty-mile round trip hike to search Beth's property again. This time, he searched the inside of the house and only found evidence of activity from days before. Nothing gave him the indication that someone had been there too recently. He did the same at Lewis's property. He had walked along the main road one last time as well to get a view of the other couple of properties that were along the road. He thought he couldn't be too careful. This group was obviously willing to kill in their search to steal other people's supplies. They had discussed it upon Alejandro's return and concluded that they must have run out of places to ransack and moved on to another town. It was time to return home.

It took about an hour to navigate down the rough four-wheeling trail and arrive at Lewis's. On the drive down, they had decided that Lewis's house would be where they all lived for now. They still worried about the possibility of the group returning and it seemed most likely that they'd return to Beth's. Plus, Lewis's crops went untouched by the large group's vehicles and tents.

After unpacking the bed of the truck and getting settled in Lewis's house, Beth, Alejandro, Juana, and Lea decided they should make a trip back to Beth's house and hopefully be able to salvage some of their things there.

Beth and Lea both seemed to be on edge ever since Will took off with Marcus. They understood, but at the same time, they both couldn't believe he would leave them behind like that. For Beth, she sometimes still thought of Will as her little boy. She knew better, but couldn't help it sometimes. Lea too easily descended into her anxiety attacks. Will had become a steadying anchor for her and now he was gone. She almost didn't know what to do with herself if she had any free time.

Alejandro made sure everyone still had weapons on them. Lewis laughed when he found out his fuel went untouched. He refueled his truck and lent it for their short journey to Beth's. If they were able to recover any of their things, the truck would make the trip back to Lewis's much easier.

Beth drove and Alejandro sat in the passenger seat with a rifle sitting partway out of the window. Lea and Juana sat in the back. They arrived after a few minutes and all started to get out of the truck. Without any warning, a helicopter passed low over the trees and then directly over the house. The sound must have been muffled enough by the trees and its low-flying altitude for them to not hear it until it was right upon them. The helicopter climbed slightly as it made a wide arc around them. It descended in a clear area and touched down.

"I bet that's Will!" Lea yelled over the loud whine of the turbine engines and still-rotating helicopter blades.

She took off full speed towards the helicopter. Alejandro hadn't gotten all the way out of the truck yet and tried yelling to his daughter. He had to pull his rifle out of the window before opening the door. A couple of soldiers stepped out of the side door of the helicopter. They were in all black garb. They looked like they were a special forces unit or possibly S.W.A.T. They all held rifles at half ready. Alejandro could see the two men yell something to Lea as she approached. The noise was too great and Alejandro was too far away to be able to hear it. Alejandro started towards the helicopter. He thought for a moment that Lea might be correct and they were bringing Will back home.

All of a sudden, the two soldiers took Lea by her arms and took her into the helicopter. Alejandro started sprinting towards them. The two soldiers took aim at Alejandro from inside the helicopter and he immediately stopped, nearly tripping. He threw his hands up in the air in surrender and dropped down low to the ground. Wave after wave of turbulent air from the helicopter's rotors blasted his face. The two men never fired. The helicopter engines wound up higher in pitch and it took off. Dust stung Alejandro's eyes as he kept them stuck on the helicopter. The soldier at the door kept his gun trained on Alejandro as the helicopter passed above the trees and disappeared out of sight.

The whole situation took place in maybe a minute or so. Quiet returned to the area. Beth and Juana ran up to Alejandro. Juana was wailing for her taken daughter.

"What just happened?" Juana cried out. "What do we do?"

Alejandro was in shock and full of confusion. He still knelt on the ground staring at the point above the trees where his daughter just disappeared, tears beginning to stream down his cheeks.

Chapter Forty

Marcus was fuming. His world had just been rocked. Marek Dominski, a man he considered a friend, was behind the Central Management Authority. Marcus realized it meant that Dominski was behind the attempt on his life. He babbled on about the country and the entire world needing to return to a more structured method of governing. He said that he was sure the country became so divided by the freedoms people were given. Marcus eventually decided to keep his mouth shut. Perhaps not talking would save him. From Marcus's perspective, Dominski was an already powerful person that was hell-bent on gaining ultimate power. The model that the CMA was acting out proved his theory.

Dominski tried all he could to find out why Marcus and this random other young man were here in Cheyenne Mountain. Were they trying to stop the bombings? Were they trying to survive the bombings? Marcus and Will kept quiet. Dominski became visually upset at their silence. Ava screamed curses at them. Dominski told them they would regret their decision and then they were left alone again in the cold cell.

Hours upon hours had passed. They weren't quite sure how long they were in the cell. It could have been a whole day for all they knew. They took turns getting whatever sleep they could on the uncomfortable bench. At times they were both awake, they had discussed in whispers the fact that it seemed the explosives went undiscovered. They had been captured with a detonator and a spool of wire sitting at their feet. Did the guards simply rush them off and not even check into what they had been doing? Had Ava completely missed it as well? She saw them both kneeling down working on something. She must have been more focused on the fact that Marcus was alive in order to blank that from her memory.

A door opened and the hallway in front of the cell brightened temporarily as light from another room was let in. The door shut behind two men that walked up to the cell door. They retrieved Will and left Marcus behind. Marcus slumped back onto the bench. He had an overwhelming sense of guilt come over him. This young man, Will, could still be safe in the woods if it hadn't been for Marcus dragging him along. Maybe he should have died in the plane crash. He placed his face down into his hands and wept for the first time in a long time.

*****

Will had a growing feeling of fear and anxiety building up inside of him. He tried to hide the feelings and appear brave to the two men that held him by his arms and guided him through the maze of hallways and up a set of stairs to a second level. They brought him into what looked like an interrogation room. It was a dull tan colored room, floor included. A single metal table sat in the center of the room with a few chairs sitting around it. Another few chairs sat along the wall by the door. They forced Will to sit down at the table. The men tied his hands behind him and secured him to the chair. Afterward, they walked out of the room. To his right, a large mirror was built into the wall. Will was sure that it had to be a piece of one way privacy glass.

The man that Marcus had told him was Marek Dominski walked into the room. Will only slightly recognized him. Marcus had expected that Will should know much more about the billionaire. Dominski sat directly across from Will.

“Mr. Richards, is it?” Dominski asked.

Will remained silent. He still tried to hide his fear. He shifted slightly in his seat and looked off somewhere beyond Dominski.

“Will,” Dominski said, “I think you are going to want to cooperate with me. What are you and Marcus doing here?”

Will kept up the stubborn act.

“I would talk to Marcus, but his anger for me seems to not allow civilized conversation at the moment,” Dominski said. He paused for a few moments hoping Will would finally give in and start talking. “I see that you are taking too many cues from Marcus. The man might have been a well-known and trusted name in news, but you should soon understand that whatever delusions he’s put in your head are just that...delusions. Is his one-man fight against the inevitable worth joining, Will? Are you really willing to put your life at risk? Are you willing to put...Lea’s life at risk?”

Will's eyes shot open wide and he snapped his head towards Dominski. The stubborn, silent look on his face disappeared. His skin reddened as anger boiled up inside him. At the same time, he was also slightly confused. How did he know about Lea? The confusion must have been revealed on his face.

"You do recall that you were speaking about Oakhurst and Lea before I came to talk to Marcus," Dominski said as an evil grin formed on his face. "I was standing right in from of you two. It doesn't take too long for an organization like mine to figure out where you lived...where Lea was hiding out."

"You wouldn't dare," Will said. "If you do anything to her or any of my family-"

Dominski cut him off, "What? What do you think you could do to me?" He lifted his arm closest to the one-way glass and twirled his forefinger around a couple of times.

A bright light was switched on in the adjacent room which revealed the view through the one-way glass. Lea sat in a chair in a room similar to the one he was in. She was watching through the glass with tears continuously streaming down her cheeks. Will could tell she had been crying for a long time due to the puffiness surrounding her eyes.

Will struggled against his tied hands that were also tied to the chair. He was attempting to stand but the bindings wouldn't allow him to do so. Dominski twirled his finger again. Will had been so focused on Lea that he hadn't seen the guard in the room. The man walked over to a switch on the wall and Will's view through the mirrored glass was cut off.

"I'm going to make this decision easy for you now," Dominski said. "You are going to tell me what you two are doing here and who, if anyone, you are working with. The Liberty Army? The American Rights Foundation?"

Will's face must have given away something when Dominski mentioned the ARF.

"That's right," Dominski said, "I know all about these stupid little groups. I'll assume you are working with one of those two. Those are the two largest. I couldn't imagine any of the small-time militia groups could figure out how to get inside here. After you tell me everything I want to know, I will spare you by letting you and your precious Lea go to one of my camps. They are such nice and homey places to live. Quite quaint. You'll both have to work, of course. It'll probably be different camps. I'll be honest, you will probably never see her again."

Will couldn't believe how arrogant this man was. How did Marcus ever consider him a friend?

"The alternative," Dominski said as he pounded a single fist down on the table, "is that you get to watch me, personally, kill your girlfriend over there." He pointed to the glass. "I'll make sure it's a painful death. Then, I'm not going to kill you. You heard me correctly. I won't kill you. That'd be too easy, wouldn't it? You'll be sent to a camp in, let's say, a remote and barren part of North Dakota. We can have you dig trenches in the frozen ground for absolutely no reason at all and then fill them back up again. All the while, you get to relive your decision to blindly follow Marcus and let Lea die."

There was spit flying from Dominski's mouth as his emotions were erupting. Will was beginning to see this man as a psychopath. Although that was already obvious from what he was doing to the country. Will's anger and rage matched what he saw in Dominski, but what could he do? Dominski had all the upper hands. Will was just some idiot tied to a chair. He had nothing. No cards up his sleeves. In fact, at this point, he had no cards at all. His mind was racing trying to figure a way out. He couldn't come up with anything. The only two options that he had been given were both horrible. Of course he would choose the one that kept Lea alive. Either way, he was beginning to think the last time he would see her already happened a minute ago. The view of her through the glass crying would be stuck in his head forever.

"Which is it going to be?" Dominski yelled at Will. He pounded his fist down on the metal table again.

Will looked over at the glass. The look of anger subsided. A look of sorrow, sympathy, and longing took over his face. He mouthed the words, 'I love you,' towards the glass. He hoped she could see it and hoped she was saying it back.

Chapter Forty-One

Marcus wiped away the tears from his face with his sleeves. Will had been taken about five minutes ago and all Marcus had done was cry. He regained himself.

"Crying isn't going to do anything," he muttered to himself.

He needed to figure out a way out of the cell and to save Will. He walked up to the cell door and tugged on it. He didn't have much hope for that plan anyway. He walked back to the bench and sat down to think. The hallway door opened again and this time, it closed quickly and quietly. Whoever just walked in made sure the door didn't make any noise as it shut. Marcus's face immediately turned to a scowl. The thought of anyone who worked for the CMA now enraged him.

"Marcus," a whisper came from the dark figure in the hallway.

"Who's there?" Marcus asked.

"Keep quiet, Marcus," the voice said, still a whisper.

Marcus furrowed his brow out of confusion now and

walked all the way up to the bars. Kenneth stepped forward. He still stayed near one end of the hallway by the door.

"Ken?" Marcus was surprised to see him. He almost became happy and then he realized that Kenneth probably knew that Marcus was being sent to his death on that flight. It was all the more evident since Ken was here just like Ava was. His scowl returned.

"You disgust me, Ken, you know that?" Marcus said. "How can you go along with these people? You probably knew that Marek was sending me to die in a plane crash. How convenient for all of you. Get rid of me and then play heartwarming stories about my life so people keep thinking you care about them right before you bomb them and their homes." Marcus cursed at Ken.

"Shut up, Marcus," Ken said in a low voice. "Would you just listen to me for once? I've been trying to get you to keep your mouth shut since this all started. If you would have never done that speech on the news this all would have worked out better."

"What do you mean?" Marcus asked.

Kenneth kept looking back at the hallway door. "I don't know what you were told, but I received the messages. It has just been impossible for me to respond."

"What?" Marcus asked, still confused. "You aren't making any sense."

"Jackson!" Kenneth was getting louder, "Marcus, I'm Jackson. I've been in contact with Thomas for years. You know those groups I always hung around that you hated? That was me spying for the ARF."

Marcus's head was beginning to spin. He almost felt like he was going to faint. He had so many emotions flowing through him recently that he was also getting a splitting headache. He stepped forward and held on to one of the cell bars.

"Are you okay?" Kenneth said. "Marcus, we need to finish this. The bomb, Marcus, where is it? Is it on a timer? Can we get out of here in time?"

"A timer," Marcus said with a sigh. "Wouldn't that have been a good idea." He shook his head. "No timer Ken...or Jackson...whatever your name is."

"It's still Ken. Jackson was a code name. What do you mean by no timer?"

Marcus took a deep breath. He knew he didn't have time for all the questions he wanted to ask Ken. "We were planning on remotely detonating it. We never got the remote detonator in time. We heard the bombing started and we came straight here. We have a spool of wire and a detonator."

"Who's the kid?" Kenneth asked.

"Kid?" Marcus said. "He's no kid. He's one of the bravest guys I know." He paused for a moment. "Apparently you are too." He gave Kenneth a half smile. "Will. His name is Will. He rescued me from the plane crash out in the wilderness in California. When he found out about what the CMA was going to do he joined up with me immediately."

Kenneth took a set of keys from his pocket. "We have to blow this place up, Marcus." He unlocked the cell door. "Come on, we have to be quiet." He motioned for Marcus to come out of the cell. "They are bombing the country in planned waves. They don't have the forces they had expected. Once a lot of the troops found out what they were going to be doing, they either abandoned the CMA or tried to sabotage the operation. It's got to be all out civil war out there right now. A lot of those guys joined up with the ARF or one of the other militias. The bombers that already went out destroyed all the major cities on the west coast. Another wave started hitting all the major cities from Florida to North Carolina. Marek only needs to give the order for the next wave."

"Why hasn't he?" Marcus asked.

"Because of you," Kenneth said. "You've got him spooked by showing up here. He thinks that the ARF and other militia forces have a way into the mountain. He's on edge with so many of his troops abandoning him. He could still accomplish his plan, though. We can stop him from giving the order for the next wave of bombing if we blow this place now. Your friend will crack for sure. He brought in his girlfriend."

"What!?" Marcus said too loudly. Kenneth shushed him. "Lea is here? We need to get them."

Kenneth sighed. "I don't think we have time. I don't see any way of doing it without getting us caught again. Marek has himself surrounded by armed guards now. Marcus," Kenneth paused, "he is feeding him a line about getting a chance to live and save his girl but he is going to kill them no matter what."

Marcus's heart sunk to his feet. How could he have brought Will into this? Now Lea was brought in and he felt like it was all his fault for telling them about the CMA in the first place.

"The bomb, Marcus?" Kenneth was urging on. "We are wasting too much time. I've worked too many years to bring a stop to Marek's crazy plans to slip up at the end."

Marcus knew Kenneth was right. He somehow had a stroke of luck that Kenneth was on his side and was able to break him out. The explosives needed to be set off. If he tried to go after Will and Lea then it was most likely that he would just get caught again and then the explosives would never get blown. Marek would continue to obliterate all the population centers around the country and then he'd have his camps full of slaves and he and all the other CMA scum leaders would get their way.

Marcus sighed. "We need to get back towards the engineering department. We placed a ton of C4 plastic explosive against the water storage tank."

"Water tank?" Kenneth asked raising his eyebrows.

"A military guy that used to work in here said there are over six million gallons of water storage," Marcus said. "It was meant for long term survival from nuclear winter. He said it should flood a couple of the floors. The explosion will trigger the automatic closing of the main blast door, which is what we want to hold the water in. The inner blast doors should still be on manual operation. There is a natural spring that fills the water tank. The water should keep pouring in and eventually fill the entire air tight mountain. Once we use the extra spool of wire, we might be able to hurry after triggering the detonation, maybe we have a chance of making it through the blast door before it finishes closing. It should bring us somewhat close to it."

Kenneth looked at Marcus as if he wasn't believing they had any chance of survival at all. He nodded his head. "Let's go."

They snuck out of the prison area and headed towards the engineering department. As they hurried along, Kenneth spoke with Marcus in hushed tones.

"By the way, I had no idea that you were working with the ARF," Kenneth said.

"Really?" Marcus asked. "I thought I was being blatantly obvious. Especially around you. You know, the whole worthless news stories so I could get to the cafe."

"Made up? What was at the cafe?"

"There was a transmitter at that table we were sitting at with Anthony."

"A transmitter? What do you mean by a transmitter?" Kenneth looked puzzled.

Marcus explained that once the CMA moved the WWNL staff to the camp and tightened their leash on him, the ARF had to come up with a different way for him to pass information to them. He divulged the process of how it worked and how stressed he had been the day he was trying to pass the information about the bombings with Anthony sitting right across from him.

"Wow," Kenneth said. "I had no idea. This whole time, even back in New York at WWNL, I was only trying to get you to walk a straight line to keep any heat off of myself."

Marcus laughed. "I wondered what was going on with you. I couldn't figure out why you were always acting weird. Wish I would've known."

"You and me both, buddy," Kenneth said.

"Look," Marcus said and pointed down the hall at the floor. They had just turned down a hallway in the engineering department. "There's our stuff still laying on the floor. It is some kind of miracle those idiots missed this."

Chapter Forty-Two

Will turned from the mirrored glass and stared down at the floor in defeat. Dominski began yelling at him again that he needed to start talking or he was going to kill Lea.

Will turned to Dominski. "We placed explos-"

He was cut off by an explosion. He felt everything shake. Dust fell from the ceiling. A ceiling tile dropped and hit Dominski on his head and shoulder. He let out a sound of disgust and brushed dust from his forehead. Blind rage engulfed his face again. He threw his chair away from him as he stood up. The chair slid across the floor as he bolted for the door. He threw the door open and ran off to the left out of sight. Alarms started to blare all over the underground bunker.

Will started working the knot that was tied to the chair up and down along the metal. He was hoping the metal chair would have a sharp enough edge to it that it could cut through the rope. He pulled and tugged with all of his might to try to get his hand out from the rope as well. Seconds were ticking by and he knew that the level below him would be quickly filling with water.

Will strained his neck to see behind him to his tied wrists. It appeared there was absolutely no progress made to the rope. He roared in anger as he pulled against the knot with all his strength. Nothing. He was probably only tightening the knot further by pulling against it. He wasn't going to be able to break free. He would spend his last moments in life knowing that Lea would also die nearby. She would most likely suffer the same drowning death that he would once the millions of gallons of water filled this level. Not only that, he would know it was all because of the bomb he helped to place.

I hope we at least stopped them, he thought.

"Lea, I'm sorry!" he cried out in the hope that she would be able to hear through the walls. "Lea?" he said puzzled.

Lea stood in the open doorway. He was still trying to come to terms with the fact that they were going to die today. How was she standing there?

"How did..." he was in too much awe that he couldn't finish speaking.

"Luckily, I wasn't tied up," Lea said as a big smile formed on her face. "I had to fight the guard to get the keys to get out of the room."

She went behind the chair and started working on the knot. Will had, indeed, tightened the knot with all of his straining. Lea reached into her pocket and pulled the set of keys she had fought the guard for. She had planned to use a key to pick into the knot. She was elated to find a small pocket knife attached to the keyring.

"How did you beat the guard," Will asked as she began to cut.

"What? You don't think I'm strong enough?" Lea asked

in a sarcastic tone.

"That's...not what I meant," Will said.

"He and the other guard were scrambling at the door to unlock it," she said. "I was pretty sure they were going to leave and close the door behind them and leave me locked in. I grabbed a chair and hit one of them over the head. The other guard had just opened the door and saw what happened. He slammed the door behind him. Almost got this knot," she said with a grunt." I found a set of keys on the guard and walked right out. Got it!"

Will's hands became free and he quickly stood up. He moved the chair and pulled Lea in. He immediately kissed her and she pulled him in more tightly. He pulled away after a few moments.

"This can wait," he said. "We better figure out if we can find a way out of here."

"Was that the bomb that you and Marcus placed?" Lea asked.

"Yep," Will said.

"How come this place didn't collapse in on itself?" she asked. "How are we still alive?"

"We found out that this place could probably survive a nuclear bomb going off inside," he said. "We joined up with Marcus's group. A guy that used to work in here said we needed to blow the massive water tank and fill the place with water. Drown everyone inside. The explosion should automatically close the main blast door."

Lea's eyes shot wide open.

"I know how we can get out," she said. "The guards were saying there's an emergency airlock exit on the next floor up."

"Let's go," Will said as he grabbed Lea's hand.

They dashed to the open door and then stopped. They were startled by a rushing flow of water running into their feet. There was already a couple of inches and it seemed to be increasing at a rapid pace.

"Do you know where that exit is?" Will turned and asked Lea.

"Just the next floor up is all I heard them say," she answered.

They turned out of the room to the left. Will subconsciously decided that the upstairs would be to the left since he remembered seeing Dominski run out of the room in this direction. They sprinted down the hallway. At least a couple of inches of water had filled the entire length of the hallway in the few seconds they paused at the doorway. Sprays of water flew up with each footfall. The lights began to flicker. They could see a stairwell just ahead.

All of a sudden, they heard someone emerge from the water and heavy strained breathing. They turned back towards the stairwell behind them that led down to the first floor. In the flickering light, they could see two bodies crawling away from the stairs. Water was rushing up around them. They hacked and coughed as their lungs fought for air. Will's first instinct was that these were CMA employees coming after them. He paused for just a moment longer. Lea, not caring to find out, tried to tug Will along. He thought in one of the dim flashes of light that he saw Marcus. He let go of Lea's hand.

"Marcus!" Will yelled. He was almost positive that it was him.

He ran back towards the men and back towards the deluge of water filling the hallway. In what seemed like only thirty seconds, the water was now up to his knees. He could see the two men push themselves up from their crawling position to keep their faces out of the water. Another dim flash of light brought relief as he saw it was Marcus.

He helped Marcus up and then turned to the other man that stood.

"I found Jackson," Marcus said through deep breaths. "He's been my boss for the last decade and my friend for the last thirty years."

Will shot an eyebrow up. "Explain later. We need to find an emergency exit up the next floor."

"I'll get us there," that man Marcus called Jackson said.

They waded as quick as they could through now waste-deep water. The water was reaching that depth where they couldn't decide whether it would be easier to keep walking or start swimming. They had decided on wading and reached Lea who stood on the first step of the stairwell.

Chapter Forty-Three

Their shoes squeaked and squished as they ran through the third-floor hallways. The lights on this level flickered some but not as much as the floor below had been. Marcus had explained who Kenneth was as they left the stairwell. Kenneth, in turn, explained that the CMA hadn't been using this floor for much other than storage so they shouldn't run into anyone.

"Marek and the guards that were with us came this way," Will said.

Kenneth cursed. "I guess we better be on the lookout then. They probably went to the same exit we are heading for."

Kenneth opened a door to an empty room. He rushed across the room to what looked like a closet door. He threw that open. The emergency airlock exit was hidden behind the door. It was wide open.

"Marek must have escaped," Kenneth said. "We have to stop him if we can. He can probably still send the command to continue the bombings. He has all kinds of safe hiding places being as rich as he is."

They slowly stepped out, checking all directions. They started down the trail when Kenneth abruptly stopped everyone.

"There," he whispered.

Kenneth pointed down the winding trail to a group of four men and one woman. It was Dominski, Ava, and three armed guards accompanying them.

"We need to get them," Marcus said angrily.

"We don't have weapons," Kenneth said holding Marcus back from charging down the mountain. He thought for a moment. "Here's the plan. You three need to cut through the trees down the mountain." He pointed further to the right of where Dominski and his group were on the trail. "I'm going to catch up with them. They still don't know that I'm not really on their side. Once we approach you on the trail, we'll jump the guards and capture Marek."

The others agreed to the plan and headed down the mountain. Kenneth ran down the trail towards Dominski. He waved his arms and yelled out Ava's and Marek's name as he neared them from behind. The three guards turned quickly and trained their pistols on him. Dominski had them lower their guns as he realized it was Kenneth. He joined them and they began a quick pace down the trail. Dominski said he had a helicopter waiting about a mile ahead.

"I'm glad you got out, sir," Kenneth said to Dominski. "You too, Ava."

Ava returned the comment and gave Kenneth a hug.

"I looked all over for you," Kenneth lied. "There's water filling the entire bunker. What happened?"

Kenneth was trying to be obnoxiously loud so Marcus,

Will, and Lea could hear them approach easily. He was relaying his made up harrowing story of escape from the mountain with excruciatingly too much detail. However, he was still beginning to worry. He thought they had walked too far and should have come across them by now. He was running out of material for his fake story. He wasn't as good on his feet as Marcus was with story telling.

"What was that?" Dominski said.

"What was what?" Kenneth answered quickly. "I didn't hear anything." He had heard something too but was trying to get them to keep moving. He was fairly certain they were in the bushes off to the right.

"Check in there," Dominski said as he pointed to the bush.

Two of the guards immediately walked to both sides of the bush with pistols drawn. Kenneth was wondering what happened to their plan. What were they doing? The guards pulled Lea from behind the bush. Now Kenneth was really confused and beginning to panic. Would he have to figure out a way to stop Dominski on his own? Maybe he would have to crash the helicopter they were heading to. He would be willing to sacrifice himself to stop this madman.

Lea had tears filling her eyes as they brought her to Dominski.

"I don't know how you got out and how you got down here but I don't care at this point," Dominski said. "Shoot her."

Marcus and Will lunged from the other side of the trail. They held small boulders and brought them down on the heads of the two guards that held Lea's arms. The third guard fumbled to get his pistol from his holster. Kenneth thrust a fist at the man. He struck him square in his temple, sending him falling to the ground. Dominski dove for the guard's pistol. Ava screamed and tripped backward onto the ground.

Kenneth struggled with Dominski to get the pistol. Will and Marcus secured the pistols from the two guards they had brought down. Kenneth landed a punch squarely into Dominski's jaw. He was temporarily stunned long enough for Kenneth to grab the pistol. A shot rang out, piercing everyone's ears.

Silence ensued. Marcus stumbled back, clutching the hole in his upper chest. He dropped to his knees. Lea noticed and screamed. Blood rushed out of the opening and he dropped all the way to the ground. They all looked over and saw Ava holding a small pistol. She must have had it hidden on her. Lea, who stood to the side of Ava, jumped at her. Lea had picked up a rock. She swung the rock at Ava and bashed it across her forehead. Ava flew back. The pistol dropped to the ground. Will trained the pistol he retrieved from the guard on Dominski who now was laying on the ground.

Kenneth rushed to his lifelong friend. Marcus's face was turning a ghostly white.

"Hang on, Marcus," Kenneth said frantically. He lifted Marcus's top half above the ground, letting him rest against him. He placed his hand over the wound in an attempt to stop the bleeding.

"Thank you, my friend," Marcus struggled as he spoke. The corners of his mouth curled up slightly. "We stopped him." His eyes shut and he let out a long breath as he slumped against Kenneth.

Chapter Forty-Four

WWNL Evening Broadcast
May 2037

"Hello everyone and thank you for joining me. I'm Marcus Braden. It was reported last month, by this network, that I had died in a tragic accident. A plane crash. The truth is that the Central Management Authority had made an attempt to kill me. I was, indeed, in a plane crash. However, as you can see now, I survived."

Marcus had sweat forming on his forehead. It wasn't from nervousness. He was still recovering from his wounds. His professionally tailored pin-striped suit hid the bandages that covered his bullet wound. His chest was still wrapped, now done by a doctor, as his cracked ribs were still healing. Kenneth stood beside the camera that was aimed at Marcus. He was worried for his friend. Marcus, however, was stubborn and wanted to be the one to tell the nation the story. Kenneth had eventually given in to the stubbornness.

Marcus relayed the story of the CMA and Marek Dominski and their long time planning and then the ultimate speedy takeover of the nation. He told of Mr. Dominski's capture and now of the life-long imprisonment he faces. He concluded with a 'Moment with Marcus.'

"My fellow citizens, our future is now in all of our hands. We will now have to decide how we will move forward. Are we to be like the end of the ancient Roman empire? Will we divide into smaller countries? Will our states become reunited? Whatever we decide as a people, we must always remember what we went through over this past year. We should also take into account the history of our world. More centralized and more powerful governments will always attract people like Marek Dominski. Those are the people that are bound and determined to rise to the top and will do it at whatever cost it may bring. As we all know, Mr. Dominski did it at the cost of millions of American lives. What about the rest of us? Why aren't we bound and determined to protect our freedom and liberty? Will we rebuild this country under the thumb of a powerful and overbearing government? Or, will we rebuild this country under the power of the people? A free people. I challenge everyone to consider these things. I also challenge everyone to take up your shovels and hammers and work together to clear the destruction. Take up your tools to work together to rebuild this country. We should all claim our part in rebuilding this land. Will we create a system of governance like our founders? Will we limit their powers and empower the people? How will we prevent what happened over the last decade from happening again? This is now our challenge. These are the tasks we must complete. I'm Marcus Braden with the Worldwide News Link and this has been 'A Moment With Marcus.'"

Chapter Forty-Five

One month earlier.

The helicopter droned on as it climbed up into the mountains. Will and Lea held hands as they watched the trees pass below them. They had spent a long day waiting to hitch a ride on a flight back to California. Thomas arranged for a flight to Fresno. From there, Thomas told them they could get a helicopter ride up to their property. They were fatigued and anxious to get back to their families.

The pilot occasionally turned back to Will to make sure they were still on the right course to get to their property. Figuring the roads from the air was a new experience for Will, but he was managing. He spotted their road from the air and pointed out Lewis's for the landing sight. Lea had told Will they had moved back to the property and then told of her experience of being taken. She wondered what her parents had thought of it.

They could see Alejandro, Juana, Beth, and Lewis come piling out of the house as the helicopter descended. Lea turned to Will with a smile growing on her face.

"I've been meaning to ask you," she said. "What was it that you said to me through the mirror when you were tied up?"

Will smiled and leaned in and kissed Lea. "I love you."

From The Author

Thank you for purchasing and reading my novel! I hope you've enjoyed reading it as much as I enjoyed writing it. Please rate this title from your favorite retailer and any other website or app you use to keep track of books you've read.

The idea for this book was born several years before publishing. I had dreamt of writing a book starting sometime in college. I have no idea where that desire came from. My degree and the field I work in is aviation. I heard a quote once that everyone has at least one book in them in their lifetime. I don't recall who to credit for that.

I took that quote seriously and began writing 'From Within' in the Fall of 2013. I wrote on and off for a few years. I had outlined my whole story, it was just a matter of getting it all down on paper (computer in the modern world). In early 2016, I decided to change directions slightly. I removed a few chapters and re-outlined the last half of the book. After removing the chapters, I was back down to about thirty pages. It was a bit depressing and discouraging, but now with a new goal at hand, I took to action. I completed writing by mid-July of the same year.

Again, I hope you enjoyed this adventure of a story. I currently have about a dozen or so other ideas in the works and seem to add more all of the time. Most are still rough ideas, but some are outlined and I've started a couple of them. I plan to keep up my new rate of writing and hopefully will be able to publish at least one book a year for you all to enjoy.

Thanks Again,

Brian Delaney

Please add me on Facebook for updates on upcoming novels.

Www.facebook.com/authorbriandelaney

Made in the USA
Las Vegas, NV
21 January 2022

41954437R00198